THE
HIKE

ALSO BY SUSI HOLLIDAY

Writing as SJI Holliday:

Black Wood

Willow Walk

The Damselfly

The Lingering

Violet

Mr Sandman

Writing as Susi Holliday:

The Deaths of December

The Last Resort

Substitute

THE HIKE

SUSI HOLLIDAY

THOMAS & MERCER

Text copyright © 2022 by Susi Holliday
All rights reserved.

No part of this book may be reproduced, or stored in a retrieval system, or transmitted in any form or by any means, electronic, mechanical, photocopying, recording, or otherwise, without express written permission of the publisher.

Published by Thomas & Mercer, Seattle

www.apub.com

Amazon, the Amazon logo, and Thomas & Mercer are trademarks of Amazon.com, Inc., or its affiliates.

ISBN-13: 9781542035347
ISBN-10: 1542035341

Cover design by The Brewster Project

Printed in the United States of America

To Brian, Bec & Kiki – the perfect companions on the hike from hell. Thankfully we all made it back down.

Few circumstances are more afflicting than a
discovery of perfidy in those whom
we have trusted.

—Ann Radcliffe,
The Romance of the Forest (1791)

Prologue

He is in much worse shape than she is. Half of his face is obscured by dried blood and muck. One of his eyes is puffed up and squeezed shut. His shorts and t-shirt are ripped. Muddied. Bloody. She knows she doesn't look too great herself. Sweat patches under the arms of her sweatshirt. Grazes on her knees. She tries to stay focused. Keep the pain at bay.

They're sitting, far apart, on the steps outside the wooden chalet-style building that allocates most of its space to an outdoor equipment shop. Only the small blue sign stuck on the wall to the right of the glassed entrance gives away what's inside. She swivels around to read it, wincing as her back protests.

POLICE

Below that, another small sign stating that tourist-season opening hours are 11 a.m. to 12.30 p.m. and 3.00 p.m. to 4.30 p.m. Three hours to wait.

She turns back around, rests her elbows on her knees. Takes in the empty street. It's still early in the village. Most people are probably tucked up in bed, while the early risers are starting on the croissants and coffee as they scroll through their phones and glance out of the windows, soaking up the views.

He coughs. 'What now?' His voice is ragged, hoarse. His breathing laboured. He needs medical attention.

She stands up, wipes a hand across her face, smearing the mud and tears that have replaced her make-up. She walks carefully around him, leans in close to the sign next to the door. 'There's a phone number here. For emergencies.'

He coughs again.

'We don't have phones, remember?'

She sighs. Walks away from him, glancing up and down the street. 'Something must be open.' She pauses. 'I could go to the hotel.'

He shakes his head. 'Not sure that's a good idea, is it? You said we need to stick to the plan.'

She hesitates. Unsure. 'Yes, but . . .' Her eyes travel over him. His injuries. His pain. After everything that's happened, maybe this is too much. 'I could go somewhere else. Get help. We need assistance now, not in three hours . . .' She walks further away from him, takes in the street filled with closed shops, hotels still sleeping, no public phones in sight. She starts to walk along the street. Her heart starts to beat faster. She could change the plan. It's not too late. Is it? She glances back. He's clinging on to the railing, trying to stand up.

He calls out to her, his voice barely a rasp. 'Don't leave me here. Please.'

She stops walking. She is torn. She turns back fully and takes a long look at him. He's broken. Maybe enough is enough. She walks back to him, sits down on the step again. Lays a hand on his arm, guiding him back down. She shuffles across, lets him lean against her. Feels his warm body against hers. His breathing slows.

'Thank you,' he whispers.

Side by side they sit, waiting. They are in this together.

2

One

If someone had asked Cat Baxendale to draw a typical Alpine village, then Villars-sur-Ollon would be it. Pointy-roofed wooden chalets, swathes of lush greenery. Pine trees as far as the eye could see and, behind it all, framing the scene, the jagged-topped mountains; majestic and looming. The August heat was stifling, but the Swiss Alps remained snow-capped all year round. In winter, the whole vista would turn from green to white. But on this blue-skied summer's day, cold weather and ski boots were the last things on her mind. All Cat could think about was a glass of chilled white wine outside one of the pretty Alpine bars, soaking up that killer view.

Cat had spent a lot of time planning this trip, making sure that every little detail was perfect. It was almost a shame that things would inevitably end on a sour note, but she'd had enough. She wasn't going to put up with the situation for one day longer. Well, two days, actually. At least this evening would be fun for them all before she lit the touchpaper.

The drive from Geneva Airport had been quicker than expected, hardly more than an hour. The tall grey buildings and advertising billboards on the fringes of the city had soon made way for open roads and parched green fields. The ascent up the mountain had been exhilarating and twisty, and often precarious, but before they knew it, they'd arrived in the village and Cat was inwardly bouncing with excitement before they'd even stopped the car.

She had never been to Switzerland before, but her year-long stint in France as an exchange student meant that her language skills should just about hold up, as long as the group didn't veer into the German- or Italian-speaking regions. Her three companions – her husband, Paul, her younger sister Ginny, and Ginny's husband, Tristan – seemed less enthused. Paul, because he'd been green with travel sickness since they'd got into the hire car, and the other two because they'd been bickering since the departure lounge at Heathrow. It wasn't unusual for Tristan and Ginny to fall out, but luckily it usually passed quickly, like a cloud on a windy day. Cat's plan would definitely lead to more than a bit of bickering, however, and the thought of that cheered her even more. Her sister, of course, remained oblivious, despite Cat's obvious glee.

'Let's just dump the bags and head out,' Ginny said, yanking her small suitcase out of the back of the car and dropping it on the pavement. 'I have an urgent need for cheese and wine.'

'We can sort the bags,' Tristan said, slapping Paul on the back. 'Can't we, mate? Sorry . . . are you going to puke?'

'You took those corners far too fast.'

'Oh, come on. You need to drive like that, ascending so high in one of these stupid little cars.' He kicked the driver's-side back tyre. 'I thought you'd ordered a four-by-four?'

Paul was gulping lungfuls of fresh mountain air, his colour slowly returning to normal. 'Cat said she did. It's not my fault they messed up the booking.'

Ginny grabbed hold of Cat's arm, dragging her away. 'There's a bar over the road. Let's leave them to it.'

Cat grinned at her, and the two of them hurried towards the cute little hut with wooden chairs and tables outside. The tables were covered with red-and-white-checked cloths, held down with metal clips. In the centre of each table was a small stone vase holding a bright-yellow flower.

'This is just perfect,' Cat said, pulling out a chair. 'It's exactly as I'd pictured.' She glanced around, soaking up her surroundings. 'I feel like Heidi.' She lifted her honey-blonde hair out to the sides in two bunches. 'Can you do plaits?'

Ginny laughed. 'I think Heidi was German.'

'Yeah, but she lived in the Alps, didn't she? I'm sure it's not that much different in the German cantons.'

'Well, let's hope we don't bump into the evil Fräulein Rottenmeier. She was horrible.'

Cat was about to start dredging her memory for the exact details of the book that she'd read so long ago, when the waiter, dressed in a typical French black-and-white ensemble, appeared by their table, an expectant look on his face.

'*Bon après-midi, mesdames. Vouz avez choisi?*' He waited a beat, then spoke again, this time in heavily accented English. 'Good afternoon, ladies. Have you chosen?'

Ginny grinned at him, holding up two fingers. '*Grandes bières. Merci.*' Her accent was terrible, and the waiter forced an indulgent smile before disappearing back inside.

Cat rolled her eyes. It was just like France then – the locals finding the tourists' attempts at their language barely tolerable. Especially tourists with terrible accents. 'I thought we were having cheese and wine?' She had been looking forward to the wine. It was typical of Ginny to change her mind. Sometimes Cat wondered how she managed to get through a day, with all her dithering and indecision.

'We need a livener first.' Ginny blew out a long breath. 'I am *so* glad to be here. One more of those hairpin bends and I thought we were all goners.'

5

'Me too,' Cat said. 'Tristan wasn't exactly taking it easy for someone driving on the wrong side of unfamiliar roads.' She paused, smoothing down the edge of the tablecloth from where the breeze had flipped the corner up. 'Are you going to tell me what you two were arguing about?' She kept the 'this time' to herself.

Ginny took a packet of Marlboros and a lighter from her handbag. 'Everything. Nothing. You know what it's like.' She offered Cat the packet, knowing she would shake her head because she hadn't smoked in years – despite her sister's attempts to lure her back to it, to 'keep her company'. Eventually, Ginny shrugged, then popped a cigarette into her mouth, lighting it quickly and inhaling deeply. 'I think he might be having an affair.'

This time it was the word 'again' that Cat added, only to herself. She tried to keep her expression neutral. There was no way her sister could know the truth about what she had planned for this trip, was there?

'*Deux bières.*' The waiter reappeared, placing two large bottles of beer and two stemmed glasses on the table, setting down a small bowl of peanuts between them. Then he was gone, and Ginny's sentence hung in the air. That cloud, again. But this time it wasn't shifting so quickly.

Cat nibbled on a peanut, crunching it hard between her teeth. 'What makes you say that?'

Ginny waved her cigarette, blew out a plume of smoke. 'A few things. I don't know, Cat. Maybe I'm overreacting.'

Cat picked up her glass, tipping it to the side as she slowly poured in the beer. 'Like what?'

Ginny drank hers straight from the bottle. 'It's so clichéd, I don't know if I can even be bothered to tell you. Late home from work. Not paying attention to me. New clothes . . .'

'Maybe he's just busy at work.' *Some of us actually do some work*, Cat thought, taking a long, slow drink. The beer was ice-cold and tasted heavenly.

'Not too busy to buy new clothes, though?' Ginny stubbed out her cigarette, crushing it hard into the metal ashtray. 'He used to always ask me to help choose his clothes.' Ginny pouted like the spoilt child that she had always been. 'God, you're so lucky with Paul. He'd never cheat on you, would he? The two of you are so bloody perfect.'

Cat kept a poker face. Ginny knew nothing about her relationship. She was far too self-absorbed to care. A classic Daddy's Little Princess, her sister had grown up to be the ultimate city boy's trophy wife. The fact that she was supposed to have an actual job helping Cat run her events company barely registered on her radar, especially over the last few months. Ginny's life was all about looking pretty and searching for the perfect recipe to wow Tristan with every night, despite the fact that he usually got home late, half-pissed, having already eaten out with clients at a posh restaurant. It was no wonder that Tristan had got bored and gone looking for some fun.

At least Paul was always home for dinner. He usually cooked it, in fact. Things had changed a lot since he'd started his new job. Since he'd been *forced* to start his new job. He was making an effort, but it was mostly in vain because Cat couldn't bear to have him near her most of the time. Even the thought of his hands on her when she knew they'd been all over someone else was enough to turn her stomach. Just one of the many things that this weekend would fix, once and for all.

Cat had zoned out of her sister's chat. It was *The Ginny Show*, as always. Her photos *did* look good on Instagram though. Festooned with her humble-bragging captions about how she knew it wasn't as good as the original, but she'd tried her best, hashtag blessed. Cat wondered what her Keto-diet yoga-bunny Insta devotees would think if they could see her now – carb-laden beer and a second cigarette on the go. Cat took another large drink. The beer was nearly gone already. Her sister's moaning was in danger of ruining her mood.

'How about we forget all that for the weekend, eh? We're meant to be here to relax and enjoy ourselves. The four of us haven't seen each other properly since your birthday party.' Cat clocked the change in Ginny's expression and smiled inwardly. *Oh yes. We will be discussing that, dear sister, along with some other very important things. But not right now.* She signalled to the waiter for two more beers, then spotted the men heading towards them from across the street, and called him back for another two.

Ginny frowned, making her nose wrinkle – but not her forehead, because it was Botoxed to the max. 'I hope this hike you've planned isn't too strenuous. I really fancy a mooch around the shops and a long soak in the hot tub.'

Tristan stood behind Ginny and placed his hands on his wife's shoulders. He gave Cat a wink. '*Au revoir*, ladies! *Mange tout?*' he said, in an awful Del Boy from *Only Fools and Horses* accent, the words making no sense in the context, but turning Ginny's frown into a smile. She really did love Tristan, didn't she? The poor cow. Tristan reached over and took a swig of Ginny's beer. 'Hope you're not trying to weasel your way out of my carefully planned hike, Wife.'

Ginny wriggled her shoulders, shaking him off. 'What do you mean *your* hike. I thought Cat was arranging it all?'

Cat shrugged. 'He offered to help. I was busy with all the rearranged event bookings, so . . .'

Ginny pulled herself completely away from Tristan, turning awkwardly to address him. 'Nice of you to find some time for my sister, when you barely find time for me.' She turned back to face Cat, crossing her arms tightly. 'You don't even *like* each other—'

'I could've helped,' Paul cut in, his face falling as he pulled out the chair next to Cat. 'I've got far more time than any of you.'

'That's because you don't have a job, mate,' Tristan said, punching him on the arm. He pulled out the chair opposite and took a handful of peanuts from the bowl, tipping them into his mouth and crunching noisily.

Paul took a breath. Cat could see from the flush rising up the neck of his t-shirt that Tristan's barbs were getting to him.

Good.

The waiter arrived, depositing the four beers, and more peanuts, on the table. The moment passed.

Paul did have a job, of course. For the last six months he'd been a part-time delivery driver, and he loved it. But Cat knew that all Tristan could see was a city boy who'd burned out, and he refused to let him forget it. Cat had agreed to keep the real reason behind Paul's career change a secret, and she had no plans to reveal it, even over this weekend. She had other things in mind to deal with that.

'You guys . . .' Ginny lifted her bottle. 'We're on holiday? Let's have some fun. Cat and Tristan have worked *so* hard to arrange this for us. Cheers!' Her voice was light, but Cat could hear the tension bubbling just below the surface. Ginny was good at painting on a smile. Cat knew that Ginny didn't want to be here. Cat knew her sister hated hiking, but she was making the effort to keep things friendly. More fool her.

Cat glanced across at Ginny and mouthed a silent thank-you. She didn't want them all arguing. Not right now. Not tonight.

They all chinked their drinks together, to a chorus of 'cheers' and '*salut*', and Cat smiled, pleased with herself for pulling this weekend together. Because there were a few surprises that she planned to deliver.

And not everyone was going to like them.

Two

Friday Night

Cat decided to slow down after the third beer. Maybe it was stronger than the lager she usually drank at home, or maybe it was the altitude. Or maybe just the excitement . . . but she felt fuzzy-headed and she really didn't want to feel rough the next day. The others, though, were definitely up for a party.

'Shall we get a bottle of wine?' Ginny tossed a peanut in the air and opened her mouth to catch it, but failed. The peanut bounced off her chest and skittered across the table.

Tristan and Paul cheered, and Ginny tried again. Failed again. Then shrugged and finished her beer. 'Wine? Anyone?'

Cat shook her head. 'I might slow down a bit, I think. That stuff is like rocket fuel.' She felt happy with the buzz it had given her, but she didn't want to push it.

Tristan laughed. 'Since when were you such a lightweight?' He stood up. 'I'll go and get us all some proper drinks.' He walked into the bar, ignoring Ginny's call to him that it was table service and the waiter would be out soon.

'I'm just nipping to the loo.' Cat picked up her bag and followed him inside. He was at the bar, laughing with the barman, and she suspected that he would ignore Ginny's request for wine, because he didn't like wine. He was equally as self-centred as Ginny. How they'd lasted this long as a couple was a complete mystery. Cat watched him pointing to bottles on the shelf behind the bar. He'd be returning with more beers, plus something stronger. It was still early, but all the more reason to kick things off now. He knew as well as she did that they had an early start.

He turned as she went to walk past him. 'You alright, babe? How about a gin and tonic? Might wake you up a bit.' He took in her frown, then laughed and squeezed her arm. 'Don't worry, Cat. Everyone will be up in time for the hike in the morning. I'm hardly going to spend all that time helping you plan it then wimp out at the last minute. Let's go hard, then go home . . . early.' He turned back to the bar and started chatting to the barman again as he poured the drinks.

'Just nipping to the loo,' she said, pointedly, over his shoulder.

The toilets were in the basement. Dark and dingy. There was only one cubicle, with the rest of the space taken up by a single urinal and a sink. She pulled down her underwear and sat on the toilet, reading some of the graffiti etched into the back of the wooden door.

Lauren pour Antoine – toujours!

Monique est une pute.

La vie est douce.

She smiled at that last one. Life was indeed sweet. Or else it would be, after this weekend. If she had a pocketknife, she'd be tempted to scratch in some words of her own: *Cat woz 'ere.*

'Cat?'

She grinned. Her head might be feeling fuzzy, but the rest of her was fully alert. 'In here.' She stood, quickly pulling up her jeans.

'Mmm,' he said, stepping in and kicking the door shut behind him with his heel. 'Nice place you've got here.' He spun her around and pushed her against the door, started nuzzling her neck. She felt his knee pressing against her crotch as his hands slid up her t-shirt, into her bra. She gasped.

'Tristan . . .'

'Come on, babe. The others are too busy guzzling their drinks. We've got a few minutes.' She let him kiss her. He was hard to resist.

He nibbled her earlobe. 'We can forget the plans, you know . . . we don't have to do this. We can just keep having fun . . .'

She pulled away from him. Looked him in the eye. 'Have you changed your mind?' She started to fix her bra, tucked her t-shirt into her jeans.

He sighed. 'Nah, you're right. It'll be good. Let's do it.' He kissed her nose then shoved her away gently so he could get out of the cramped cubicle. 'You better go back up first. Don't want to blow it.' He winked, letting his eyes drop down then back up to her face. 'Although . . .'

She slapped him lightly on the arm, then squeezed past him to wash her hands in the tiny sink. Luckily, no one else had come down to the basement. She hurried back up the stairs, a stupid grin making her cheeks ache as she remembered the graffiti.

Not just Monique who's a slut.

Pre-empting the drinks that she knew would be on the table, she stopped at the bar and asked for four shot glasses, then filled them from the water jug. She carried them back outside, where the others were drinking from fresh beers. A slew of shots were lined up in the middle of the table.

'Where the hell have you been?' Ginny said. 'We thought you'd run away.'

Not yet, Cat thought, placing her fake shots down next to the others. 'I knew Tristan would buy something vile, so I got these for myself.'

Ginny wrinkled her nose. 'Oh god, is it that horrible aniseed stuff? Trissy's bought us all tequilas. Did you bump into him in the toilet?'

She shook her head. 'Just vodka.'

'Thought you were slowing down?' Paul said.

Cat ignored him. 'So what are we waiting for?' She picked up the first of the water shots and knocked it back, grimacing in a way she hoped was convincing.

If anyone suspected, they didn't show it.

A few seconds later, Tristan was back. He grabbed one of the drinks. 'Whoohooo!' he shouted, slamming the empty shot glass down on the table. He licked his lips and grinned at her.

Cat raised her second shot in the air, and grinned back.

Three

The bed sagged slightly as Tristan rolled over and pushed himself into Ginny's lower back, an arm snaking over and inside her vest top. She wriggled away towards the edge of the bed. Her head was banging, and she definitely wasn't up for anything that her very insistent husband might have in mind. She closed her eyes tighter. Tristan huffed and rolled back, and a moment later the bed creaked as he swung his legs off the other side and disappeared into the bathroom, muttering something under his breath. Ginny heard the squeak of pipes as he wrestled with the taps. Then the shower started running, and the door slammed shut.

She could imagine what he was doing in there. There was a time when the pair of them would be at it like rabbits at all times of day or night, but, as time went on, she seemed to find herself more distracted, more tired. Less up for it. She couldn't even say why, because it wasn't like she had a high-powered job like his to tire her out.

Ginny gingerly shuffled up the bed, propping herself up on the pillows, and grabbed the pack of paracetamol and the bottle of water she'd thankfully had the foresight to leave by the bed. As she tipped her head back to swallow the pills, the room spun and a wave of nausea swept over her, only subsiding when she managed to suck in a few long, slow breaths.

Right, so mixing the drinks had been *her* idea. The rest of them had protested, saying they needed to be fresh for the morning, and that it was the night *after* the hike they could get properly stuck in and let loose. They'd be well up for it, Paul had said, after all the exertion of the hike. But then Tristan had bought the shots – some supposedly good-quality tequila, and definitely the wrong thing to drink the night before a five-hour hike. He was used to it, though, being much more of a regular drinker than any of them. Ginny *had* been surprised at Cat suddenly going along with it, lining up a row of vodkas for herself. Her sister was such a bore these days, with all her healthy eating and exercise. OK, yes, Ginny did spend a lot of time taking pretty photos of healthy food and she did have a devoted following who loved the way she made it all look so easy. But funnily enough, Insta life wasn't real life, was it?

Ginny spent hours making those dishes, but she often survived on cheese and toast because it wasn't about the eating; for her, it was the charade of the perfect household. It was no wonder she didn't have any time to do the boring little work tasks that Cat tried to get her to do.

Cat was good at her job, but it didn't really interest Ginny particularly, so most of the time she didn't bother to do what her sister asked. It's not like Ginny needed the money, what with Tristan's ridiculous income – and there was her secret little fund squirrelled safely away. Just for her.

Tristan appeared out of the bathroom, towel around his waist and a healthy pink glow in his cheeks. He was smiling. Clearly he'd forgiven her for spoiling his fun earlier.

'Are you not getting up? We're meeting for breakfast in ten minutes. We need to go through the plan for the day.'

'Ten minutes? Why didn't you tell me?' Ginny leapt out of bed and into the bathroom, pausing for a moment with a steadying hand on the towel rail as the room spun again. 'You could've left the shower on for me at least.'

'See you down there,' he called, and the door slammed shut behind him.

She swallowed back her irritation and blasted herself with ice-cold water. It caused her to momentarily stop breathing, but it was the only way to clear her head and get on with this absolute pain of a day. Why had she let Tristan talk her into it? She'd told him point-blank that she had zero interest in hiking in the Alps, and his attempts to suggest that the scenery was worth it and that the fresh air would do her the world of good had just made her laugh. She was not a fresh-air kind of girl. She much preferred driving to walking, and if she managed to even turn up at the yoga studio once a week, it was a miracle. She always made sure to snap a couple of pics for Insta, though. She looked good in her expensive workout gear, even if she only used it to sit around drinking coffee in.

Then he'd changed tack . . . telling her there were world-class massage therapists, and a hot tub that contained some sort of mountain spring water that would make her look younger. Something to do with the minerals, he said. Good shops, too, he'd said. Designer gear you won't get back at home.

That had swung it. She'd even agreed to let Cat take her shopping to get the clothes and equipment they needed for the weekend. It was quite possible that Cat had something else up her sleeve. After their showdown at her thirtieth a few months ago, Ginny had kept expecting some further fallout – but her sister had been uncharacteristically *fun* last night.

Well, whatever. Ginny had given in. The magic mineral spa would at least provide some new fodder for her followers, even if she had to filter the fuck out of herself for the foreseeable, to make it look like the water had indeed performed miracles.

When she made it down to breakfast, half an hour later, the other three were smiling and laughing; a table full of croissants and cheeses and fruit in front of them. Ginny sat down and grabbed the coffee pot, slopping liquid over the sides of the cup and into the saucer as she attempted to pour with a shaking hand.

Cat raised an eyebrow over her glass of orange juice. 'Sore head, love?'

Paul looked at Ginny with sympathy. 'I was a bit rough too, but the food has sorted me out. It's so nice to be able to help yourself to a lovely breakfast buffet again, isn't it? I've really missed all this.'

Cat nodded. 'It's weird though, isn't it? I was so desperate for normal things, then when things started to normalise, it was almost like it never happened. I was lucky with the business, with most people postponing their events rather than cancelling. But it's been non-stop trying to fit everything in lately. I'm so glad of this break.'

'Well, *I'm* just glad all that working-from-home nonsense is over,' Tristan cut in, taking a bite out of a croissant. 'Worst eighteen months of my life, being stuck at home with the missus.' He laughed hard and pinched Ginny's arm, to let her know he was joking.

She gave him a weak smile. 'Wasn't a barrel of laughs for me either.' She picked up a hard roll and ripped it apart, pulling out the soft centre and stuffing it into her mouth. Actually, she'd quite enjoyed the lockdowns. They had given her plenty of time to come up with new ways to grow her followers. It wasn't like she spent much time with Tristan anyway. He spent most of his time in his office at home with the door locked. He slept on his sofa bed in there most nights, too – citing late-night meetings. She had a feeling he was spending more time chatting on Messenger, but he never left his phone unattended for long enough to even attempt to snoop. 'Can we drop the pandemic chat? We're all still here, aren't we?'

Cat looked bemused, and Ginny was surprised yet again at her sister's overly cheery mood. How could she be so damn chirpy at this hour?

'I'm so glad I switched to water when you lot started on the shots,' she said, reading Ginny's mind. 'I felt a bit funny after the beers, actually.'

Typical Cat. Always so bloody sensible. Ginny should've known that Cat wouldn't drink shots. She'd pulled that trick before.

'Forgive *me* for trying to have some fun,' Ginny said, more harshly than she intended. She was pissed off that Cat had made a fool out of her with the fake shots. Not that the men seemed to have noticed or cared. She rubbed her temples. The headache was still lingering, and she felt like she hadn't slept a wink.

Cat flinched. 'Someone got out of the wrong side of the bed.'

Tristan squeezed Ginny's arm. 'Come on, Ginny-Gins. Get yourself sorted, eh? Wait until you see the mountain views . . . this hike is supposed to be spectacular, you know.' He paused. 'And not *too* challenging.' He pulled a map out of his back pocket, unfolded it and smoothed it out across the table, shoving the breakfast things out of the way. 'There's a great halfway point here. This little lodge restaurant has excellent reviews.' He pointed at a brown square on the map that meant nothing to her. Patches of green and grey, and broken brown lines. *How on earth is he going to navigate us like this?*

'Isn't there an app for this? I can't believe you actually bought a *map*.'

He clapped his hands together. 'Well . . . as you know, I agreed to help Cat with the planning, and we thought it might be fun if we did something a bit different. Proper old-school. Map, compass. Not a lot else. No apps . . .'

'No phones,' Cat continued, still smiling. 'Some time for the four of us to reconnect. Properly chat without distraction. It's been so long since we've all been away together. Everyone's lived their lives online for so long, it's going to be amazing to be back to nature, to—'

'Are you both mad?' Ginny stared at them both, then turned to Paul. 'Are you having this? No phones? What if we get lost? What if one of us gets hurt?'

Paul opened his mouth to speak, but Tristan laid a hand on top of Ginny's and gave Paul a small nod, his gesture saying *leave it, I'll deal with it.* 'Take a chill pill, Gins. We're doing it because it'll be fun.' He glances at Cat. 'We didn't expect you to have a full-on panic attack over it.'

Ginny pulled her hand out from under his. 'I just think it sounds a bit irresponsible. Especially for *Cat.*' She picked up a glass of water and took a sip. Her heart was racing, and she was trying hard to regulate her breathing. 'Since when did the two of you get so chummy, anyhow? There's helping to plan and there's being in cahoots . . . what are you both actually up to?'

'Come on, Gins,' Cat said. 'There's no conspiracy. I mentioned the idea to Tristan back at your birthday party and he said he'd like to help. Besides, it's a bit rich calling us irresponsible when you were knocking back the shots too last night.' Cat leaned in closer, lowering her voice. 'Do you need something to calm you down a bit? The hangover is probably making you feel anxious. You've got your pills, haven't you . . . ?'

Despite wanting to kick up more of a fuss, mainly to get out of the whole thing and spend the day admiring the view while she soaked up the healing powers of the outdoor hot tub, Ginny found herself nodding and reaching into her purse. She was glad to have a good private GP at home who knew when she needed the right things to pick her up or calm her down. Valium was exactly what she needed right now.

Cat watched her intently as she popped the pill into her mouth and gulped it down dry. Ginny felt a little uncomfortable under her gaze. It wasn't like her sister to be so interested in her pills. Cat was one of those people who would wait for her head to burst open before she took a paracetamol.

'Want some?'

Cat bit her lip. 'Actually, do you mind? I might not take it now, but it might come in handy later if things get a bit hairy up there.' She laughed.

Ginny frowned as she handed Cat a blister pack with a couple of tablets in it. It had better not get hairy. They'd promised her this was going to be a gentle hike and worth her while. Cat better not be lying to her, in an attempt to humiliate her later. If she tried anything, Ginny would bloody kill her.

Four

Cat was happy to drive. It was only a short trip from the hotel to the starting point of the hike, but Ginny complained for most of it about how irresponsible they were being not taking their phones, and how she was sure it wasn't a good idea for her to go to high altitudes with a headache and dehydration. It was always 'me me me' with her. Had been since they were kids. And yet Ginny still seemed to sail through life getting what she wanted without having to work for it. Cat had started to think recently that she should take a leaf out of her sister's book. Maybe being demanding *did* get you what you wanted in life.

Not today, though. Today, for once, Ginny was being overruled.

The sun was already beating down, so Cat pulled into a parking spot close to a bank of dense pines in an attempt to keep the car cool.

Ginny was still rabbiting on as Cat turned off the engine, but Cat had decided that ignoring her was best for now or the hike wasn't even going to start. She suppressed a sigh as she rubbed her eyes with her knuckles, pressing hard into the sockets.

'It just looks so high,' Ginny whined under her breath as she unclipped her seatbelt.

Tristan jumped out of the car first, shading his eyes with his hand as he looked up at the mountains that surrounded them. 'We're only ascending about a kilometre, Gins.' He uncapped a bottle of water and handed it to her. 'Most of it's a nice, simple climb . . . and the hard bits will be worth it for the stunning views.'

Ginny glared at him and gulped down half of the water. 'I could look at the views from the hot tub—'

Paul snapped, cutting off her whine. 'For god's sake, the hot tub will still be there when we get back.'

Cat took his elbow and steered him around to the back of the car to get their rucksacks out, keeping her voice low and struggling to keep her annoyance in check. She could do without Paul acting up too. 'Someone else have a bit too much last night, did they? Thought you said you were fine?'

'I *am* fine,' Paul hissed. 'I'm just sick of her whining. Last night it was all about her, that stupid story about the mix-up at the hairdressers and how she has to wait weeks for another appointment and how it ruined her week because her roots are showing for her weekend away. I mean, come on. Has she got nothing better to worry about?'

Paul grabbed the bags out of the back of the car and dumped them on the ground. Cat was a little surprised at him being so grumpy. They all knew what Ginny was like, and they all knew that she would be fine once they got going. Although, it was true that she did like to make any drama very Ginny-centric. Cat glanced over to find that Ginny was now out of the car and still looking miserable. Tristan was standing with his hands on his hips, staring over at her and Paul. Had he overheard? He turned away, but not before Cat caught him smirking in Paul's direction.

Ah. So that was it. The constant ribbing last night about how Paul couldn't hack it in the City and was now a kept man had got under his skin, despite his protestations otherwise.

Cat hoped it wasn't going to be one of *those* days. They hadn't even got their rucksacks on their backs and the bickering had started. She had far bigger issues to deal with than hot tubs or Tristan's needling of Paul.

'Right, come on, everyone. This is stupid,' Cat said. 'Ginny – come and get your bag. Tristan – can you show us the route, please? Make sure we all know where we're going . . .'

He pretended to look hurt, before fixing his face into one of his annoying grins. 'What – you don't trust me?'

Cat glared at him, then threw her rucksack over one shoulder and marched across to a large board with a map on it. *Bienvenue à Solalex*, it said. *Tour de l'Argentine*. There were several photographs of the route, showing sheer silver rock faces interspersed with picturesque Alpine meadows.

Ginny appeared beside her. 'What does it say?'

Cat shrugged. 'You know my French is rusty,' she said. It was nothing of the sort, but she didn't want Ginny to know that. She pretended to struggle with the words. 'Welcome to Solalex. The other bit is just the name of the trail. It's a loop around the Argentine mountain. We start and finish here.' Cat peered closer at the smaller font in the legend beneath the map. 'Says it's moderate difficulty.'

Ginny sighed. 'I suppose it *might* be fun. Tristan said there was a nice place to stop for lunch, didn't he?'

'A perfect place.' Cat took her sister's hand and gave it a squeeze. 'And I brought some extra walking poles. I didn't think you'd have any . . .'

Ginny turned to her and laughed. 'Walking poles? Well of course I don't have any walking poles.' She looked down at her feet. 'I don't even have proper boots, but Tristan said these would do.'

Cat looked down at Ginny's designer-brand, perfectly white trainers. Did they actually have a *heel*? She frowned. 'I guess they'll have to. I really wish you'd let me buy you those boots when we bought the shorts and tops . . .'

Ginny picked up her rucksack and took off across the grass, wiggling her hips. 'Those boots were *ugly*, Cat. You should think yourself lucky I'm not in flip-flops.'

Cat shook her head at her, in a 'what can you do?' gesture, like her sister was some errant schoolgirl instead of a thirty-year-old woman. She was never going to grow up.

Paul scrunched up his face. Cat knew he'd never particularly been a fan of her sister. But if it hadn't been for Tristan meeting Ginny on a blind date, and then Tristan asking her if she had any friends to introduce to his workmate, then Paul and Cat would never have met and he'd probably be quite happy somewhere else right now, without Ginny pissing him off. She knew he only put up with Ginny because she was her sister. Cat had often thought that if she'd been just a friend, Paul would've convinced her to dump Ginny years ago.

Ginny stopped by a bench and sat down, taking her phone out of her pocket.

'Oi,' Cat shouted, 'bring your phone back, Gins. We're leaving in a minute and I want to lock them in the glove box.'

Ginny stomped back towards the car and held out the phone. 'I've messaged Lauren to tell her we're going on this stupid hike and if she doesn't hear from me by this evening, to call the police.'

Tristan overheard. 'You've done what? You know what Loopy Lauren's like – she probably bloody will and we'll end up with a rescue squad and a massive fine for wasting police time.'

Ginny laughed. 'I'm joking. I didn't message her. God, can you imagine?'

Cat felt a small flutter of worry in her stomach. Ginny's best friend, Lauren, was twice as flaky as Ginny, and would take massive pleasure in alerting the authorities if she didn't hear back at exactly the specified time. Once, when she and Ginny had been on a weekend in the Cotswolds and realised the gentle walk they'd taken was too long, she'd called the police and asked them to take them back to the hotel because they were worried about heat exhaustion.

'Oh dammit – it won't send.' Ginny held her phone up in the air. 'I can't believe there's no reception here.' She held out her phone to Cat. 'Actually, I don't think she's even around. I think she was flying out to Australia today.' She frowned. 'I wish I'd bloody gone with her.'

Cat took Ginny's phone. Good. Lauren was out of the picture, it seemed. She held out her hand, and Tristan and Paul dutifully handed their phones over, too. She left them all to it for a moment, Ginny starting up some other story that would no doubt infuriate Paul further. He'd been quiet since his earlier outburst and Cat was hoping the fresh air would calm him down.

Cat slid into the passenger seat and opened the glove box, depositing Paul and Ginny's phones inside. She held Tristan's phone in her hand; it was smeared with fingerprints. Twisting around in her seat to make sure the others were all still distracted, she opened his up and scrolled for a moment, marvelling at his lack of security. Then she checked her own phone one final time, tapping out a quick message before sliding both phones in beside the others and locking the small compartment. She lifted the central armrest and dropped the key inside, covering it with a bunch of leaflets, then climbed back out of the car.

'Right, are we all set?' Tristan was standing with his hands on his hips. He had the map around his neck on a lanyard.

Cat's fingers went to her own neck, to the small round silver pendant on a leather cord. It had come on a thin silver chain but she'd thought it would snap. Besides, she liked the leather more. She wasn't really a sparkly jewellery type, but the pendant was also a fitness tracker – she'd got it to replace her usual wrist-worn one.

This one had GPS and measured elevation as well as steps. She turned the pendant over in her fingers for a moment, then slipped it inside her t-shirt to make sure it was safe.

'Ready,' Cat said. She held out a hand, almost took hold of Paul's out of instinct, but then stopped herself. He looked pleased for a moment, before his face fell as she quickly stuffed her hands into her pockets.

'Cat . . . are we going to talk about whatever it is that's bothering you? Are you going to tell me what I'm supposed to have done?'

She forced a smile. 'Sure. Later.'

Paul shrugged, then walked on ahead. She headed over towards Tristan – who took Ginny's elbow, and the four of them headed off towards a gravelly path. Ginny was chattering again, but they'd all zoned her out now. Tristan was pointing off ahead, at something Cat couldn't yet see from her position behind him.

As they reached the peak of the short incline, two men appeared, heading directly for them. They looked a bit older than them, maybe in their mid-forties, and they had the gear and the kind of rugged, weathered faces that suggested they were seasoned hikers. They were both carrying rucksacks with walking poles strapped across the top and, as they drew closer, Cat caught their warm body scents of sweat and pine.

'*Bonjour*,' called the one in the red jacket, which, closer up, she could see was deeply soaked with sweat. The men stopped walking and took in their little group. 'You speak English?'

'Yep, hello,' Cat said, stepping forward alongside Tristan and Ginny. 'We're over from London for the weekend. Lovely day for it.'

The one in the blue t-shirt grimaced. 'Have you done this route before?'

They all shook their heads.

'Hmm. Well, it's a bit tricky today.' Blue T-Shirt nodded towards his companion. 'We've done it many times, but today got a bit hairy.'

'Regulars, are you?' Paul asked. He'd hooked his fingers into the belt-loops on his shorts, and was rocking back and forth on his heels.

Red Jacket nodded. 'Yeah, I suppose we are. We're both from Northampton but we live in Geneva. We work for the WHO.'

'Oh wow,' said Ginny, sidling closer. 'That must've been so exciting with all the crazy pandemic stuff going on? What's the real story about the virus? Was it—'

Tristan cut her off. 'Is there a problem with the route? I looked it up and it seemed to be doable for a bunch of amateurs like us.' He laughed, but the two men didn't laugh back. They looked tense. Stressed. Not like two men who'd just enjoyed hiking a trail they'd done several times before.

'Personally,' Red Jacket said, 'I'd choose a different one if you're not regular hikers. I mean, sure, the views are incredible. But there are huge swathes of the trail hanging loose today, on the trickier parts. You'll be fine on the gravel like this, and through the meadow. But the stepped part up the face is slippery, and there've been a couple of small rock falls overnight, so you really need to be careful.'

'I slipped,' Blue T-Shirt said, turning sideways and lifting his shorts to show a nasty graze. 'I was lucky,' he added, with a wry smile.

Cat adjusted her rucksack on her back; it felt heavier than before. The burden of the hike adding weight all of a sudden. 'Rock falls? Like avalanches? I thought they only happened in the winter?'

Red Jacket looked her up and down, his eyes lingering too long on her tight t-shirt. 'Not anymore. Don't you listen to Greta? Climate change is genuinely causing problems. The permafrost is melting, meaning that rocks are dislodged. We've had a few bad slides lately, down as far as the road.' He gestured down towards the road they'd driven in on. 'The main road was blocked off for a day just last week, while it was cleared.' He shrugged. 'It's lucky no one's been killed yet.'

'There's a lot of work going on,' Blue T-Shirt continued. 'Putting netting up, that sort of thing. But that's for the roads. Up here, it's more of a gamble.'

'Maybe we should choose a different path,' Ginny said, looking at Tristan. 'I'm honestly not sure I'm up for this. You said it was a casual walk – this sounds like a bloody rock-climbing expedition!' The fear was evident in her voice. This wasn't just her usual whine about wanting to spend the day in the hot tub. *Well, tough*, Cat thought. It was about time Ginny moved out of her comfort zone. She'd had life far too easy for far too long.

Tristan pulled the map out of the plastic covering and unfolded it. The hikers gathered around him, closer. Blue T-Shirt ran a finger across the map. 'This is the part that's down today. Someone from the Refuge will probably come and try to clear it later, but you can avoid it by going here . . .' He pointed at another part of the map and Tristan nodded.

'Fine,' Tristan said. 'So just a bit of a detour? The rest is OK?'

The two hikers looked at each other. Red Jacket spoke. 'Technically, yes. But as we said, it all just feels a bit looser today. You know . . .' He looked at Cat again, and she really didn't like the lecherous expression on his face. 'Maybe I can go with you? As a guide? I was only heading back home to go out with some friends, but that can wait . . .'

'I don't think so,' Cat said, fixing him with her gaze. 'We'd prefer to go it alone.'

He ran his tongue over his lips. 'Sure. It was just a thought.'

Blue T-Shirt looked confused for a moment, sensing the change in the atmosphere. He slapped his companion on the back. 'We do need to get back, actually. But look, the sun is heating the rocks now. We had a really early start. It was all still slippery with dew. You'll be fine if you keep to the trail, and avoid that one part I mentioned.' He paused. 'Just be careful, OK?'

'Of course,' said Tristan. 'Careful is my middle name.'

Five

Careful was *not* his middle name. His full name was Tristan Frederick Lytham, and he was certainly not known for being careful. *If* he was careful, then Ginny wouldn't have found that receipt in his jacket pocket for a night at the Berystede Hotel near Ascot, on a date when he'd claimed he'd been two hundred miles away in Manchester at a work conference. If he'd wanted to invent an accurate middle name starting with C then 'cliché' would be one of them, and another option would rhyme with 'hunt'. Not that Ginny would ever say such a word. Not out loud.

When Cat had suggested this weekend away, Ginny's first thought had been to make up an excuse. Any excuse. Because the last thing she wanted was her perfect sister picking up on there being something not quite right between her and Tristan. Ginny was certain that Cat had never liked her husband. So she had been more than a little surprised when he said he'd been helping her sister plan this hike of hers.

Although, thinking about it more, it wasn't the first time Cat had misled her over a relationship. There had been that guy they'd both fancied when their parents had taken them to Spain that time. Cat was fifteen and Ginny thirteen. The boy had liked them both, and Cat had convinced Ginny that he wasn't good enough for either of them, dragging Ginny away from the beach. And then, later, Ginny had gone back to the apartment early and found Cat and the boy in the alleyway outside.

They'd sprung apart as if they'd been electrocuted, and Cat had come up with some bullshit story. Ginny had shrugged it off. It could never have been more than a holiday romance anyway, and she was sure the boy had liked her more. I mean, of course he did – Ginny was much prettier than Cat. She spent far more time making herself look good so that boys would like her, while all Cat did was wash her face with soap and smear on a bit of lip balm.

There's no way the boy could have liked Cat more . . . clearly Cat had done something to persuade him to be with her instead. But that couldn't be the same here, could it? Tristan couldn't possibly be interested in Cat. Was it more likely that Cat had realised that she needed to get on with Tristan for Ginny's sake?

It was typical of Cat to want a weekend like this. She couldn't help but do something rigidly planned out. It came from her job, Ginny supposed. Cat was such a planner, when everyone else would have been happy enough spending a weekend in Brighton, drinking beers from plastic pint glasses on the pebbled beach. It was no surprise to anyone that Cat had become an event planner. She was always planning things as a kid. Mapping out her life. Trying to map out Ginny's too. A lot of the dubious choices Ginny ended up making were purely to prove her sister wrong. Cutting off her nose to spite her face, their grandmother would have said. Even their parents got fed up with Cat's constant planning. God rest their souls. If only they could see her now.

Thankfully, the fresh air seemed to have calmed her raging hangover and she was finding the first part of the hike quite pleasant. Plus, she thought she was looking quite good in her shorts and t-shirt. Cat had insisted she got proper walking gear and had dragged her into one of those horrendous outdoors shops full of horrible fleeces and ugly shoes; the latter she had flatly refused to try on.

Cat and Ginny had bought almost-identical outfits – navy shorts with side pockets and pale-blue t-shirts. Ginny had done it on purpose, seeing what her sister had hooked over her arm and taken to the changing room – and she'd been slightly miffed when Cat hadn't said anything. Normally she hated it when Ginny copied her. Clearly Paul had got the same memo, as he was wearing something very similar to Tristan's beige-shorts-and-black-tee combo. From the back they looked very similar. In fact, the casual observer might think the group was two sets of twins.

She giggled to herself at that, trying to get rid of the dodgy sexual connotations it had conjured up. She pulled her necklace out of her t-shirt, admiring the sparkling green stone. She'd found it in a box when the inheritance had come through, just after her thirtieth birthday four months ago. Wearing it was her little treat to herself. The first of many. Cat hadn't noticed it yet, despite it being a ridiculous item to wear on a hike – but Ginny was scared it might fall off, so keeping it inside her t-shirt was the best plan. She was planning to casually flip it out later, when they were sitting down. See what Cat had to say about it then.

Anyway, she was feeling a lot better now. After her initial nervous chatter, she'd found herself quietening down and the four of them walked in silence, at peace with their surroundings. She'd already forgotten about the two hikers from the WHO and their portentous warnings of rock falls. In fact, the only thing on her mind was the start of a grumbling stomach. Breakfast was hours ago, and she'd only managed coffee and half a dry roll.

'Hey,' Ginny called, picking up her pace a bit to catch up with Tristan, who was striding ahead. 'How soon until we stop for lunch?'

Tristan took her hand and pulled her alongside him. 'Jesus, Ginny. We've barely started. Another hour. Maybe two?'

'There's some snacks in the bags, Gin. Hang on.'

She heard Cat's footsteps stop behind her, the sounds of draw-cords being slackened, Velcro unstuck. She turned around to find her sister brandishing a bruised banana in one hand and a bag of sugary sweets in the other. 'Will these do you?'

Ginny took the sweets. 'Don't suppose you've got anything nice to drink other than water in there.' She nodded her head towards Cat's rucksack.

Cat laughed. 'Ginny, you're carrying the drinks. Have you forgotten you've got a bag?'

Ginny frowned. She actually had forgotten. Tristan had handed it to her and slid the straps over her shoulders and she hadn't even thought to ask what was in it. She hadn't considered that they would actually need much for a few hours up a mountain. Just as well she had others here who were better at organising things than she was.

She shoved some chewy sweets in her mouth and undid her own rucksack, taking out a can of Coke. She flipped the ring-pull and drank greedily, before carrying on walking. She heard Cat muttering something behind her. Then Paul stopped, cupping an ear with a hand. He had a huge grin on his face.

'Do you hear that?'

They all stopped and listened. It sounded like . . . bells. Tinkling gently in the breeze.

'What the . . . ?' Ginny started.

Paul walked quickly up a short incline and disappeared around a bend. 'Oh wow,' he shouted. 'Hurry up, you guys – this is so cool!'

They all picked up the pace and hurried after him. Ginny got there first, energised from the sugar, and burst into laughter as soon as she saw the source of Paul's wonder.

A herd of creamy-brown and white-patched cows were ambling close to the wire fencing. They were bedecked with horns and cowbells hanging from their necks, jangling as they walked, making that glorious sound.

'Oh my god,' Ginny said, clapping her hands with glee. 'Cat – what was it you said in the bar last night about Heidi? This is amazing. I didn't think cowbells were an actual thing.'

Tristan laughed, squeezing her shoulder. 'How else do you think the herders can keep track of them all, Gins?' He waved an arm, indicating the expanse of the meadow. 'Look how far they've got to roam.'

Ginny shrugged. 'How am I supposed to know things like that? Anyway. This is so cool. Wait a sec until I take a photo . . .' She pulled her rucksack off her back and starting rummaging in the pockets. 'Where's my phone, I . . . Oh.' Her face fell as she remembered. 'You didn't think of that when you took away our tech, did you, *Catatonia*?'

Her sister looked annoyed for a second. Ginny knew how much she hated that nickname. She'd started calling her it in primary school – suggesting that Cat was so boring that she sent people into a stupor – and it had stuck, despite all Cat's attempts to change it. She'd even gone through a phase of demanding that people call her by her full name – Catherine – to try and shake off the annoying moniker, but that just made Ginny more insistent on using it at every opportunity. She wasn't even sure why she was using it today, but Cat's smugness had been pissing her off since they got off the plane.

Cat gave her a sarcastic, tight-lipped smile, then pulled a small box out of her pocket. She held it up and directed it at Ginny, then clicked a button on the top. 'Perfect picture of all the *cows*, Ginny. I'll make sure to send you a copy.'

Ginny started laughing. 'Is that an instant camera? I haven't seen one of those in years. Didn't even know there were still places to get photos developed.'

Cat put a hand on a hip, then snapped another photo. 'Like I said, *Sweet Virginial*. I've planned everything out. You don't need to worry your pretty little head. Just keep putting one foot in front of another and we'll make it to the end.' Cat spun around and started walking again. Paul shrugged at Ginny, then followed after his wife.

Ginny watched Cat as she walked away. God, she was so pathetic. The Sweet Virginial nickname had never stuck, even at school. So like her to dredge it up now to try and make it work.

Tristan was waiting for Ginny, an amused half-smile on his face. 'You two,' he said, pulling her by the straps of her rucksack and leaning in to kiss her on the forehead. 'Give it a rest, eh?' He pulled back. Smirked. '*Sweet Virginial*, though. I *do* like that.'

Ginny glared at him, then kicked a stone and it shot across the path and into the grass. Bloody Perfect Cat and her stupid plans. She decided to keep away from her sister for a while, before she said something she might regret.

Six

Sunday Morning

Captain Thierry Pigalle stares down at the couple who are slumped on the steps outside his police station. He is not even meant to be working today, and was looking forward to a long, leisurely lunch with his wife – who queued for thirty minutes yesterday afternoon in order to pick up the best cut of beef from the extremely busy *boucherie* in Aigle. He contributed to the planned meal by selecting one of the best reds from their cellar – a vintage Château Tour Massac Margaux chosen from the vineyard on their summer holiday in 2012.

He stares at the couple – the woman with her tangled hair and dirty face, the man with wounds that are hopefully not as bad as they look, because they look bad. Very bad. He stares at them, and he blows out a long, slow puff of air through his nostrils – and he knows that he will not be getting away from here at 12.30 for his lunch, and likely he will be here right through the usual closure period, and will remain here past the usual end-of-business time of 4.30 p.m.

Merde!

Shit indeed. These damn tourists who refuse to stay on the marked paths and think they know how to navigate these mountains. His lieutenant was supposed to be here today, covering the usual mind-numbingly boring Sunday shift, where usually not one person crosses the threshold – unless they've accidentally turned right instead of left into the shop next door that shares their main entrance. There are not supposed to be two injured, disorientated tourists making the entrance to his workplace look untidy.

'*Bonjour*,' he says. Then, tentatively, '*Ça va?*'

They are clearly not fine, but he's at a loss for words.

The woman speaks. 'We . . . we got lost on the mountain. The . . . *Argentine*? Our friends . . .' She pauses and turns to her male companion, who is staring back at Thierry with glassy-eyed confusion, then looks away.

Thierry feels a prickle of unease. This is going to be considerably worse than he first thought – and his first thought was bad enough. He glances around, expecting to see another couple slumped elsewhere, but there is no one. 'Where are your friends, madame?'

She starts to cry, her face falling to her chest as huge, wracking sobs cause her shoulders to shake. The man tries to put an arm around her, but she flinches and his arm falls back down by his side. He groans. Broken ribs, perhaps. *At best*, Thierry thinks.

Thierry's knees crack like starting pistols as he crouches down to hold himself at eye level. 'Madame?' Sympathetic now. Thoughts of his leisurely day long gone. 'Where are your friends?'

She shakes her head. Rubs a hand across her face, tears smearing with snot and dirt. 'I don't know,' she says. Stares back at him, finally meets his eye. 'I don't know.'

Seven

Cat realised she needed to dial it back a bit. She'd been doing well, not letting Ginny's foibles get to her, but she was getting fed up with her sister's pathetic teenager act. Paul had been quiet since they'd stopped to take photos of the cows, his enthusiasm for the day out clearly waning, and they'd barely even started. Cat had to keep reminding herself that this was meant to be a fun weekend, not a slog. They were meant to be enjoying themselves. There would be plenty of time for misery later on, if all went to plan.

She picked up her pace and caught up with Tristan, who'd been marching ahead but had recently slowed. They'd been on a seemingly endless path for a while now, and although the views of the mountains in the distance were nice to look at, Cat had expected them to have reached the other side of this meadow, heading towards the gentle descent into the valley for lunch. This was how Tristan had explained it all at breakfast, but it was taking longer than she'd expected.

'Hey,' she said, putting a hand on Tristan's arm. 'Are we close to the restaurant yet? Only, I'm starting to get hungry, and it doesn't seem to be anywhere in sight . . .'

Tristan huffed and pulled away, making a sudden change of direction. 'Guys, I think this way will be quicker. If we can get over that crest over there, we'll make it over and down into the valley in half the time.' He left the path and started walking across the grass. There was a plain, then a dip where Cat could just make out what looked like a small lake, then a steep rise on the other side. Cat wasn't sure that this was the right way, but she trusted that Tristan knew what he was doing.

Paul caught up. 'Are you sure about this, T? Those hikers told us not to veer off the path.'

Tristan stopped and turned. His face was slightly pink from exertion and the harsh, beating sun. 'They were overreacting. It's fine. Come on.' He started walking again. 'I'm hungry too. And I'd kill for an ice-cold pint. Come on.'

Ginny jogged past Cat and Paul, catching up with Tristan and grabbing his hand. She started chattering away, but Cat couldn't quite make out what she was saying. For someone who'd had no energy earlier, she seemed to have perked up.

Paul, on the other hand, was completely flagging. 'This is taking far too long,' he said, pulling Cat back by the elbow and keeping his voice low. 'We set off at ten. This is meant to be a five-hour hike. We're three hours in and we haven't even had lunch! Why the hell did you go along with his madcap plan of using a bloody paper map, for god's sake? We're clearly lost, and he hasn't a clue how to get us back on track.'

Cat shrugged him off. 'Calm down, will you? He knows what he's doing.' She was trying to sound confident, but she wasn't so sure anymore. Tristan seemed tense. Why *had* he chosen to ignore the hikers' advice about not veering off the safe paths?

Paul shook his head. 'He clearly doesn't. But he'll continue to barge on regardless. This is what he *does*. Don't you remember the last time we went away? The weekend that he and Ginny organised that was an absolute bloody disaster?'

Cat remembered it well, but had tried to put it out of her mind. They'd hired a boat and sailed through the Norfolk Broads. Tristan had insisted on being the captain, getting pissy when anyone else tried to have a go. Ginny had done all the shopping, except she'd ordered a load of ridiculous ingredients – truffle butter, some exotic vegetables that no one knew how to cook. And far too much booze. They'd all been starving and blind drunk and it was a wonder none of them had ended up drowning. Both she and Paul had vowed never to travel with Tristan and Ginny again – but then the pandemic had happened, and all that unfolded afterwards.

And this weekend was important. To Cat, if no one else. Once things had returned to normal – or the new normal, at least – Cat's life had spiralled out of control in ways she'd never imagined. Paul's work nightmare, then Ginny's thirtieth, and then, of course, the affair. That was quite unexpected and a lot more fun than she'd imagined. Until the revelation about the money that Ginny had done her out of.

Cat had spent the whole of the pandemic worried about her business, wondering how life would be afterwards – and then as soon as the world opened up, Paul had shown his true colours with his colleague and Ginny had simply done what she'd always done. Thought about herself. Cat was sick of people thinking they could walk all over her. She was sick of being the nice, sensible one.

Hence the showdown that she had been planning ever since.

'It'll be fine,' Cat said, shaking away her thoughts and trying to keep up the pretence that she was having fun. 'Once we all get fed and watered, we'll laugh about this bit, and how Tristan clearly can't read a map, and . . .'

She let the sentence trail off. Paul had already marched off ahead towards the others, leaving her on her own. What was his problem today? As far as he knew, the whole point of this trip was for him and Cat to take their minds off things back home. That's what she'd told him it was for. But clearly Paul wasn't able to do that. She knew he was frustrated about his work situation. The only person he could talk to about it was her, and she'd purposely avoided talking about it since she uncovered the truth. It was exhausting. Being here with Ginny was supposed to be fun, but she was nothing but a constant annoyance, like a buzzing fly trapped behind a window.

'Guys, wait up, will you?' Her dawdling had left her far behind them now, and she was finding it harder here to walk faster, with the uneven grassy mounds and the larger loose stones that lay hidden in the brush. How had they all gotten so far ahead of her?

She started power-walking, using her arms to propel herself faster. Her breath had quickened, and she was starting to feel a bit light-headed. 'Ginny!' She raised her voice as much as she could while she was struggling to catch her breath. It came as a surprise that she felt like this. She considered herself fit. Fitter than Ginny, certainly. But then Ginny hadn't been left behind and forced to practically run across the hillside. Plus, Ginny was fuelled by sugar.

Cat finally caught up. 'Gins . . .' She was panting, hands on her thighs as she leaned forward, trying to slow her breathing. 'Ginny . . . can I have some of those sweets? And a drink of something. I'm struggling here.'

'Oh, damn. I finished the sweets.' Ginny dropped her rucksack on the ground. 'There's still drinks though, hang on.' She rummaged in the bag and pulled out a can of drink. 'Only Diet Coke left. That do you?'

Cat grabbed it and popped it open, then drank greedily. The liquid burned down her throat. She paused for a second, then drank more. They were all staring at her. 'I could've done with something sugary.'

Ginny shrugged. 'Sorry. I didn't think you did sugar these days.'

Cat had got her breath back, but she was shaking now – a mixture of hunger and rage. 'The sweets were meant as an energy boost for the hike.' She glared at her sister. 'For all of us.'

Ginny said nothing, but she had the grace to look mildly chastened. 'Don't worry – it's all downhill from here. Look!' She took Cat's arm, started dragging her towards the others. Cat let herself be led, but inside she was fizzing with rage at her sister's selfishness. But now was not the time to be angry.

Ginny kept hold of her as they made it to the crest of the hill. 'Look,' she said, pointing to a small wooden chalet, far down in the valley. 'There's the restaurant.'

Cat stood on the ridge and looked down. The descent was steep, the path looking overgrown and rugged. Not a well-trodden path. Not a path for a bunch of day-walkers. Especially after what the hikers had said. She looked up at the mountains that loomed large in front and all around. Then back down to the valley. She felt a rush of dizziness taking hold again. Bright lights flashed in front of her eyes, then faded away again. A kestrel swooped down as if from nowhere, hanging gently over the open mouth of the valley.

Waiting.

She took a step back, feeling her legs start to wobble. Her body felt small all of a sudden. Insignificant. Then a feeling of a weight pressing down on her, behind her, on top of her . . . maybe they should turn back. Maybe she should forget about what she had planned for later. Was bringing everything out into the open really going to solve her problems?

She felt her foot catch on a rock, her ankle twist – and then she was falling. *No*, she thought, pinwheeling her arms, trying to lean back. Trying to get herself together. Stop herself falling. *No, this is not happening. No . . .*

Eight

Ginny grabbed Cat by the shoulders and yanked her back to safety. The momentum threw them both down hard, Ginny falling backwards on to the grass and pulling Cat down on top of herself.

'Oof. Jesus, Cat,' she managed, as she wriggled herself out from underneath. She rolled over on to her knees and pulled Cat up into a sitting position, cupped her chin with one hand. 'What the hell happened there? I thought you were a goner.' Her mind jolted back to the precarious drive up the winding mountain roads, where Tristan's Formula One-style corners had scared the life out of her. Now this. Such a near miss. Her heart was thumping in her chest, but Cat still seemed to be away with the fairies. What if Ginny hadn't managed to grab her? It didn't bear thinking about.

'Cat? What the—' Paul thundered over the lumpen grass and crouched down next to his wife. He turned to Ginny, who had moved away a bit, trying to give her some space. 'What happened?'

Ginny shook her head. A wave of nausea had hit her now. Her body reacting to the shock of what almost was. As much as her sister was a pain in the arse, she didn't want her falling off the edge of a mountain.

Cat was staring ahead, glassy-eyed. Her body was shaking gently. She opened her mouth to speak, but no words came out. She blinked, then started to cry. Tristan was crouching down beside them all too, taking things out of his rucksack.

'Here, take this.' He ripped open a small foil sachet and handed it to Cat. 'It's an energy gel. I use them when I go running sometimes. I threw a few in the bag, just in case.'

Ginny frowned. He hadn't offered any of those to *her* when she'd been struggling earlier. Hadn't even mentioned he had them when Cat asked about the sweets.

'Nice of you to remember.' Her voice was curt. Her momentary concern for her sister was gone now that she was clearly OK and Tristan was fussing over her.

Tristan ignored Ginny. He was still leaning in close to Cat, his hand over hers, holding the sachet to her mouth, squeezing it in. Paul sat on the other side of Cat. He tried to put his arm around her, but she shoved him away.

Interesting.

Ginny felt like she was surplus to requirements. As usual. She stood up and started to stretch out her arms, throwing them wide and leaning back. 'I took a bit of a hit there, *Catastrophe*. You knocked the wind right out of me.'

Tristan looked up. 'You seem fine now.'

'I think Cat's fine now too,' Paul said. 'Can you check the map again? See how long it'll take us to get down there? Maybe we can get someone there to give us a lift back to the car park. It's totally normal to hitch in the mountains. I think we've had enough for the day, don't you?'

'You should've used an app, Trissy,' Ginny said. She'd found another packet of sweets, hidden at the bottom of her bag. She took a couple, then handed the bag down to Paul.

'Jesus. I told you, I know what I'm doing,' Tristan said. He grabbed a couple of sweets from the bag that Paul was offering. 'The apps are no good for this kind of thing anyway. Didn't you read that article about Ben Nevis? Idiots using Google Maps being directed to walk off a cliff. Like those Uber drivers who can't read road signs, and drive you in circles because the app said so. Technology is making people stupid, guys. You need to stop relying on it all the time. I've got this, OK?'

Cat finally spoke. 'Can you maybe just check again, Tristan? I don't know why I'm feeling so weird, but I could really do with a proper rest.' She paused. Popped one of Ginny's sweets in her mouth. 'I think we all could.'

Ginny watched her sister as she chewed the sweet. She did seem fine. Maybe she hadn't been about to fall after all. Maybe this was just her way of getting some attention. Cat always did have to make more of an effort than Ginny ever did.

'Fine.' Tristan pulled the map out of the plastic wallet on his lanyard and opened it out again.

Ginny was watching him. Taking in his facial expressions. Tristan was a decent liar, most of the time. But as that receipt had proved, he was clumsy. And in these situations, his face gave him away.

He frowned, tracing a finger down the map, then glancing down at the supposed route into the valley from where they sat now. Then he was back on the map. And his angry-impatient face switched to a possibly-made-an-error face. She knew it well, and she smiled to herself anticipating how he was going to get himself out of this. One thing that Tristan really, really hated was being wrong – and what he hated even more was having to admit it.

'O . . . K . . .' he said, at last. 'Slight change of plan, I think.' He looked up, briefly catching Ginny's eye, then looking back down again when he registered her smirk. 'This descent looks pretty hardcore and I'm not sure we're quite tooled up for it.' He pointed at Ginny's trainers. 'Those things, for a start, will not make it down this way.'

'You told me they were *fine*. Now you're saying it's my fault we can't go down this way? How about if you hadn't brought us the wrong way in the first place, and then maybe Cat wouldn't have nearly died, and—'

Tristan stood, his nostrils flaring. 'Shut up, Ginny. You didn't want to come in the first place, did you? You're loving this. I made a mistake, OK? Are you happy with that?'

'No, I'm not happy. I'm bloody starving.' What the hell was he playing at?

'OK, OK. Let's just sort this, shall we?' Paul stood up and walked over to Tristan. 'Can I see the map? Maybe I can help?'

Tristan looked uncertain for a moment, still desperately battling to keep control. But in the end, he relented. 'We need to head back up the way we just came, past the lake. That's where we veered off track. Then we round that small peak, and we'll be on the proper path again.' He shrugged. 'Then it's just a winding route down to the Refuge. I'm thinking less than an hour—'

'Less than an hour? How many hours are we already out by, Tristan? I thought we were meant to be back at the hotel drinking champagne in the hot tub by four. It's three now, and we're—'

'Ginny, will you shut the hell up about the damn hot tub? We're on an adventure now. Deal with it.'

Ginny raised an eyebrow at Paul's outburst. She was about to answer back, but decided she quite liked seeing Paul wound up like this. It was exciting. Maybe it *was* an adventure. She was regretting being childish about the trainers though. Of course she'd known that they weren't really suitable. She'd gotten away with it so far, but from what Tristan had said at breakfast, there were a few trickier parts towards the end. Hopefully she'd be fine.

Paul pulled Cat to her feet. She looked a bit brighter since having the energy gel and a few sweets. Less shaky, but still a bit pale. *Oh shit*, Ginny thought, *I hope she hasn't got a bug or something.* She could do without that getting spread between the four of them. She had a new set of recipes to start on Monday and a huge Waitrose delivery arriving. Last thing she wanted was to be feeling ill.

The four of them made it back the way they'd come, then found the turn where Tristan had led them a merry dance. He was right, it was plain sailing after that, if a bit sore on the quads as they began their long, steep descent. Ginny stayed at the back, happy not to have to talk to anyone for a while. Tristan took pole position, his control regained. Ginny watched Paul and Cat as they followed close behind him. They were talking too quietly for her to hear, but they were engrossed in conversation about something. Paul occasionally took hold of Cat's elbow, making a big show of helping her – although she seemed much better now and frequently shrugged him off, like she didn't want him touching her at all.

Ginny recalled her earlier doubts about Cat's near miss, but she pushed them away. Cat had always been more subtle when she wanted attention. She wasn't one for theatrics. That was Ginny's department, and she was good at it. In fact, she had a nice little show planned for later, well rehearsed and ready to go live. Even Cat being ill wasn't going to spoil it. There was something she intended to say, and she was looking forward to the reaction.

By the time they reached the restaurant, Ginny was humming a little tune. She wasn't sure why, but Survivor's 'Eye of the Tiger' had popped into her head and was setting the scene very nicely indeed.

Nine

Even though it had been in her line of sight as they descended, seeing the restaurant up close was like discovering an oasis in the desert. Cat stopped in front of the wooden building and took a deep breath, letting it out slowly. The relief was palpable. She looked down at her hands. They'd stopped shaking, but she knew she needed something to eat and drink, and a proper rest before they carried on. She had no idea why she'd suddenly felt so strange up the mountain, but she was thankful for Ginny's quick action. Maybe she wasn't so useless after all. Cat vowed to try and be less hard on her – at least for the rest of the day. She wanted to go with the flow, be more like her sister, but there was a knot in her stomach today that she couldn't quite shift. She tried to put herself in Ginny's shoes – think about how she would react if she was facing the issues that Cat was right now – and she knew that Ginny would be ruthless. Despite her sister's ditzy little games, when she was unhappy about something, she made sure that everyone knew about it.

Cat followed the others inside. The Refuge de Solalex was a typical Alpine chalet. Two peaked buildings with a cluster of wooden benches and tables outside, some topped with umbrellas.

In the background, the majestic mountains. Picture-postcard stuff. Despite their journey so far, it was worth it for this. She hoped the food was good – but the way she felt right now, she'd probably eat the leather from an old shoe.

They took a table in the corner, by a window. Dark, shabby-chic tables and stools. The wooden walls of the chalet were adorned with a high shelf filled with copper pots; the space below was decorated with old-fashioned snowshoes hung on the walls, amidst some cheerful paintings of people drinking at tables just like the one where the rest of her group sat. The menu was written on a small blackboard on a stand. Ginny was holding it up, frowning as she read. No doubt being picky about what was on there.

Cat sat down on the stool next to Paul. He was reading his table mat, which contained drawings and historical information, in English and in French. She glanced around the room then towards the small bar area, where a few rugged-looking men sat on high stools, laughing with the bar staff. The place wasn't busy – probably because it was well past lunchtime – and the waiters were taking their time to clear tables and chat with some of the customers. Thankfully there was already a carafe of water and four glasses waiting for them. Cat poured herself a drink.

Tristan stood up. 'I'll go to the bar.'

Cat attempted to wave him back down. 'It'll be table service. They'll be here in a second.' She picked up the menu from where Ginny had sat it down. 'What are we all having?' She took a long drink of her water, then refilled her glass.

Tristan ignored her and walked across to the bar.

'What's *tartiflette*?' Ginny asked. 'Is it a quiche? Says it comes with *salade verte* – which even I can work out is green salad . . .'

'It's a sort of creamy potato dish, with bacon and cheese. You'll like it, Gins. Bit warm for summer, but perfect to replenish us. I think I might have that.'

'What else is there?' Paul hadn't looked at the board. He preferred Cat telling him what there was, because she knew what he liked. She used to think this was quite sweet, but now realised it was more to do with his weakness and indifference. Traits that had only come to light very recently, and neither of which were appealing.

She held back a sigh. 'There's a steak sandwich with fries – when it says *sandwich*, it'll be a chunk of baguette of course. Um, a local sausage with fries . . . and some sort of fish stew. Plus chef's salad, which I think usually has cubes of cheese and ham in it. That's the most summery thing on the menu, I think.'

Tristan appeared back at the table, a grinning waitress in his wake. Cat had to hand it to him, despite his often acerbic nature, he always managed to charm the ladies. He had the looks. Messy black hair, athletic body. Strong, sexy arms. She could see what Ginny saw in him. She used to think he was a complete prick, but she'd seen another side to him lately. He'd been the right choice of person to help her organise this trip, and he definitely enjoyed spending time with her. More than he enjoyed spending time with his wife – which was a bit of an issue. She wondered if she was just the latest in a long line of his little 'obsessions'.

'*Bonjour!* What would you like?'

Cat ordered for herself, Ginny and Paul. Then looked across at Tristan. He set the blackboard back on the table. 'I'll have the *tartiflette*, too. And we need four large beers.' He grinned at the waitress. '*Merci beaucoup.*'

Ginny scoffed as the waitress hurried away with their order. 'Listen to you, fancy-pants. "Thank you very much!" She's not going to shag you, you know.'

Tristan rolled his eyes and took a sip of the water that Cat had poured. 'How you feeling, Cat?' He leaned over to the side and undid his boots, sliding his feet out then shoving his boots under the table. There was a slight waft of sweat, then it was gone.

Cat took another drink. 'A lot better now. I'll be better still after I get some food. I should've eaten more at breakfast. Or brought some more snacks—'

Paul picked up a glass. 'To be fair, we thought we'd be having lunch about three hours ago—'

'To be fair,' Tristan cut in, 'some of us didn't exactly do much to help with the planning of this trip, and if everyone hadn't been walking at snail's pace, we would've been here ages ago.'

'Except you got us lost, Trissy, didn't you?' Ginny laughed, just as the waitress arrived, depositing the beers and a basket of bread on the table. She looked at them, bemused, then hurried off again.

Ginny looked down at her placemat, tracing a finger around the map, and Cat caught the look that Tristan gave her when she wasn't looking. There was pure venom in there, and it made Cat's stomach somersault. Then Tristan turned to her and winked. He picked up his beer and downed half of it, before slamming it down on the table. '*Salut!*' The cutlery rattled, and Cat noticed a couple of the men from the bar eyeing them with interest.

'We're here now,' Cat said. 'I'm sure Tristan had the best intentions when he led us down that path.' She picked up a piece of bread and gnawed the hard crust. 'Right, so do we know the rest of the route? How long will it take us to get back?'

Tristan took another drink of his beer before replying. 'It looked like a decent shortcut. We don't want to be scrabbling around this mountain all bloody day, do we? Anyway, we're back on track now. You can all stop stressing.'

'I thought we were going to try and get a lift back down to the car park?' Paul said. 'You were in a bad way earlier, Cat. I think we should call it quits and enjoy our evening back in the village.'

'Quits? You're good at that, Pauly. Better at quitting than you were at your job, that's for sure.'

Tristan's voice was like ice. Cat's stomach did another loop-the-loop. Why was he being so antagonistic? He needed to keep it together, like she was trying her best to do. 'Tristan—' she started.

Paul cut her off. 'For god's sake, Tristan. Give it a rest, will you? Why do you care so much that I left? Plenty more filthy lucre for you now that the team is one man down, eh? I'm perfectly happy with my decision . . .' He let his sentence trail off. The waitress was standing by the table, three steaming dishes on a tray.

'*Tartiflette?*'

Cat pointed to her place, then Tristan's opposite, and Ginny's next to his. She gave the waitress a 'sorry about them' smile. But she felt anger bubbling hard in her chest. This wasn't meant to happen. They were all supposed to be having a good time. She was going to have to pull Tristan aside and rein him in a bit before he ruined the whole thing.

'Steak sandwich will be here in one minute.' The waitress scurried off again, and Cat could hear her mutter something under her breath about annoying tourists, and some swear words that Cat remembered from her time in France. The French didn't have many swear words, but depending on the inflection, one particular word could be used in a variety of ways. She felt like swearing herself. Tristan's needling was becoming physically painful.

She dipped her bread into the sauce in her dish, swirling it around, then blew on it before she took a bite. She recalled from past experience that the sauce had a tendency to be radioactive, and she didn't fancy burning the roof of her mouth. She hadn't warned the others, though, and a moment later, Tristan was cursing under his breath and downing more of his beer. She tried not to smirk at him and instead side-eyed Paul, and saw that he'd noticed too. He looked pleased. This was good. Best for Paul to believe that she was still on his side, and it stopped Tristan upsetting everyone for a minute.

The waitress reappeared and placed the steak sandwich down in front of Paul, checked if they needed more beers – which, of course, they did – then left them to it.

'*Merci bien*,' Cat said, automatically. She scooped up a forkful of potato.

Ginny looked up. 'What's the difference between thanks with a *bien* and thanks with a *beaucoup*? I don't remember that from school.'

Cat shrugged. 'The first is less formal, but they're kind of interchangeable. To be honest I hadn't heard the *bien* version until I lived in France.'

'Oh yes, of course you lived in France. What was that though, ten years ago? More?'

'Ten, yes. I was twenty-two. My final year at uni. I thought about trying to get a job there for a while, do you remember?'

'I do remember. I also remember some of the stories you told me from your year there, when you weren't such a square.' Ginny's eyes flashed with amusement and Cat felt the knot in her stomach pull tighter. There were many stories. And she really didn't want them being told today.

'I remember that bloke you were into . . .' She looked around at Paul and Tristan, making sure she had their full attention. 'We called him French Frank. You know, like the old currency?' She laughed hard at her own joke. Classic Ginny that she felt the need to explain it too.

Tristan laughed loudly. 'Did you come up with that one all by yourself, Gins? Bit intellectual for you.'

Ginny's cheeks went red, and she crossed her arms, clearly annoyed at her big moment being ridiculed. A smattering of laughter wafted over to them from the direction of the bar, and Cat turned to look. The two men there were huddled together, looking at something on a phone.

'Frawwnk,' Ginny continued, trying to get everyone's attention again. 'Ee was very sexy, *non*?' She giggled. 'Did you ever show me a pic, Catkins? I don't think you did . . . Thinking back, I've only got your word for it that he was sexy. But considering what you did, I'm going to give you the benefit of the doubt. Unless, of course, you were so blind drunk you couldn't tell what he looked like.' She giggled again.

Cat dropped her fork into her half-eaten lunch with a clatter. 'Shut up, Ginny.'

'Oooh,' Tristan said. 'This sounds juicy.'

Even Paul was intrigued. 'Indeed. What exactly did you do, Cat? Something naughty by the sound of it.'

'It was a long time ago.' She really didn't want Ginny saying any more about it. It was long ago, and Ginny didn't even know the full story. She only knew the bits Cat had told her. Cat hadn't told her sister that Frank had been her tutor. Her very *married* tutor. And she certainly wasn't going to bring that up now. It had been a brief, intense fling. Too intense. And she'd broken it off before anyone got hurt, although she knew that he had ended up splitting with his wife anyway, then gone off to teach in Asia.

Cat pushed her stool back, the wooden legs shrieking across the floor. 'I'm going to the toilet.'

Ten

He watched them as they entered the restaurant. He was facing the other direction, but he could see everything from where he was sitting, via the mirror behind the bar.

Best seat in the house.

He liked to watch. And watching those who had no idea that they were being observed was the best part of all.

There were two blondes. He'd always liked blondes. But although the two of them were similar – same generic shorts and t-shirts in the same boring colours, same hairstyles, similar features – it was the one who was holding court that he liked the most.

She was talking them through the menu, and the others were hanging on to her every word; trusting that she knew what she was talking about. He liked that level of self-assuredness in a woman. He liked the way her mouth moved as she spoke. He liked her lips; her wide, expressive mouth. Her bright, intelligent eyes.

He pretended to be interested in his companion's conversation, but he was only half listening. He was mostly thinking up ways of how he could initiate a conversation with the better of the blondes.

He didn't have to wait long.

He heard the screech of her stool against the floor as she stood up from the table and headed towards the toilet.

His companion was dull, like most of the people in this bar. He'd spent a month in the area now, hiking the trails, helping out with some of the forestry clearances. It'd been a change from his usual way of life but it wasn't something he intended to do for much longer. It had already served its purpose. He felt like every day he'd spent here had been building towards this moment.

He was looking at his companion's phone, some pathetic video on YouTube that he had to pretend to find funny, when he sensed her behind him. He looked in the mirror again, and there she was.

He turned to her and smiled.

She gave him a half-smile back. Barely there, but enough. Like she was nervous. But that was alright.

She had a beautiful smile. A beautiful face. A beautiful body.

She was perfect.

Eleven

Saturday Afternoon

She left them laughing at the table and locked herself in the single cubicle – her mind going back to the night before, to the toilet in the bar, pushing Tristan away. What would Ginny think if she knew about that?

No doubt Ginny was already spilling the beans about Cat's experiences in France in her absence. But Cat doubted that Ginny's half a story would really interest the others that much. Ginny was shit at anecdotes, even if they were her own – so a second-hand one with the vital details missing would have no impact whatsoever. Anyway, it had happened a long time ago. When she was a different person. Before her sister's inadequacies got Cat sidelined from her own family. Her parents having to spend their time coaching Ginny – who'd failed her exams – into the next phase of her life. *Poor Virginia*, they'd said. *She never had your brains, Catherine.*

More like she did, but she chose not to use them. Ginny had always wanted to be looked after. Saw herself as a princess, destined never to lift a finger except to admire her perfect manicure.

And she'd got away with it for years, until their parents had died, crashing into a bridge at the bottom of the winding, single-track lane that led to their house – and nothing had been the same again. Cat hadn't found out until much later that the reason they weren't paying attention to the road was because they were distressed after learning that Ginny had been lying to them.

Ginny had spent several years convincing their parents that Cat didn't care about them, didn't need them, didn't want anything to do with them. And all the while Cat had felt like she was being frozen out . . . because instead of asking Cat, they had believed all that Ginny told them. They had believed that when Cat didn't call, it was because she didn't care, and not because she was busy working, building her business; living a life that Ginny seemed unable to create for herself while she waited around, expecting Prince Charming to come along and scoop her up.

Cat hadn't found out any of this until a few months ago. When Tristan told her.

She stopped by the bar on the way back from the toilet to ask for a round of coffees. One of the men from earlier got up and went to the toilet. The other was facing towards the bar again, gazing down at his espresso cup, but Cat could see his eyes lift as he caught a glance of her in the mirror behind the bar.

He turned to her, his eyes dropping briefly to her neckline, where she was rolling her pendant between her fingers. His gaze went back to her face and he gave her a lazy smile. 'Enjoy your lunch?' he said. His eyes were green and intense. He spoke French, but his accent was light.

She pushed the necklace back inside her t-shirt. 'Yes. Thank you. Back to the hike soon though. We're on the last part of the loop now, I think.'

His gaze had become unnerving, and she was glad when he turned back to the bar. He picked up his coffee and took a sip. 'The last part may be a little tough. Hang in there.' His friend had returned and was sitting on the stool to his other side. Espresso Man swivelled around to face him and the two started talking again, rapidly in French. Too fast for her to pick up. But then he turned back and said something else, his voice low, so that the other man didn't hear. Something that he wanted only Cat to hear.

'*Je te veux.*'

Something that she understood perfectly.

I want you.

She was shaking by the time she made it back to the table, trying hard to act normal, while the man's words were still ringing in her ears.

'I ordered us some coffees,' she said, fighting against the wavering of her voice. 'Then I think we should get going.'

Paul put a hand on her arm. 'What did he say to you? The man at the bar?'

'Oh, he definitely said *something*,' Ginny piped up. 'I saw him speak, but I couldn't hear. He was practically salivating.' She smoothed her t-shirt over her chest. 'Although I'm not sure why he'd prefer you over me.'

Cat pushed Paul's arm away and sat back down, ignoring both him and Ginny. 'He just said to be careful on the last part as it's a bit tricky.'

Tristan was smirking at her now. 'Ginny was just telling us how you shagged that Frank bloke in a nightclub toilet. Classy, Cat. Very classy.' He shifted in his seat. 'Sounds like you have a thing for toilets.'

Ginny's face was triumphant. Cat said nothing. Let Ginny have her moment. It was hardly a shocking story – it just seemed so because they all thought she was the straight-laced, sensible one. None of them knew that the real scandal was that Frank had been married, and in a so-called position of power as her tutor. She could reveal that, and they could have something to really get their teeth into.

But now was not the time.

Because she was too busy wondering what to do about the fact that, under the table, out of sight of the others and with that same ridiculous smirk on his face, Tristan was running his foot up the inside of her thigh. Did he want to be caught? She was frozen in place, unable to shake him off without drawing attention to what he was doing. But as much as she wanted to kill him right now, she was grateful to him for the distraction.

Twelve

SUNDAY MORNING

Pigalle stands behind the front counter, watching the woman as she paces back and forth across the waiting area of the police station. The space is sparsely furnished, with only a couple of padded bench seats in the far corner. On the wall to his right is a large fish tank in an alcove. This was his own attempt at making the waiting area more interesting, although as he watches now, he thinks perhaps it gives off the wrong message. In the tank, small orange fish circle aimlessly. In the room, the woman does the same.

The man is sitting on one of the seats, tending to his wounds with equipment from a first-aid kit that Pigalle provided earlier. He wanted to take them both to hospital, urging the man that he needed help; but the man refused after the woman made it clear that he wasn't to leave this place.

'We must stick to the plan,' she'd said.

And neither of them offered any means of identification, not even their names. Pigalle can't force them to reveal who they are, although he is of course deeply suspicious of them now. They asked for help, and yet they refuse to help themselves.

This is *un signal d'alarme*. A red flag, flapping hard.

Whatever their plan is, it is a mess. They must know that now. He knows what they are thinking: they've come this far, and they can go further. As far as it takes.

But what are they hiding? Where are their friends? Why will they not speak – and let him get on with his job and back to his day instead of them all hanging around here in silence.

It is infuriating. But Pigalle is a calm man, known for his patience. So he will wait. For now.

He walks out from behind the counter and stops next to the fish tank. A tiny golden seahorse is bobbing close to the front glass. He taps the glass and it turns, swimming away in its curious fashion.

The woman comes to stand beside him. Her face is wrinkled in disgust. She peers at the tank and visibly shudders. 'I hate them,' she says. 'Their weird snouts and googly eyes. The way they float along upright, when all the other sea creatures are horizontal. They creep me out.'

'You know they are meant to symbolise strength and power,' Pigalle says. He doesn't understand how she can hate something so magical.

She shakes her head. 'They're a bad omen. Awful things have happened every time I've seen one.' She looks away. 'My sister used to find my phobia hilarious. She was always buying me seahorse-related gifts. Loved trying to trick me into looking at pictures of them on the internet, by sending links supposedly to other things.' She pauses, looking like she wants to say more, but stops herself.

This is very interesting, he thinks.

'Is it your sister that is one of the missing?' Pigalle asks.

They are interrupted by the man. Pigalle balls his hands into fists, digging his nails into his palms. Just when he thought he might be getting somewhere . . .

'Any chance of some help here?' The man is groaning as he tries unsuccessfully to wipe away dried blood from the wounds on his chest. From the way he's holding himself, and his pain when he coughs, Pigalle thinks it likely that he's broken at least one rib. But as long as he can still breathe, it's the cuts they need to deal with first. The woman goes over to him and takes the box of alcohol wipes from his hand. Takes one out, rips open the packet.

Pigalle observes.

'This is going to hurt,' she says. There is some glee in her tone.

The man's mouth curls into a half-smile. 'I think a little sting while you patch me up is the least of my worries, don't you?' He grimaces as she applies the wipe, although she is seemingly being gentle. The man's chest is a mess. Pigalle still can't work out why they are refusing to go to the hospital.

Pigalle takes a step closer to the pair.

'Just to let you know, madame . . . I have called with my colleague. He will be joining us soon. In the meantime, may I assist?' He leans in towards the man. 'This is looking very nasty, *non?*'

The woman shakes her head. 'It's fine. I can sort it.'

The man snorts. 'I knew your addiction to *24 Hours in A&E* would come in useful one day.'

The woman ignores him, but she rubs the wipe harder across his chest and he lets out a little yelp of pain.

Pigalle looks from one to the other. Shrugs. If they want to play this little game with themselves, then so be it. 'Very well,' he says. 'In that case, I will make another call to the embassy in Bern. Hopefully someone will be in the office now and, soon, they can join us.'

'Thank you,' she says, taking another alcohol wipe from the box. Rips it open. She turns to Pigalle. 'Like I said before, we're not talking to you until we get embassy assistance. However long that takes.'

Pigalle nods. It might take a while. But he's determined to get to the bottom of what has happened – with or without their help.

Thirteen

The path ahead was narrow and winding, and, as they climbed higher out of the valley, the drop to the left became steeper. Ginny was feeling buoyed by the rest and her little bombshell at the end of the meal. Cat's face when she returned from the bar had been a picture. She hadn't really meant to tell the story, but something about being in the little Swiss-French bar had reminded her of it. Not that she'd been there, of course. She'd asked Cat if she could visit her while she was studying in France, but Cat had said she was too busy and she needed to spend her time with the other students.

As if. French Frank hadn't been a student, had he? Although, saying that, Ginny can't remember if she ever knew how her sister had actually met him. No, just like always, Cat thought she was too clever to hang around with her stupid little sister. She'd only told her about the nightclub encounter one night in Soho because they'd ended up both being invited on the same night out, and Cat had drunk too many tequila slammers and decided to spill all. She'd quite liked this Frank, apparently, but he'd turned out to be a bit of a shit.

'You had to bring that up, didn't you, Gins?'

Cat had moved away from Paul's side and held back a bit, sidling up to Ginny. The path was barely wide enough for two, and Ginny didn't feel particularly comfortable being doubled-up like that, so she moved ahead leaving Cat close behind. The two men were a good bit further ahead, out of earshot.

'Oh, come on. Why are you so bothered? It's not even scandalous, really. It's a funny story. It was ten years ago. You were young, free and single once, you know. Everyone's got a dodgy sex tale to tell.'

'Yeah, and usually they're reserved for the participants to tell, are they not? Anyway, you don't even know the full story and I'm glad now that I didn't tell you anything else about it. Would you like it if I told Tristan the stuff you used to get up to before you met?'

Ginny huffed. 'I'm not sure he would care. I don't think he would even care if I started a few new tales now.'

'So you're still convinced there's someone else?'

Ginny could hear Cat's breath coming out in short puffs behind her. 'I told you. Just suspicions at this stage.' More than suspicions, but it wasn't time to divulge details just yet. Not until she was sure.

'Why don't you just ask him, Ginny.'

Ginny stopped walking, and Cat slammed into the back of her. Ginny turned to face her sister, their faces almost touching. 'I will ask him when I'm ready to ask him, OK? What's it to you, anyway. You didn't even like him until . . . until he became your BFF for planning this stupid trip.'

Cat took a step back. 'Christ, Ginny. That's a bit harsh. I was only asking because you brought it up. You're the one who mentioned it last night, and then again today. You clearly want to talk about it.' Her voice softens. 'You can talk to me, you know?'

Ginny rolled her eyes. 'You're so full of it, Cat. Your holier-than-thou attitude is becoming a bit wearing.' She wanted to say more, but she wasn't sure why. She wasn't even sure why she was so intent on picking a fight this weekend. Cat hadn't actually done anything wrong. She hadn't done anything different to usual. She'd actually been *nice*. Ginny was starting to think that maybe her suspicions were wrong. She knew she'd been spiky. She was about to apologise, but, before she got a chance, Cat shoved past her and marched off ahead. Ginny wasn't having this.

She took off after her sister, grabbing Cat by the arm and pulling her back. 'Just what the *hell* is wrong with you?'

Then she noticed Tristan was in front of them, his face registering alarm. 'Ladies, ladies . . . what exactly is going on here? We thought you'd got lost.' He had made his way back down the hill, Paul following close behind. 'Sorry if we're going a bit too fast.' He looked from Ginny to Cat and back again, frowning. 'Maybe you two should set the pace for a bit?'

Ginny looked at Cat. Shrugged.

'Go on then!' Cat snapped.

Ginny adjusted the straps on her rucksack and started walking again, Cat walking by her side as the path widened. It had turned from a loose beige gravel to a section of flat, silvery rocks. Ginny looked up, shielding her eyes from the late-afternoon sun. The silvery rocks seemed to stretch far off into the distance. It was starting to get steep. She slowed down. 'Sorry,' she said, eventually.

Cat said nothing.

Close behind, she could hear the men chattering. Sounded like they were getting on well, now that Tristan had stopped trying to wind Paul up. Tristan had always been good at switching his mood around when it suited him. She was trying to do the same, but it seemed Cat wasn't biting.

'Cat? I said I'm sorry.' Cat still said nothing. Ginny decided to carry on talking, hoping Cat would join in eventually. 'I finally got a recipe for that weird vegetable. The kohlrabi? Remember, I took one with us to Norfolk and I didn't have a clue—'

'Oh, shut up, will you? Let's just get to the top of this bit in peace.'

Ginny turned her head so hard she almost gave herself whiplash. 'No need to be such a bitch, *Catty*-Cat. I'm only making conversation.'

Cat's eyes flared. 'It's always the same with you, Ginny. You think it's fun to humiliate me, don't you? Using *my* interesting stories to make up for the fact that all you have is a boring drivel of a life with a bunch of vacuous followers and a husband who doesn't give two shits about you. You never ask anything about my life. You never get involved in any of my work—'

'Jesus. Calm down, will you? It was just a stupid story. Anyway, I'm meant to be a silent partner, remember? I said that from the start . . .'

'No, you didn't. When I started the business, I told you I needed help. I told you I could use your social media expertise. You said you were happy to be involved. But you've left me high and dry. Then you spend your time messing about with ridiculous recipes, and—'

'I gave you the money, Cat. That's what you really wanted, was it not?'

Cat stopped walking. Ginny stopped too. The men were almost on top of them now.

'Girls? Everything OK?' Tristan looked amused, but there was steel in his eyes. He could quite easily flip again, Ginny knew.

'Cat?' Paul sounded concerned.

Ginny felt the heat rising. She could see from Cat's face that she was ready to explode. 'Cat . . .'

'And where exactly did that money come from, hmm?'

Ginny swallowed. 'I don't think this is really the time—'

'Oh, what better time, *little* sister.' Cat snorted. 'Perhaps the others can help me to understand why it was you who was left in charge of the inheritance, as the younger sibling. Why it was you who decided to keep it all for yourself . . .'

'I gave you what you asked for, Cat.' Ginny's voice rose an octave. 'I *told* you, you can always ask me for more . . .'

Cat shook her head. 'Why should I have to ask you? It should have been an even split.'

Ginny lowered her voice. 'You didn't contest it at the time.'

'I was fucking *grieving*, Ginny. While you were deciding what to spend the money on . . . while you were already designing yourself a brand-new kitchen. *I* was grieving.'

Ginny was lost for words. She knew her sister was right, but she'd always hoped that she'd gotten away with it. She had been left all the money to distribute as she saw fit. Cat was well within her rights to be angry. But now wasn't the time, or the place. So Ginny said nothing and walked on ahead.

Fourteen

Cat dug her nails into her palms. She wanted to scream. But instead, she kept quiet and watched Ginny march on ahead, Tristan following close behind his wife. What the hell had he been thinking, touching Cat's leg like that in the restaurant? Thankfully she didn't think that Ginny had had any idea it was happening, but if these were the kinds of stunts he was pulling, it was no wonder Ginny thought he was cheating. Because, of course, Ginny was right. Bringing up the inheritance had been a way to deflect from talk of sex in toilets and affairs. It would all come tumbling out soon enough, but it had to be on Cat's terms.

That was the plan.

Cat blew out a long, slow breath, trying to calm herself down.

The path veered off into the mountainside, taking them away from that steep drop down into the valley, and across another meadow. Paul caught up with her, took her elbow. She shrugged him off.

'What's got into you? Why bring all that up with her now? She's hardly going to give you a sensible explanation when we're eighteen hundred metres up a mountain and we're all bloody knackered.'

Cat sighed. Paul was right, for once. She had to get her head sorted. There was no point in getting worked up when they still had so much walking to do. 'I don't know what's wrong with me. I feel a bit funny. I have done since that dizzy spell back by the lake, when we took the wrong turn.'

'It's the altitude, probably. And the heat. That sun has been beating down on us all day, and none of us has drunk anywhere near enough water. It's no surprise you feel weird. I think we all do—'

'The rest of you are just hiding it better, are you?'

Paul shook his head. 'Hardly. Ginny's been enjoying winding you up and Tristan's been doing the same with me. I have frequent urges to push them both over the side of the mountain.'

Cat's stomach flipped. She forced out a laugh. 'And then what?'

'We'd walk back down to that restaurant, have a few beers and ask them to give us a lift down to the car park. We'd tell them the others went on ahead. Plenty of time for us to grab the car and be out of here before anyone realised what we'd done.'

'It's an interesting plan, but I don't think we'd get very far. We're hardly master criminals, are we?'

'Who needs to be a master criminal when you've got the perfect place to make a murder look like an accident? Those hikers warned us early on . . .'

'You've been watching too many crime dramas.' She paused, trying to think of a way to change the subject. Because as much as it was meant to be a bit of fun, to lighten the mood, it had disturbed her that he'd said it, even in jest. 'Let's catch up with the others. I'll try to keep a lid on it with Ginny.'

'Well, at least until we get back to the hot tub.'

'Good point. We could drown her in it.'

Paul started laughing, and couldn't seem to stop himself. It was out of proportion to what she'd just said. But she laughed along with him, keeping up the charade. She was not happy to be in his company, and she had a feeling that he also felt uneasy in hers – like he knew that Cat had a plan and he wasn't going to like it. He couldn't have failed to notice that she had pulled away from his every attempt at being physically close to her. He'd seemed distracted. Distant, for a lot of the day. Gluing himself to Tristan's side, despite all the ribbing. It was almost as if he didn't want to talk to Cat. But of course, she knew why. And she was fed up with it being brushed under the carpet.

She decided to give him one last chance.

'We should talk about it, you know,' she said.

Paul's laughter stopped abruptly. 'Not here.'

She sighed. 'Not here. Not now. When, then? And where? I've tried and tried at home but all you do is change the subject. When the allegations were first made, you couldn't bloody stop talking about it. Begging for reassurance from me that you would be OK . . .'

'That's when I thought it was going to be a straightforward thing. It just dragged on so long . . . and I don't want it in my head. And it *is* in my head, I can assure you. Do you really need it in yours?'

'All you can do is keep telling the truth, Paul. It's her word against yours. And you say you didn't do anything—'

Paul stopped walking and grabbed her by the wrist, pulling her close to him. 'Are you doubting my innocence now? Is it not enough that fucking Tristan keeps asking me what happened at work and why did I really leave, because I never seemed like the burnout type? He's getting close to the truth, Cat. I don't want him knowing about this. Do you not understand?'

Cat pulled herself away. Rubbed at her wrists. So he was going to continue to lie about it? Cat knew exactly what he had done to his work colleague. How he'd forced himself on her. Humiliated

71

her. And he had no idea that she knew the truth. She'd done a good job of defending him. Because she actually had believed him. Until the photos that he forgot to delete showed otherwise. Well, that was fine. It made everything she had planned for later so much easier to deal with.

'Oi, you two? Have your feet stopped working?' Tristan yelled. He'd stopped up ahead. Ginny was standing beside him with her hands on her hips, her face squinting up at the sun.

'Coming,' Paul called to them, giving Tristan a little wave. 'Come on,' he said to Cat. His voice was gentle now, and that just annoyed Cat more. He thought she was still on his side. But he was very wrong about that. They started walking, Cat keeping her distance from Paul but trying not to make it look too obvious to the others.

'This isn't over, Paul,' she said, under her breath. 'I am sick and tired of liars. I'm fed up with people thinking that they can get one over on me, somehow. Like I'm this soft touch, just because I like to do things properly and I don't like to fight.' She sighed. She was wasting her breath. 'I think you're right about the altitude and the heat, though.' She picked up the pace and Paul carried on beside her. They were close to the others now. 'At least I don't feel sick anymore.'

Ginny overheard. 'Oh . . . you felt *sick*? And dizzy? And you switched to water last night while we all carried on with the shots? Wonder what on earth could be wrong with you, Kitty-Cat.' She looked pointedly at Cat's stomach, smirked. Then turned away and carried on walking.

Tristan raised an eyebrow at her, but said nothing. She hoped he hadn't picked up on Ginny's insinuation. Paul gave her a brief glance then turned away. She thought he looked uncomfortable, and it made her feel uneasy. She was thirty-two years old. Would it be the worst thing if she was pregnant? They'd always said they didn't want children, but that had been a few years ago, and now everything had changed. She laid a hand on her flat belly, wondering what might be going on deep inside.

Would a pregnancy ruin her plans? Maybe. Maybe not. She glanced around at the others. It was too soon to tell.

Fifteen

He took his time following them up the mountain. He knew exactly where they were going. He had to walk slowly to keep a safe distance behind them. He didn't want them hearing him. He was enjoying himself too much for this to end.

He wondered what would happen if she spotted him. Recognised him. Would she raise the alarm? Or would she carry on walking, hoping for the best. Hoping that there wasn't really someone tracking them along the trail.

They should walk faster. They'd run out of daylight before they made it to the end, and how would they manage to follow the trail then?

Maybe he should change his plans a little. Maybe he should walk out on the track, like them. Make them aware of his presence. Offer to guide them back down. He was getting frustrated, only catching glimpses of them through the trees. He wanted to see more of the blonde. The confident blonde. Not the whiny, skinny, moaning one.

But no. That wouldn't work. He had to stay hidden.

For now.

He pushed his way through the trees, staying away from the track. Walking carefully, trying to make as little noise as possible. He stopped for a moment, listening. There were other sounds. Animal sounds. There could be anything out here in the woods.

He smiled at the thought.

Conjured up the blonde's face.

He couldn't wait to see her again.

Sixteen

SATURDAY, EARLY EVENING

Ginny was fed up talking to Tristan. She regretted going too far with Cat, but she had just been trying to liven things up. They'd been out all day on this bloody mountain in the baking heat, and apart from some pretty scenery and an average lunch, Ginny had been bored stiff. Surely they all knew this was not her idea of fun? Was it any surprise she'd had to make her own?

She sighed.

Cat had caught up and was looking a bit hot and sweaty. And stressed. Was there something up with her and Paul? The Perfect Couple? What a scoop that would be. Cat had been ominously quiet when Ginny had made her little hint at pregnancy. Too close to the truth?

Christ, Ginny, have a word! She couldn't help herself.

'Sorry about earlier, Cat. I'm just bored . . .' she said when Cat arrived by her side. They were still on the meadow, but, from what Tristan had told her, the next part was going to be harder. Those silvery rocks from before were about to make a reappearance as a tricky, slippery set of steps, he'd said. But this was the bit with the amazing views. Almost like walking up the Grand Canyon, he'd said. She remained unconvinced so far. She was still hoping they'd make it back in time for the hot tub.

Cat still hadn't said a word. 'Cat?' Jesus, was she going to ignore her for the rest of the trip now? She looked at her sister, who, in turn, had her gaze fixed over on the thicket of trees that joined the meadow to the steep side of the mountain. 'What is it?'

'Did anyone else hear that?'

Cat had stopped walking again. Ginny sighed. At this rate they were never going to get back to the hotel, and the hot tub would definitely be closed for the night. So Plan B would obviously be to get mightily pissed in the bar, because what the hell else were they going to do on this absolutely shit trip? She wished more than ever that she'd put her foot down and refused to come. And now Cat was playing silly buggers about some noise in the trees.

'Hear what?' Ginny said. She was so pissed off now. 'Honestly, can we just get a move on? Tristan said we've got another hour, if we stay on course. Then we've got to drive back, get changed . . . the hot tub closes at seven-thirty.'

'Again with the hot tub,' Paul muttered.

Ginny ignored him. She hadn't quite realised until today what an absolute bore her brother-in-law was. 'Cat?'

'There's someone in those trees,' Cat said, pointing. 'I saw something moving.'

'Jesus Christ, Cat,' Tristan said. 'It'll just be some animal. A deer or something. We should leave it well alone and get through this section. As I told Ginny—'

There was a rustling sound. Unmistakable. Ginny's ears pricked up. Even if it was just an animal, were they safe? Did deer come out and attack humans for disturbing their habitat?

'I heard it,' Paul said. 'Tristan's right. It's an animal.'

There was a crunching sound, then. Like something big and heavy crushing lots of small twigs. If it was an animal, it was something big.

Ginny felt goosebumps prickling up her arms. 'Oh god, do they have bears here?' She moved closer to Tristan. 'Bears eat humans, you know. I saw a programme—'

He squeezed her around the waist. 'There are no bears here, Gins. Honestly. Can we just keep walking, guys? Please? I know you all think it's my fault that we've taken so much longer than we were meant to, but we're on the home straight now, I promise. If we could just . . .'

Tristan's voice trailed off. They were all watching the trees. It wasn't an animal. There was some*one* in there. Ginny was sure she'd seen a flash of clothing, and now she was convinced she could see a pair of eyes. Watching.

'Trissy, let's just go?' Her heart started to thump hard in her chest.

'Probably just another hiker,' Paul said. His voice was full of bluster, but he still sounded unconvinced.

Cat took Ginny's hand, and she was grateful. A small symbol of solidarity, despite all the bickering. 'If it's another hiker, why wouldn't they just come out of the trees and walk the path with us,' Cat said, squeezing Ginny's hand harder. 'Why would anyone be skulking around here, trying to scare us? There's no one there. Like Ginny said . . . let's just go?'

'The girls are right,' Tristan said. 'Let's get a move on, shall we?'

'Maybe there's another route?' Ginny squeezed Cat's hand back.

'Or maybe whoever it was got disorientated. Aren't we overreacting a bit here?' Paul started walking towards the trees. 'Hello? Anyone there?'

Ginny held her breath. There was no sound coming from the thicket anymore. The rustling had stopped. 'Maybe . . . maybe we imagined it.' She tried to laugh but it sounded forced. 'I think we're all just far too tired . . .'

Cat let go of her hand and walked across to Paul, who'd stopped some way from the trees. He might be a pain in the arse, but Ginny was glad he hadn't ventured any further. It was probably nothing. She must've imagined seeing the eyes. The light playing tricks on her.

But she was sure she hadn't imagined the flash of a reflective stripe on a bright-red jacket. And she was pretty sure that, despite her protestations, Cat had seen it too.

Seventeen

SATURDAY, EARLY EVENING

Cat tried to pull Paul back from the trees, but now it was his turn to shrug off her touch. He looked furious. 'This is getting ridiculous now. We should go back the way we just came. Back to the restaurant. It's going to be dark before we make it to the bottom.' He turned to Tristan, his eyes narrowed. 'This is your fault, you arrogant prick. If you'd just let the rest of us see the bloody map.'

'Woah there, cowboy. Let's back up a bit.' Tristan puffed out his chest and took a step closer to Paul.

Cat shot in between the two of them, holding out a hand towards each one in an attempt to keep them apart. She had no idea why the pair of them were getting so worked up. 'Guys . . .' She couldn't remember ever seeing Paul this riled up. She didn't think that Paul and Tristan would actually become physical, but it might be a close call.

'I just want to go home.' Ginny was crying.

Paul and Tristan had stayed apart, but their faces revealed all. Cat knew that Tristan had been in fights in the past – usually after too much to drink – but he had that fire in him now and it scared her. Paul's anger would fade soon, if she knew anything about her husband at all. Which in recent months had proven doubtful.

Maybe it would be good if the pair of them laid into one another. It wasn't how she wanted things to unfold, but it might be the easiest option. She was starting to have second thoughts about her plans, but they'd come too far now. They just had to keep going.

Cat moved away from the men, and across to Ginny. She was still crying, her shoulders shaking with the weight of her sobs. Cat actually felt sorry for her for a moment, despite the bickering and the fact that she was a monumental pain in the arse and a total drama queen. And, of course, there was the money.

It was really all about their parents' money, and the years of betrayal that it represented. But just as she was about to say some soothing words, Ginny turned on her, a finger pointed at her chest.

'This is your fault, *Catastrophe*. None of us wanted to come up here and do this stupid bloody walk. It's far too much. We're not hikers. Those two we met at the start clearly thought we were off our heads.' She jabbed her finger into Cat's chest. 'You need to get us out of this.' Jab. 'Now.'

Cat stepped back. 'Get your fucking hands off me, you little cow.'

'Ladies, ladies . . .' Tristan was there, dragging Ginny away.

'Come on, Cat. This isn't helping.' Paul tried to pull her away. Cat felt another flurry of light-headedness, the same as when she'd slipped on the rocks earlier in the day. She gripped Paul's hand, hating the feel of his skin.

'I'm sorry,' she said. Was she, though? Mostly she was just tired, and struggling to find the energy to carry on with all of this.

Paul sounded confused. 'What are you sorry for? You haven't done a thing wrong.' He paused. 'Other than asking Tristan to help you plan this. I'm not sure what you were thinking . . .'

No, and I won't be telling you, either, Cat thought. She called on her reserves and gave him a weak smile. 'I think I was a bit ambitious with the plans. Ginny's right, for once. We're not really hikers.'

They walked ahead, leaving Tristan and Ginny to catch up with them. Cat was sick of the arguing, but she had to stay strong. It would all be worth it in the end, when she was back in the village. The point of the trip was to right some wrongs, and she'd already set the ball rolling by mentioning the money to Ginny. They'd continue it, and it would be sorted. Then she would confront Paul, and that would be dealt with too. It really was that simple. She just had to remember that.

She let go of Paul's hand, wiping away his sweat on her shorts. She had to keep it together. She had to find enough strength to make it to the end.

'Guys, wait up,' Tristan called from behind. 'We need to stay together.'

They were coming to the end of the gravel path, heading away from the trees and towards the steep drop. Cat had felt safe on the wider, meadow-type area – and she was starting to feel a bit nauseous at the thought of being so close to the edge again. But there was no other way that was obvious to any of them, so she'd just have to get on with it. She let the others overtake her, slowing her pace just a little. Taking a few calming breaths, after a moment the squeamish feeling passed.

They passed another cluster of trees, and this time, the rustling was unmistakable. She had seen a flash of a red coat earlier, but hadn't said anything to Ginny. She recalled that one of the hikers they'd met earlier in the day was wearing red. And he'd spent too long looking her up and down, too. She really hoped it wasn't him in the trees, following them. She didn't need any added complications.

Her heart was fluttering. She stopped walking. 'Who's there?'

The others turned towards her. 'Oh, what *now*?' Tristan said. 'Not this again.'

He looked her hard in the eye; she felt that he was trying to tell her to drop this. To carry on. This wasn't part of the plan. And he was right – it wasn't. But there was definitely someone watching them.

'There is someone . . . Right. There.' She pointed. 'In those trees.'

Tristan swore, then yanked the straps of his rucksack off and dropped it on the ground. 'Right . . . I've had enough of this shit.' He marched into the trees, pushing branches aside to make way. 'Hello? Who the fuck's there? Come out, come out, whoever you are . . .'

The rustling came closer. Tristan was deep in the trees, hidden from sight. Cat was watching Paul, wondering what he was going to do. She was about to head over to the trees herself. But then a man burst out from between the branches right in front of them. A man who wasn't Tristan.

Ginny screamed.

Eighteen

Pigalle is sitting in his office. His lieutenant, Sébastien Marchand, arrived a few minutes ago and is scrolling through his phone. Pigalle has purposely turned up the TV in the office and left the door ajar so that he can keep an eye on the couple and also talk about them when required.

The man is pacing the room now, getting restless. Pigalle has already told them twice that it will be at least two hours until someone can help them. At least.

These tourists . . . they do not understand the roads around here. Pigalle has lived here all of his life. Forty-five years. He has seen all of the things that the weather can throw their way. But it is becoming more common that the summer is as bad as the winter. Landslides caused by melting snow from up high. Not enough defensive support in place. They are working on it, but they cannot predict all of it. And it is just very bad timing that the rocks have fallen down on to the main road from Bern when these people so desperately need to meet with someone from the embassy.

The embassy was not pleased to have to send someone out on a Sunday. But tough. If he has to work today, someone else can damn well work too.

Pigalle is not pleased, either, that the tourists are refusing to talk without an embassy representative. It is their right, of course, but it is not convenient. It makes him instantly suspicious when someone exercises this particular right. They have come to the police, yet they do not want to be helped?

He asked them again about their missing friends, and the man seemed keen to explain, but the woman glared at him, and he shut up. So, she is in charge. She is the one he needs to try and break down. Unless they want to be here all day.

Pigalle is thinking about what he can do to try and gain the woman's trust when the door to the station swings open and his wife marches in. He did not see her pull up in the car. She must have parked further up the street.

'*Voilà*,' she says, dropping a paper bag on the counter.

He goes through to greet her. '*Merci*, Sandrine.' He smiles but she doesn't return it. She looks harassed. But still beautiful, as always. She is dressed in her favourite designer workout clothing, her face gently flushed.

'You've been to your class?' he says.

'Yes, yes. But I left early to go back home and get this for you after you left the message. I couldn't concentrate knowing you were waiting.' She returns his smile, eventually, and her eyes light up.

Pigalle knows that she can never stay mad at him for long. Even if he has ruined their lunch, their afternoon together, and now her exercise class – which she has left early, to go home and make lunch for the tourists. She wouldn't be Sandrine if she refused his request.

She blows him a kiss, and then she is gone, leaving a soft fug of expensive perfume and an underlying whiff of cigarettes. Pigalle notes this for use later, when she complains about him smoking. They are both meant to be giving up, but they are both still smoking in secret. He's not sure why they are bothering with the pretence anymore.

He's grateful to her, for bringing them food and drink. He hopes the tourists appreciate the effort. Séb comes out of the office and inspects the bag, then starts to remove the items. Four sandwiches, four drinks. Two large bags of potato chips.

'Lunch,' Séb says to the tourists, holding two sandwiches aloft.

The man stops pacing and comes to the counter. He picks up the sandwiches.

'Thank you,' he says.

The woman comes and takes the drinks and the chips. '*Merci*,' she says. They both retreat back to the seats and start to unwrap the sandwiches from the brown paper.

Pigalle watches them eat. The man bites on the sandwich and pulls hard with his teeth as if he is attempting to eat a chunk of raw meat, instead of bread and ham. He unwraps his own sandwich and takes a bite. OK, so maybe the bread is from yesterday. But it still tastes better than any of that awful sliced stuff the British are so keen on. He's been to London a few times and been deeply unimpressed by the attempts at cuisine.

He takes another bite, chews slowly.

The couple – if they are a couple – are not talking to each other. They are eating in silence, occasionally taking a sip of their drinks. The man puts his sandwich down and opens the bag of chips.

Crisps – that's what they call them, isn't it?

Pigalle doesn't like them, but he knows that Séb will happily eat his share from the other bag that's been taken through to the office.

The woman is facing the window. The man leans in towards her, holding the bag of crisps. Pigalle retreats into the office, but keeps watching. Keeps listening. They might think he can't hear them over the TV, but this is one of his little tricks. He has excellent hearing. Sandrine often says he could hear a pin drop on a beach. He is also excellent at lip-reading.

'Maybe we should just leave,' the man says, quietly. 'They're not keeping us here. They don't think a crime has been committed.'

She talks to him without turning to face him, her voice a low hiss. 'Keep your voice down.'

The man frowns. He glances across at the door to the office, which is still ajar, but Pigalle is careful to keep him out of his line of sight. The sound of the football match on the TV is leaching out into the reception area. 'The captain said it could be hours before the embassy send someone. Why don't we go back to the hotel? Get cleaned up properly.'

'Are you insane?'

The man sits back in his seat. He looks pained.

Why don't they go back to their hotel? Pigalle wonders. He's really not sure what their game is. If there even *are* others, out there.

Missing.

But something bad has happened, he can't deny that. Their injuries are enough.

The woman is still staring out of the window. Pigalle takes another bite of his sandwich. He wants to know what she's waiting for.

Nineteen

SATURDAY, EARLY EVENING

Ginny's scream died in her throat as the man started to walk towards them. She recognised him. She was almost certain that he had been sitting at the bar when they were having their lunch. He was brushing down his red jacket. His hair was messed up from being ruffled by branches. A moment later, Tristan came crashing out of the trees behind him, swearing as a branch pinged back and smacked him in the face.

The man clearly saw their horrified expressions, and he raised his hands. Ginny wasn't sure yet if he meant them harm, but he wasn't moving fast and he was saying something that she didn't understand.

'I am sorry,' he said, eventually, after meeting their blank stares. His accent sounded French, and she took in his jacket and knew she was right.

'You were in the restaurant.'

Cat came up beside her. 'I don't think so.'

Ginny whirled around to face her sister. 'He was. You spoke to him when you came back from the toilet.' What the hell was Cat playing at now? She turned back to the man. 'Didn't she? You spoke to her.'

'I think you are mistaken,' the man said. 'I am very sorry if I scared you all, I was . . . ah, taking the restroom.'

Tristan laughed. 'You mean you were shitting in the woods? Seriously, mate . . .'

The man looked embarrassed. 'I am shepherd, up here. I am on my way to my hut, but I was away for too long.'

Ginny stared at him. 'You mean you were walking up here from the restaurant and you were following us.' She crossed her arms. The fear from before had dissipated now at the bizarreness of the situation. But she wasn't convinced he was telling the truth. He looked very like the man she'd seen in the restaurant earlier, but then she had only seen him from the table, and Cat seemed sure it wasn't him. Why would she lie? That jacket though – she could've sworn she saw it hanging on a hook near the bar. But there were other jackets there too. And why was he even wearing it? She was sweating in a t-shirt. Bloody locals.

'No harm done,' Cat said, smiling at the man. 'We just got a bit spooked. It's been a long day.'

'And it's going to be longer still if we don't get back to the hotel soon,' Ginny muttered. She didn't like the way Cat had looked at the man. Like she did recognise him, but she didn't want the others to know. But that made no sense.

Ginny ran a hand through her hair. It felt lank and greasy. She was not feeling at her best right now, so it wouldn't be that much of a stretch for her to think she recognised this man when she didn't. She tried to think about the hikers from the start of the day, and realised she couldn't quite picture their faces. One of them had worn red too, hadn't he? She was tired. She was getting mixed up. And did it even matter if he was the man from the bar or not?

She let out a long, slow sigh. She could kill Cat for bringing her up this godforsaken mountain. The trainers she was wearing were rubbing on her heels and she knew there were blisters, but she didn't want to tell the others and have them belittle her even further for wearing the wrong gear. Besides, that was Tristan's fault. He must've known her shoes weren't suitable. Had he not told her on purpose or was he just too distracted with his other bloody woman? She was finding it hard to tell if he was actually enjoying being here, or just enjoying having a dig at her and many digs at Paul – although he didn't seem to be picking on Cat. Funny that.

The man gave Ginny a small nod. 'There is a shorter route. You might want to take this.' He frowned, thinking to himself. 'Maybe thirty minutes to the bottom, once you take the steep climb of fifteen.'

Tristan took out his map. 'Right, can you show us?'

The man took them all in. 'The climb is quite steep . . . you will all manage it though, I hope.'

'We'll manage it,' Paul said, muscling in to get a look at the map.

Eventually, after much pointing and shrugging between the three men, the shepherd – if that's really what he was – gave them a little wave and headed off back the other way. 'I will find my sheeps,' he said. '*Au revoir.*'

Ginny suppressed a giggle.

'Let's go.' Tristan and Paul had already started walking.

The boys didn't seem too bothered about the shepherd. They hadn't seemed to recognise him. It was definitely her tired mind playing tricks. Wasn't it? She pulled Cat back beside her. 'Are you *sure* that's not that bloke from the restaurant? Seems a bit weird. He definitely looked familiar.'

'Did you even see him properly, Gins? He was never facing you in there. I talked to that man at the bar, remember? That shepherd guy is definitely not him.'

Ginny shrugged. She didn't know why she felt so bothered. Neither of the men in question had done any of them any harm. She tried to push it out of her mind, and carried on walking.

The path snaked out on to the side of the mountain and Ginny gasped. 'Wow. This is incredible.' They were high above the valley floor. The mountains opposite were harsh and jagged, but a vision of natural beauty that literally took her breath away. The sky seemed to go on forever, a bright, clear blue with not a cloud in sight. Then she saw the route they were taking, and felt a flurry of nerves. It *was* steep. And her feet were already ragged from the friction on her heels. And still, a little niggle of doubt came back to her.

'What if he's following us and waiting until we get tired before he comes to rob us . . .' She paused, eyeing the path ahead cautiously. 'Or worse – he could be waiting to find the right moment to kill us.'

'Don't be ridiculous,' Cat said. There was a hint of incredulous laughter in her voice, but to Ginny, it sounded forced. Unflappable Cat was definitely flapped. Being stalked and murdered on a mountain was definitely not part of the plan. But Cat had a plan. Ginny was sure of that. She just couldn't work out exactly what it was.

Ginny took a deep breath and braced herself for the climb.

Twenty

Saturday Evening

Cat was enjoying the view. But then her gaze travelled to the steep rocky path that lay ahead. Tristan had mentioned this part earlier, but she'd thought they were avoiding it. The rock was smooth slate-grey, and formed a series of long, flat steps that ate into the side of the mountain like the teeth of a zip. Although each section was flat, and the height of each step didn't seem too much, it was the sheer length of the climb that worried her. The summit was high, and the climb was going to be a tough one. They'd never make it up there in fifteen minutes. She hoped Tristan knew what he was doing, letting them take this route. They only had about one and a half hours before sunset, and they were struggling enough without having to descend in darkness.

This was *not* part of the plan.

She took it easy on the first couple of steps, but even so, she could feel her heart rate start to increase. Another wave of nausea hit her, and she stopped for a moment to pull a bottle of water from the side pocket of her rucksack. She gulped down a quick drink, then shoved the bottle back into her bag. When she looked up again, the men were more than halfway towards the top. Ginny was a couple of steps ahead. The men appeared to be deep in conversation, not thinking about the two of them trailing behind. 'Ginny, wait up.' Her heart was thumping now, despite the rest and the water, and she felt sicker than before. Was it something she'd eaten at breakfast? But hadn't the others had the same? She took her rucksack off and opened the other side pocket. She pulled out the small strip of pills that Ginny had given her at breakfast. It was time she took one herself.

She wasn't usually one to take medication unless she really needed it, but she was starting to get worried about her racing heart. She'd been so calm, planning all this for so long. But planning was one thing – the reality something very different. She popped a pill out of the packet and swallowed it dry.

When she looked up again, Ginny was standing a few feet away, hands on her hips. 'What is it?' She huffed out a breath. 'I made it nearly halfway in these stupid trainers, with half the skin of my heels being rubbed off, and here you are, in all the gear, puffing like an old woman. What the hell is wrong with you?'

Cat stumbled, grabbing her stomach as she dry-heaved. Swallowing that tablet like that had been a bad idea. Then another wave of nausea hit her, and this time it wasn't stopping in her gullet. She pitched forward and vomited on to the thin strip of parched grass at the edge of the stone path.

'Ew, gross.' Ginny took a step back. 'Are you ill? Oh god, have you got that norovirus or something? I really don't want to catch that, it sounds absolutely awful.'

Cat stood up and wiped her mouth with the back of her hand. 'I notice you haven't actually asked me if I'm feeling OK? You just want to make sure you don't get it. That's typical of you . . .' Her sentence trailed off as she felt another lurch in her stomach and doubled over to puke again. 'Urgh. I actually don't know what's wrong with me. I keep getting these little waves of dizziness then this urge to be sick, and it had mostly gone away until now, when I stupidly swallowed that tablet dry.'

Ginny stared at her. Her mouth curved into a smirk. 'You're preggers, aren't you? I called it earlier – you not drinking late like us . . . these weird symptoms . . . it's all stacking up.' She rocked back on her heels, looking pleased with herself. Then winced and rolled forward on to her toes. 'Jesus, my feet really fucking hurt.'

Cat shook her head. *There she goes again*, she thought, *it's all about her.*

'You should drink some water,' Ginny said. 'I'll call on the boys. Get them to come back. You should have Paul with you.'

Cat just nodded, glad that her sister had found a little compassion at last. She sat down on the path and Ginny strode off. She looked uncomfortable in her painful shoes, but she kept on, calling out and waving, trying to get the attention of the others.

Cat took a sip of water, and hoped the nausea was under control for now. Her heart rate had slowed, and she felt much calmer. She was starting to understand why Ginny popped so many pills. It really must make her life much less stressful.

Cat looked up at the next part of the walk. Was she actually going to make it up this sharp incline? Should she be exerting herself like this, if what Ginny had suggested was true? It couldn't be, could it? She was on the pill. Had been for years. That was the one medication that she had no qualms about taking. As for if she even *wanted* kids – she and Paul hadn't broached the subject of pregnancy since early on in their relationship, when people had those sorts of conversations. It was as if they both instinctively knew that neither of them really wanted it.

It was just not something that ever crossed her mind. Cat hadn't thought for a moment that she might be pregnant, and after what had gone on at home, she wasn't at all sure she wanted a baby. At least, not with Paul.

Not after what he'd done.

But more than that . . . she'd barely let Paul near her since he'd been accused of assaulting his work colleague. So if *he* was the father, it was going to be big news for them both.

Twenty-One

Sunday Afternoon

Pigalle and Marchand have retreated to the back office and turned the volume up on the TV. The football is on. It's PSG vs Marseille, but Thierry has never really been much interested in football. Annoyingly, Séb, being originally from Paris, is a PSG fan and has decided that watching the match is a reasonable compensation for having to come into work on a Sunday.

'We're not in here to watch this shit. You do realise that, don't you, Séb?' Thierry sighs and rolls his seat away from the desk, swivelling around to watch the other screen. The computer monitor is flicking between the reception area and each of the interview rooms. Later, he will fix it so that all three screens are visible at the same time, but it involves some fiddling with the settings, and he can't quite remember how to do it. They don't usually have to worry too much about the CCTV in this place, because nothing ever happens. The bigger police station in Aigle is where most of the action takes place. They've been talking about closing this small branch altogether, and Thierry hopes that they will, so that he can ditch this job and retrain in mountain rescue instead. Sandrine thinks this makes no sense because it will cause him to have to work more, not less, but Thierry is only forty-five and he's not sure he can stomach another twenty years of this dull existence.

'Goal!' Séb jumps out of his seat and punches the air.

Thierry swivels back around to face him. 'Look at them, Séb.' He's pointing at the man and the woman in the reception area. 'Look at their body language . . . *Merde!* Can you fix this so it just shows the reception?'

Séb leans over and clicks the mouse a few times. Thierry can smell stale alcohol and fried bacon wafting through the other man's shirt, and the faint undertone of a spicy deodorant he's used in an attempt to block out the other aromas. Thierry wrinkles his nose. 'Out last night, were you?'

'Marianne took me to that new place in Ollon. Barbecue and cocktails. Might've had a few too many.' He glances at Thierry. 'Don't worry, I walked in.' He rolls his seat over next to Thierry. They both watch the screen.

The man is peering into the fish tank. His mouth is moving, but they can't hear what he's saying. The woman is sitting on the sofa by the window, her face turned away from him. Her arms are crossed and she is hunched into herself, as if trying to roll into a little ball.

'Why are they not telling us what happened to their friends?' Séb zooms in on the man's mouth, but the man is no longer talking. Just staring at the fish. He stands up straight, and his expression looks pained. He walks slowly over to the other sofa and sits down, then he leans back and closes his eyes.

Thierry frowns. 'And why don't they want to go to the hospital? Or even their hotel? I don't like this. Not at all.'

'They were on the Argentine, right? They said that much.' Séb picks up his phone and starts scrolling.

'So she said, but she's said little else so who knows. Who are you calling?'

'My friend Albert works up at the Refuge. He will have been there yesterday, all day. If our couple were there, and the "missing" couple, then he'll have seen them. I can ask if there was anything strange—'

'Ah . . .' Thierry raises a hand. 'Our couple. They mentioned their friends. They didn't say they were a couple.'

'I just assumed.'

'Yes, so did I. But maybe our couple are not a couple at all. Maybe that's got something to do with why they're being so cagey.'

Séb zooms in on the woman on the screen. She's glaring at him, her face directly on the camera, as if she knows they are watching her. Thierry half expects her to give them the finger.

Séb smirks. 'My god, that face. If they *are* a couple, then he's done something very, very bad.'

'Or *she* has,' Thierry says.

They wait, listening to the tinny faraway ring of the phone, then there's a click, and someone answers.

Thierry sees something interesting on the monitor. The woman is shouting at the man, her arms gesturing wildly. He wishes now that they didn't turn the TV up so loud, but the remote is broken and by the time he locates the stupid little switch to lower the volume, she'll have finished what she's saying. He keeps watching, his interest piqued. He'd probably be able to hear her if the sound was off, but then they wouldn't have had the opportunity to talk about the couple without being heard. The walls are far too thin in this place. He zones out of Séb's phone conversation, still watching the screen. Then smiles and gets up from his seat, just as the front door of the police station swings shut. He nods to Séb's phone. 'You deal with that. I'm going to have a chat with our lady on her own.'

Twenty-Two

Saturday Evening

Ginny stood with her arms crossed, looking over Cat. She'd managed to get the boys' attention, and they were on their way back down. Slowly and reluctantly. The sky had changed from the bright blue of the day to a darkening indigo as night crept in. Goosebumps skittered across the skin of her arms, and she hugged herself tighter. She was torn between feeling sorry for Cat, hating her for this further delay, and a growing sense of despondency about the whole situation. They were going to be navigating the descent in the dark. No question about it now.

Cat was still sitting on the ground, legs crossed, taking small sips of water. Ginny sat down beside her and unlaced her trainers. She pulled them off gingerly, and unpeeled her socks from her heels.

'Oh shit,' she muttered. 'Maybe should've just left them as they were.'

The skin was shredded. What were once blisters had already rubbed off, leaving bloodied red-raw skin beneath. She winced at the pain, the fresh air hitting the delicate flesh and making them sting even more.

'Jesus,' Cat said. She turned away and made more dry-retching sounds.

'Please don't be sick right next to me.' Ginny rolled the socks off completely, exposing her bare feet. She gently prodded the soft pads of flesh under her toes, where more blisters had formed – they felt like small, deflating balloons. She blew out a breath. 'Tell me you have plasters in your bag?'

Cat turned back to her. The retching had thankfully not taken a liquid form this time, but her sister's tired face was clammy and slightly green. Cat nodded, then started opening pockets on her rucksack.

Ginny leaned back on her elbows and looked out at the mouth of the valley beneath. So much air. So much space. And below, a dizzying descent to oblivion. Or to the restaurant, at least. Although it was so far away from them now, she couldn't quite believe they'd climbed so high.

A bird that looked like a buzzard swooped overhead, then dived deep below them. She thought back to the bird they'd seen earlier, on the other part of the mountain, where the rocks had slipped and Cat with them. Things could have ended very differently back there.

'Do you get buzzards here?' she asked Cat. 'I thought you only got them in the desert where they ate dead camels.'

Cat nodded. 'All sorts of things like that. I saw a kestrel earlier. Buzzards are really common in Europe. Not just in the movies.'

Ginny bristled at her tone. Cat was always patronising her. She couldn't help it if she didn't know as much as her clever-clogs sister. Mum and Dad had told her it didn't matter anyway. That there were other ways to become successful in life. They were supposed to love both of their daughters equally, but she'd done her best to make herself the favourite. Dropping in little anecdotes here and there when she visited them for Sunday lunch and Cat didn't bother to go – loads of people booked her for events on Sundays, she'd whine – and they'd let it go and spend all their time with Ginny, and that had suited her just fine. They knew Cat didn't really need their help – hence the reason they'd changed their will to favour Ginny.

Ginny had always been good at getting what she wanted. She just hadn't expected to get it so soon. She still couldn't believe that her parents were gone. She missed calling them. She missed asking them things. They were the ones who had always given in to her. It was much harder with everyone else.

But Ginny had wanted Tristan from the moment she'd spotted him in the Perception Bar in the W Hotel in Leicester Square. She'd been on all sorts of forums, trying to find out the best place to meet a 'man of means', as her forum buddies were inclined to call the likes of Tristan – rich, good-looking, seeking a stay-at-home wife who didn't ask too many questions. She'd been fine with the whole set-up until recently, when his recent – presumably current – dalliance started to take up too much of his time. She worried that he'd grown bored of her now, that he was on the lookout for wife number two. It happened, the forum buddies said, more often than not. Sure, she wouldn't have to worry about money. But she didn't like the thought of being rejected for a new model.

Cat handed her a box of plasters, just as the boys arrived back beside them. Neither of them looked happy.

Ginny peeled the backing off one of the large plasters and carefully positioned it over the worst of the burst blisters. 'Just give me a minute,' she said. Already forgetting that the reason for the return was not her, but Cat.

'What's up with you, Cat?' Tristan crouched down beside them both. 'You've been a bit out of sorts all day.' He paused. 'Do you think you can see this through?'

Paul snorted. 'Have you looked around, Tristan? I don't think any of us has a choice, do we? Given we've no way of summoning help.'

Tristan ignored him and laid a hand on Cat's shoulder. 'Do you need a hand?'

Paul stepped in, brushing Tristan out of the way. 'I think I can help my own wife, thanks.'

Ginny watched Cat's expression as her sister's eyes flitted from one man to the other. 'You might as well tell them,' Ginny said. 'They'll find out soon enough.' She rolled her socks back on and carefully slipped her feet into her trainers. It was better. Not perfect, but it would do. She could walk the rest of the way and still keep some of the skin on her feet.

'Tell us what?' Tristan said. 'What's wrong with her?'

'Cat?' Paul was crouched down beside her now, but Cat was already pushing herself up off the ground.

'I'm fine.' She glared at Ginny. 'She's being ridiculous. Let's just go, shall we?'

Ginny smirked. 'I'm being ridiculous? You're the one who hasn't bothered to tell their husband that they're going to be a daddy.' She flexed her feet inside her trainers, checking for friction. Much, much better.

'You what?' Paul was standing now. He looked from Ginny to Cat and back again. The sheer panic on his face was hysterical. 'Cat?'

Ginny started laughing. 'It's what happens when a man and a woman love each other very much.' She held up one hand with her thumb and forefinger in an 'o', then started prodding the forefinger of her other hand in and out of the hole. 'Didn't they teach this at your school?'

Paul had paled. *Oops!* Maybe this was something they'd decided never to do, and silly Cat had decided to trick him by stopping her contraception. This was one of the suggestions on Ginny's forums for when it looked like the straying husband was going to stray away for good. No man wanted to look like a shit and leave a pregnant woman. It's something she was considering herself, if she didn't get some answers from him soon.

Tristan was shifting from one foot to another. He also looked deeply uncomfortable at this turn of events. That was interesting, too. Had the men been talking about this? Oh god! Maybe Paul was planning to leave Cat. Maybe that's what all their secret little man-chats had been about, in amongst the play-fighting.

'For fuck's sake, Ginny.' Cat took Paul's arm. 'Look, I don't even know if this is true. I haven't done a test or anything. I hadn't even considered it until Ginny started banging on about me being sick and dizzy, and maybe—'

'Like I said before, it's probably just the heat and the altitude.' Paul's voice was stony.

Tristan changed his expression to something more cheerful. 'If it is true, it's bloody brilliant news. Cat will make a top mum.'

Paul stepped away from Cat. His face had gone from shocked pale to angry red. 'It'll be altitude sickness, that's all.'

'Oh, come on,' Ginny piped up. 'This could be just what you two need.'

Paul turned to her. He had his hands balled into tight fists, and he looked very much like he was ready to explode. This was not the reaction she'd expected at all. Cat was looking confused, and a bit sheepish. Tristan seemed to be flitting through a series of emotions – the current one being embarrassment. There was really nothing worse than becoming embroiled in another couple's domestic, and as domestics go, one half being unhappy to be expecting a child was as good as it got.

'She can't be pregnant,' Paul said, through gritted teeth.

Ginny laughed. 'Why not, silly? The pill's not one hundred per cent effective. Accidents happen.' She paused, watching his face. 'Oh . . . wait. Are you saying you don't have sex anymore?' She looked at Cat, unable to keep the gleeful smirk off her face. 'Only takes one go.'

'Just leave it, Ginny,' Cat said.

But Ginny knew she had stumbled on to something big. And there was no way she was letting it go.

Twenty-Three

He'd made a mistake getting too close to them. But it had been hard to resist. He could smell her scent as he tracked the group.

He knew the trails well.

Thought he was deep enough in the woods to stay out of sight. But the younger one had heard him. Spotted him. And running away would have freaked them out even more. He'd decided that revealing himself was the better option. Some bullshit story about being a shepherd. What the fuck did he know about sheep?

Well . . . they were followers, right? Liked to cling together in their little flock. Be told what to do, where to go.

The blonde wasn't like that. She was determined. She wanted to break away from the others.

But did she know there was a wolf in her midst?

He hoped so.

He looked forward to seeing her again.

Twenty-Four

SATURDAY EVENING

Cat felt sick again, but not the squirming nausea from earlier. This was a different feeling altogether. Like a snake had wound its way around her insides and started to squeeze the life out of her. She was staring at Paul, who was rubbing his eyes with his fists. She caught Tristan's eye where he stood behind Paul. He looked mortified. Ginny, of course, was gleeful at this new development.

Putain, as the French would say: a word covering all the swearing bases.

She swallowed back bile. It might only take one, but there most definitely hadn't been a chance in recent months for even that. Paul was the last person she wanted to have sex with at the moment.

He was staring at her, and she knew he was thinking the same thing. But he could hardly say anything about it now, could he? He didn't want Tristan and Ginny to know what he'd been accused of at work. He didn't want them to know that he and Cat had been sleeping in separate rooms for months. Last night in the hotel was the first time they'd been close for a very long time, and Cat had made sure to keep to her own side of the bed.

She couldn't bear the thought of having sex with him. So it was definitely not his baby. This was a spanner in the works that she really had not anticipated.

Paul had stopped rubbing his eyes. He sounded contrite. Maybe there was a little bit of hope left in him that they could save their relationship, somehow. 'You told me early on that you weren't interested in kids—'

'I was twenty-four years old. I probably *wasn't* interested at that point. But that didn't mean I wouldn't think about it later. We've never talked about it since, but I just thought—'

His anger came back hard. 'So you just thought you'd get yourself knocked up by someone else? Just in case you fancied it after all?'

'Woah, hang on.' Tristan stepped closer to Paul, laying a hand on his shoulder. He flicked a worried glance at Cat. 'What are you talking about—'

'Gosh!' Ginny said. 'I didn't peg you as the affair type, Kitty-Cat.' She smirked, then frowned – her mouth hanging open as her mind whirred. 'Oh, hang on . . . is this what the *real* scandal was about French Frank? Was he married, Cat? Well, well . . .'

Paul ignored her. His expression had changed. 'You know, Cat, you were acting really strangely after you came back from that event you did last month.'

Cat took a breath. She tried to laugh but it came out as a pained sniff. 'What event? What are you talking about?' She glanced across at Tristan, hoping for a reprieve. One of his wise cracks. Anything. But he was looking at her with a low-level expression of horror that made her stomach swirl. She turned to Ginny, whose amused face had turned as hard as the smooth, silvery rock they were standing on.

'Surrey,' he said. 'Some event planning conference, you said. Networking.' He shook his head. 'You stayed an extra night.'

Ginny stepped closer to Cat. Cat could smell the sweat seeping through her t-shirt. 'Was it in *Ascot*, by any chance?' She stayed where she was but turned her head towards Paul. 'The Berystede Hotel?' She turned back to Cat. Her eyes were shining with hatred.

Paul looked confused. 'I, um. I'm not sure. Maybe.'

'Give it a rest, Ginny.' Tristan moved around, reaching out for Ginny's arm.

She shrugged him off. 'Get the fuck off me.'

Paul looked from Cat to Ginny. 'What's going on here? What have I missed?'

'It's nothing, Paul. Ginny's getting confused with something, I think.' She looked her sister in the eye. Prodded her chest, as Ginny had done to her hours before. 'This. Is. Not. All. About. You.' She punctuated each word with a prod. Ginny moved back slightly with every single one, but she kept her hard eyes trained on Cat's.

'You stupid bitch!' Ginny spat in her face.

Cat wiped the spittle off her cheek. 'You're disgusting, Ginny. A disgusting, stupid little girl who values money over love, possessions over friendship. You'd rather spend your life being praised by fellow vapid losers on Instagram than have a meaningful relationship with anyone. You might've had our parents fooled, but you don't fool me.' She started prodding again. 'You. Are. Pathetic.' She was so close to Ginny now. And Ginny was dangerously close to the edge.

'Woah, come on.' Tristan took Cat's arm and tried to pull her back, but Cat wasn't having it.

Ginny stood her ground, but Cat could see she was fighting back tears. 'I feel sorry for you, Paul,' she said. 'Are you hearing all this? My perfect sister isn't quite so perfect after all. Who knew?' She turned to Tristan, her face distorted into a sneer. 'As for you . . .'

Cat swallowed. This was not meant to happen. Everything had spiralled out of control so quickly, there was no time to consider the next move, but all Cat knew was she couldn't let Ginny continue with what she was about to say. She couldn't let her sister ruin everything.

Not this time.

'Shut up, Ginny.' She took a step forward again, their faces almost touching. She could smell her sister's stale breath. Ginny took a step back and Cat stepped in again, staying with her.

'Want to make me?'

Cat's hands came up instinctively, palms flat on her sister's chest. On the warm, sticky skin above the neck of Ginny's t-shirt.

'Cat . . . for fuck's sake!' Paul's voice shook. 'Stop it.'

Tristan yelled right into her ear. 'No!' He grabbed her arm.

But it was too late.

Cat shifted her weight on to her heels, her hands staying on Ginny's chest. Their eyes locked. She was no longer thinking as she gave her sister one firm push.

And then Ginny was gone.

Twenty-Five

Sunday Afternoon

The woman is sitting on the steps outside the police station, smoking. Pigalle watched as she flagged down a passer-by and asked for a cigarette. The teenager who stopped gave her three cigarettes, and she's already on the second. She inhales hard, then chokes on the thick smoke. She looks like someone who has not smoked for a while. Interesting that she has chosen now to start again.

'I like to take a coffee when I smoke. Thought you might too?'

Pigalle sits down beside her, and hands her a white mug filled to the brim with thick, dark liquid. It smells almost like tobacco. 'It's a little strong, but it helps clear the mind,' he says.

She accepts it with a grateful smile. 'Thank you,' she says. He follows her gaze as she looks back to the road, and the wide pavement where people are milling around, going about their day. She is probably wondering if she can trust him.

'I'm afraid it is going to be some time longer before your embassy assistance is here.'

She sighs. 'It's been two hours already. It's only one hour to Bern by car, isn't it?'

Pigalle lights a cigarette just as she stubs hers out on the bottom step, grinding the butt with her heel.

He blows out a plume of smoke. 'Maybe two hours, with these roads. And maybe Sunday traffic. But there's been a problem on the road. A . . .' He pauses. 'How do you say it . . . the falling rocks?'

'An avalanche? Aren't they a winter thing . . .' Her voice trails off, as if she is remembering something. She shakes her head. 'We met a couple of hikers at the start. They were telling us we should take a different route. Said there had been some rock falls . . .'

'Yes, a rock fall,' Pigalle confirms. 'Luckily no one has been hurt, but the road is currently blocked. They will have to turn back and find another route, I think. Or perhaps they will wait for the team who will come to clear the road—'

'And how long will that take? For them to clear it?'

He shrugs. '*Je ne sais pas*,' he says. He smiles. 'I don't know.' He flicks his cigarette into a drain. 'How long is a piece of string – that is what you say, is it not?'

The woman swears under her breath, then holds out her hands in front of her. They're shaking. 'No more of that coffee,' she says.

Pigalle stands up and walks to the bottom of the steps, then turns to face her. 'Are you OK, madame? You don't look so good. Maybe it's time for you to tell us more about what happened? We don't have to wait for the embassy, we can—'

'I know. I know!' She stands, and she is taller than him now, from two steps up. She balls her hands into fists. Takes a breath. 'I'm sorry.' Her chest sags. 'I just want to make sure that everything is documented correctly . . . and I . . . I don't want to go to the hotel or do anything else until they come. In case there's evidence . . .'

He stands up straighter in front of her. 'Evidence, madame? Of what? You said your friends are missing . . .'

She shakes her head. 'Yes. No. I mean, yes, they are. It's just that . . .' She glances around towards the window of the station, where the man is standing, looking out. His face is stony. Pigalle follows her gaze.

'You are scared of him, madame?'

She turns back to face the road. Pigalle watches her carefully. She swallows. 'Yes,' she says, quietly. 'Yes I am.'

Twenty-Six

Saturday Evening

Tristan watched in horror as Ginny's small body flew into the air like a ragdoll. Her eyes were wide in shock, but it took a moment before she screamed. The sound dissipated quickly as she disappeared off the edge of the mountain. The momentum knocked Cat backwards and she landed hard on the flat stone, with an 'oof' as the breath left her lungs.

'Jesus fucking Christ, what have you done?' Paul stepped to the edge and looked over. 'She's gone. I can't even see her.' He stepped back, whirled around to face Tristan. 'Mate . . . I don't even . . .'

Tristan felt a million emotions at once. There was horror, of course. Then there was fear. Fear for what was going to happen next. Shock, yes. Because it was not supposed to happen like this. And finally, relief. Because it was done now, and there was no going back.

Stick to the plan.

He walked to the edge and looked down. Ginny was nowhere to be seen. It was a straight drop. A long drop. There was no way of knowing how far she'd fallen, or where she'd landed. There were other paths below, more treacherous ones – for climbers rather than hikers. There were trees. And jagged, unpassable rocks. Probably other hazards too. It didn't bear thinking about.

Ginny was gone.

Another feeling washed over him. A small, tingling thrill. He put it down to the adrenaline that had obviously just spiked hard. He looked over at Cat. She was sitting with her knees pulled up to her chest, her arms wrapped around them, her face pressed down. He couldn't see her face, but her shoulders were moving and there was a muffled sound of sobbing. Paul was standing above her. He had his hands on his hips and he was looking, open-mouthed, up at the sky, breathing hard.

Tristan was good at containing his emotions when he had to. He'd wavered earlier, when Ginny had announced Cat's pregnancy like that. He'd thought he knew all parts of the plan, and then that particular announcement had swung in and punched him in the gut. Should Cat even be on this hike? How pregnant was she? He tensed his body, then forced it to relax. He hated that Cat had this effect on him, but she really did.

Get a grip, Tristan.

He looked down at his hands. They shook slightly, but he flexed them and took a few breaths and got himself back under control.

Your wife may be dead, Tristan.

He hadn't factored in how this part would feel. Planning everything, discussing it all, talking about the future – he'd felt removed from that, somehow. Like he was dealing with a work project for a client, telling them how to invest their money, removing the potential sentimentality of dealing with the fact that the client would need to die for the funds to be released to their children. But as the day progressed, he'd felt nervous. Until now. Because now he felt nothing.

People die, Tristan.

114

Yes. Yes, they did. He unhooked the straps of his rucksack and lifted it off his back, laying it on the ground next to the others. Then he opened up the bottom zipped compartment and took out a rope, a couple of carabiners, a belay device and a cam. He opened the compartment above and took out his climbing belt. He was thinking about Ginny as he stepped his feet through the foot-holes in the belt. He knew she was convinced he'd been having an affair, but all those late nights weren't anything to do with that. The late nights were spent at the climbing centre around the corner from his office, where he'd been training for the last three months. Training for a moment just like this.

'What are you doing?' Paul bent down and picked up a carabiner. 'Since when were you a rock climber?'

Tristan shrugged. 'Did some at an away-day thing. Must've been after you left. I got into it.' He took the carabiner from Paul's hand and slid the end of the rope through, knotting it into a figure-eight. Then he clipped the carabiner on to his belt. 'I brought the kit today thinking me and you might have a bit of fun with it.' He blew out a breath. Shook his head. 'Never imagined I'd be using it for this.'

Paul stared at him. 'Mate, I know you've always been good at taking control. But you have to be in shock right now. Your wife just fell off a mountain. Do you really think you should be doing this?'

Tristan ignored him. He wasn't in shock. He felt more in control than ever, and it was giving him a real buzz. He was looking around for a rock to tie the rope around, but there weren't any on this section. This is why it wasn't meant to happen here. He sighed. Looked over at Cat, who still had her face buried in her knees. Cat had let her emotions get the better of her. The pregnancy had come out of left field. Questions would be asked, later.

But there was nothing they could do about it now.

He refocused on his task. Using a cam was risky. He'd done it in the climbing centre, when the worst that could happen was that he could dangle off his safety rock after dropping a few feet. But using it in real life was a risk. If he got it wrong, if he chose to place the spring-loaded hook into a crevice that wasn't strong enough, the device would pop out and the rope with it. *Bye, bye, Tristan.*

That was definitely not part of the plan.

And ultimately, he was going to a lot of effort for something that was purely for show. He doubted the rope was long enough to drop him as far as where Ginny had gone, and even if he found her, he had no intention of bringing her back. He just hoped to god she was dead, because if she wasn't, then she was in horrible pain somewhere down that mountain, and despite everything, he really did not want that.

Wanting rid of her and wanting to actually hurt her were two different things. Although, thinking about it more, he felt a flicker of excitement imagining her fear.

It was a shame that it had happened the way it did, as there were a few things in Ginny's backpack that he wanted for later. He'd packed everything in there that morning, knowing she would never bother to look beyond the main compartment with the drinks in.

He knelt down and looked over the edge, feeling his way along the rock, probing the cracks and crevices to try and find the best place for him to hook on. He lifted his head too quickly, and the vast space swam in front of him. He leaned back for a moment, steadying himself. Cat's sickness was likely the altitude and tiredness after all, and he was just catching up.

Shit, Cat.

'Are you sure about this?' Paul's voice seemed to be coming from far away.

He zoned it out.

This was dangerous. Too dangerous. But he had to do it. He had to look like he cared enough to try and get Ginny back, even though it was impossible. He found the right size of crack and slid the cam in, pushing it deep, making sure it was in tight. Then he released the trigger and it sprung open, wedging itself into position. He tugged on it. It felt solid. But he wouldn't know for sure until he slipped off a toehold and found himself dangling off the mountain, and by then, it would too be late to do anything about it.

Bye, bye, Tristan.

He just had to hope he didn't slip.

Twenty-Seven

'Cat, please. You need to talk to me.' Paul tried to prise Cat's arms away from where they were tightly gripped around her knees, but she was not budging. She had retreated inside her shell, and she was staying there. He walked to the edge and crouched down, keeping his weight back on his heels as he peered over. It was getting harder to see much now, in the twilight. The rock where Tristan had wedged his climbing equipment was just below, and Paul could see the rope snaking down until it disappeared from sight. He watched as it rippled. Heard the shearing sound of rope on metal as Tristan unravelled another length. He watched the section of rope as it hung loose for a moment, then tightened once more.

Somewhere far beneath, way out of sight, Tristan was gripping on to the rock face with his fingertips, searching for his wife. His *wife*. Paul's sister-in-law. Who was more than likely dead.

Paul shook his head. How could this trip have gone so badly wrong? He peered over a bit more, hoping to see a ledge somewhere below, somewhere not too far, where Ginny might be lying – hurt, badly injured, but alive. Hopefully alive.

What was that saying – 'hope is the last thing to die', something like that?

'Paul?' Cat's voice was quiet behind him. He turned to her, and saw that she had finally unfurled. Her face was puffy and blotchy from crying. 'Paul, I'm scared.'

He went over to her and sat down beside her, taking her hand and squeezing it tight. 'Shh. It's going to be OK. Tristan will find her. She'll be OK.' It was a stupid lie, as most lies tended to be. But he couldn't think of anything better to say at this point.

'I've killed her, Paul.'

Paul felt a chill run down his back, right between the shoulder blades, where sweat from their earlier exertions now lay, damp and sticky. Cold. They were all going to get cold now. They were never meant to be up here in the dark. The mountain weather was perfect during the day, as the sun shone, but at night, at this height, they would soon start to struggle. Had any of them even packed anything warm? He hadn't. Like Ginny, he'd actually expected to be back in that bloody hot tub before sunset.

He squeezed Cat's hand harder, but said nothing else. There was no point in platitudes now. And the revelations that had kicked this all off could be dealt with later. Besides, she hadn't admitted to an affair. And they didn't even know yet if she was pregnant.

They sat together, as the sky darkened above. There was barely a sound, except the occasional screech and whirr of Tristan's rope sliding through the metal loop that was attached to the ridiculously small peg that was stopping him from plummeting down into the valley after his wife.

Somewhere in the distance, a bird squawked.

Cat started sobbing again, and he put his arm around her.

There was no way to know how they were all going to deal with the fallout from this. They'd have to wait for Tristan to return so they could work out a plan. Hopefully, someone from the restaurant might've seen him descending. Maybe he'd tried shouting to them. Paul hadn't heard anything, but from the amount of time he'd been gone, Paul thought Tristan must be far down the mountain.

There was a faint clink of metal as more rope rattled through the loop. It was nearly dark now. If he didn't find Ginny soon . . . Paul shook his head, trying to dislodge the thought. He wasn't ready to accept the fact that Ginny was most probably dead.

And Cat – his wife, Ginny's sister – had caused her death. It had been an accident. She was upset. She hadn't meant to push Ginny. Things had all just got stupidly out of hand. He wished he could turn back time – not just to before this horrible thing happened, but to months before . . . when he'd acted like an absolute idiot at work and lost Cat's trust for ever. Sure, she'd stood by him. So he would stand by her now, too. No matter what happened.

'I just want to see if I can spot Tristan,' he said, moving away from his wife. She'd stopped sobbing and was sitting eerily still. There was a rustling sound from the trees behind them, and he turned, but of course there was nothing to see. The densely packed pines were impenetrable in this fading twilight. That sound again: small, light, fast. A rabbit, probably. Or a fox.

He knelt down at the edge of the path. 'Tristan? Are you there?' He was whispering. He almost laughed to himself. Why did people start to whisper when it got dark?

He could barely see anything past the first rocky slope. The rope whirred. Tristan had been very brave to head down there like that, in the dying light. Very brave, but very foolish. Did he even have a torch? Paul shuffled back and opened the side pocket of his rucksack. No torch. Not on his packing list. He'd packed exactly what Cat had told him to – she'd said everyone had a list and the point was that they would all share in carrying all the things they needed, instead of everyone bringing the same thing. A good idea, sure. But he'd have liked having a torch right now.

The only thing in his rucksack not on the list was his classic red Huntsman Swiss Army knife – a present from his dad for his twenty-first birthday, and something he never travelled without. It had everything on there to saw wood, strip wire, open bottles and tins, and, of course, cut pretty much anything – but it didn't have a bloody torch. He'd bought one of those tiny lights that help you find your keys in the dark and clipped it on to the keyring. He'd hoped that maybe one day the company would update the tools to add a torch – he'd rather that than them spending time making the casings wooden or camo instead of the classic red. He did like things to look traditional, but tradition wasn't helping him much right now. He took the knife out and slipped it into his pocket. Then he went back to the edge. 'Tristan?' He shouted it now, and his voice echoed in the empty darkness. Something in the bushes scurried away.

Paul peered over the edge again, but it was useless. If he couldn't see Tristan, how was Tristan going to see Ginny? He thought about what he'd said earlier to Cat, joking with her about her annoying sister. Suggesting they tossed her over the edge. Fuck . . . could he have put that thought in Cat's head? Some subliminal command that he'd had no plan to make? He took the Huntsman tool out of his pocket and flipped out one of the knives. *Sharp enough to cut bone*, his dad had said, laughing. *In case you need to survive in the wild.*

He held the knife out and it glinted in the moonlight. The rope whirred, and another intrusive thought popped into his head. He could cut the rope. See how good a climber Tristan really was. If he was good, he'd make it back. If he slipped . . . then he'd be with Ginny after all.

Stop it, Paul. What the hell is wrong with you?

It was shock, he knew. Cat would be horrified if he said any of this out loud, but sometimes his thoughts really did reveal his true soul. He flipped the knife back in. Cat still hadn't moved. She was staring straight ahead, watching him, the whites of her eyes the only things visible now.

He thought about Ginny, and what she'd been saying before she . . . before she fell. He shook his head. No. Ridiculous. He was overtired and his thoughts were in overdrive, like some kind of waking nightmare.

'Was it in *Ascot*?' she'd asked.

Cat's conference *had* been in Ascot. He remembered now, because he'd suggested he head over on the Saturday and go to the races – he'd checked, and there was a meeting on – and stay with her that night in the hotel. It'd be fun, he'd thought. But she'd turned him down. Said it would be all work and no play.

Which was bullshit, of course. What kind of work conference has no play?

But then he'd forgotten all about it. Gone down the pub instead. He'd been secretly pleased the next day, when she'd said she was staying an extra night. He went out for a Sunday sesh too. Regretted it on Monday morning. Perils of being a delivery driver. But it'd been fun.

But now . . .

'Cat? What was Ginny going on about? Before she fell?' He was still holding the Huntsman. 'Cat? How did she know about Ascot? You said she never took on anything to do with the work bookings . . .'

'Paul . . .' she started, but then she didn't carry on. There was a rattle of metal, then that shearing sound of the rope being pulled. Tightened. Pulled. Breaths. Grunts. Shearing. Something hitting against rock. He turned back towards the edge. A hand appeared, reaching. Then another.

Tristan was back.

Paul slipped the knife back into his pocket and went to help him to safety.

Twenty-Eight

Saturday Evening

Tristan pulled himself on to the flat rock. He had one foot up, ready to push himself to standing, when Paul stepped over and outstretched a hand. Tristan took it and climbed back to safety, then headed straight across to where Cat sat.

He crouched down in front of her. 'Are you OK?'

Cat gave him a small nod. He could barely see her now. The light around them had turned to a dark granite, with only the glint of the moon for company. The silvery rocks they'd been climbing were all but black.

Paul pulled him by the shoulder and Tristan turned to face him. 'What?' he snapped, and he saw Paul flinch. 'Sorry,' he said. 'Jesus.' He stood up, rubbed his eyes with his palms. 'This is a nightmare.'

Paul snorted. 'Are you for real? Where's Ginny? What happened down there?'

Tristan rubbed his hands up over his forehead and into his hair. Pulled it a bit until it stung. 'I couldn't see her. The light was already too far gone.'

'You were gone ages. You must've seen her. I don't understand.'

You never will, mate, Tristan thought. 'She's gone. There's no way she survived that.'

Cat let out a small sob and he turned around and crouched back down to be close to her. 'Hey. Come on. It was an accident. We need to stick together here.'

Paul pushed him from behind and he fell forward on to his knees. He tried to twist around into a sitting position, but keeled over a bit before righting himself.

'An accident? Are you mad?'

Cat was properly crying now.

Paul loomed over him. He stank of sweat and fear. 'Why the fuck do you care more about Cat than your wife?'

Tristan sat up and looked up at Paul, with his big, sweaty face too close to his. 'Why do you care more about Ginny?'

'Stop it,' Cat said. Her earlier despair seemed to have faded away. She almost seemed like she was enjoying watching them fight.

Tristan couldn't be arsed with all this. He'd just exerted himself far too much with that climb down and back up, and for what? He was never bringing Ginny back up with him. He was glad the cam had held the rope, and even gladder that he'd only slipped once, and hadn't had to test its capabilities too much.

'Look,' Tristan said. 'Ginny is gone. We're not getting her back. Yes, that is going to be a lot to process, but for now we need to look after Cat. And we need to get ourselves down this mountain and we need to alert the authorities, OK?' He took a breath. 'It doesn't surprise me that you're letting your emotions get the better of you here, mate. I know you couldn't hack it in our real world of managing the funds of the ludicrously wealthy, and all that entails. But you need to man the fuck up here, now. Your wife needs you.'

'You really are a heartless prick.'

Tristan stood up to face Paul. He could see the fight was going out of him. He knew Paul was struggling with what had happened,

125

and he wasn't getting the reactions he'd expected. Even Cat wasn't too bothered anymore. She had stopped crying, but she was still looking at him and Paul, waiting to see what was going to happen next. Paul had probably expected Tristan to care a bit more about his wife, but the truth was, he hadn't cared much about Ginny for years. Possibly ever. He'd done his best at playing the 'decent husband', but it didn't come easily, and when pushed to extremes today, it seemed like his carefully constructed mask had slipped. It was unfortunate, but couldn't be helped. Cat had always been the better prospect. He should've dumped Ginny and moved on to Cat the moment they'd met, instead of inflicting snivelling Paul on her.

Tristan glanced down, and realised that he hadn't unclipped the rope from his belt. Jesus, what a rookie mistake. He hadn't wound the rope up yet either, and if it slid for any reason, he'd be pulled off the side with it. He eyed Paul, seeing if he'd noticed. He wouldn't put it past him to toss the rope off the side. Paul might pretend to be a good guy too – maybe he was one, deep down – but there was something more to him. Something that he was doing his best to conceal. Tristan didn't buy his burnout story for a minute, which is why he kept bringing it up. Something else had definitely happened to make Paul leave that six-figure job with crazy perks and bonuses. Maybe Cat would tell him later. Once this was all over.

Or maybe he needed to ask himself why he even cared?

He held out a hand to Cat. 'We need to get going, Cat.' He glanced around, taking in the trees to one side, the sheer drop to the other. 'Come on.' He saw Paul out of the corner of his eye, fiddling with the pocket of his shorts. He hoped there wasn't anything in there that was going to cause them any problems. He had a feeling that Paul was about to lose it.

Cat stood up. She took a couple of steps, glanced at Tristan, then stood next to Paul. She looked nervous, but her eyes were shining with excitement.

Paul turned into one of those Eagle Eye Action Man dolls, with the little button at the back that made them look side to side. Him. Cat. Him. Cat.

Cat looked at her feet. 'Ginny . . .' Another small sob escaped her.

He wanted to shake her. Tell her to get a grip. But there would be plenty of time for that later. She threw him a look from under her lashes. A smirk. Jesus, she was faking. Tristan felt the first stirrings of a hard-on.

Paul was oblivious. Kept his gaze fixed on Tristan. 'It's true, isn't it?'

Tristan deflated. Paul was so fucking tedious. 'Is what true?'

'The conference in Ascot. Cat's conference.'

'God, this is boring. Can we just get going please? Or we might as well all throw ourselves off this fucking mountain.'

Paul moved away from Cat, who was looking at her feet again, shoulders moving gently as she cried. Jesus, would she ever stop crying? Or maybe she was laughing. Christ, Tristan couldn't wait for this to be over so he could be alone with her.

'You were there, weren't you?'

Tristan said nothing. He unclipped the rope from his belt. But not the usual way. The usual way would be to unclip the carabiner from the belay device, then take the belay device off the belt. Then pack them back in the rucksack with the neatly coiled rope.

Paul spoke louder, as if that would help him get the answer he wanted. 'You were there, Tristan. Weren't you?' He turned to Cat. 'He was, wasn't he?'

Cat lifted her head at last. She was doing a good impression of looking distraught. Tristan caught her eye, and hoped she understood.

'I'm sorry, Paul,' she said, her voice hard as stone. She stepped away from him, crouched back down at the mountainside, as far from the edge as she could. She dropped her head, and hugged her knees again. But she wasn't crying now.

'What the—' Paul started, but he didn't finish. He turned back to face Tristan, just as Tristan swung the rope, with the heavy steel belay device attached, catching Paul hard on the side of the head. There was a soft, meaty crunch as the metal slid through flesh and connected with his skull.

Tristan wiped away a piece of something warm and wet from his cheek. Paul was still looking at him as he toppled to the side, landing with a thud at Cat's feet.

'Tristan . . .' he tried, still staring up at him. His eyes were full of confusion. One side of his head was matted with hair and blood.

Cat flinched, but she kept watching, and a slow smile spread across her face. Tristan licked his lips. And with a grunt of exertion, he bent down low, put his hands on Paul's chest, and rolled him right over the side of the mountain.

Twenty-Nine

Sunday Afternoon

Thierry leans back in his seat. The infernal football is still roaring out of the TV, because now it seems the volume button is stuck. Séb makes to pull the plug out of the wall, but Thierry holds up a hand to stop him.

'It's still better to keep it on. So, tell me what your friend Albert had to say . . . Wait' – he sits forward – 'is he that one you had to arrest for drunk driving last summer? After that crazy barbecue?'

Séb shakes his head. '*Non.*' He laughs. 'That was Adrien. And I didn't actually arrest him. I just had to stop him from driving down the mountain to find more beer at 2 a.m. You know he's not normally like that, don't you? He'd been having a tough time—'

'Yes, yes.' Thierry waves a hand in front of his face. 'Albert, then. Maybe I don't know him?'

Séb pulls on his small, neat beard. 'I think maybe you don't. He's quite new to the area, actually. He moved here from Lyon. I met him in the supermarket one morning and we got chatting . . .'

Thierry laughs. 'You weren't in the supermarket in the morning. Unless I give you an early shift, you don't get out of bed until midday.'

'OK, maybe it wasn't the morning. Anyway. He says yes, there were some Brits in yesterday. Two men, two women. They had a late lunch.'

'Ah. So anything unusual? What time was this?'

'Maybe 3 p.m. Albert says he saw them come in – one of the women looked like she was about to faint, but the others were fine.'

'OK . . . this is not very interesting, Sébastien. Did anything interesting happen? Anything unusual? Were they fighting? What did they look like?'

Séb shrugs. 'Albert says he went out the back after that. He was sorting out the beer. Doing a stocktake.'

Thierry slaps his hand on the desk. The noise of the TV is driving him insane. He glances at the monitor; the man and the woman are sitting on opposite couches, not speaking.

'Did anyone else see anything? Who served them? Can Albert talk to the other staff?' He sighs. 'We're really not getting much of a picture here.'

'Maybe we should send out a couple of searchers, just in case . . .'

Thierry feels himself getting ready to explode. Takes some calming breaths to counteract it. Sandrine has warned him about his stress levels and his blood pressure. She won't even let him have salt anymore. The witch. Thierry gently punches his fists together, five times. It helps calm him. He looks at Séb. He talks slowly and calmly. 'I can't authorise any searchers when we don't know who we are searching for. Or where.'

'OK. Yes.' Séb looks at his phone, as if it might give him more answers. 'Oh . . . Albert says he is trying to call the staff who were on yesterday, to see if anyone remembers the four Brits. Problem is, they are not picking up their phones. There were three of them. A woman and two men.' He raises an eyebrow at Thierry. 'Albert thinks the three of them went off to party somewhere. They're probably passed out . . .'

Thierry wants to scream now, but he doesn't. Instead, he closes his eyes tightly for three seconds, then opens them. Repeats that three times. Another of his little tricks. He doesn't even know when he started getting so easily wound up. He used to be a calm man, until Sandrine took up all those new activities and he was never entirely sure where she was or what she was doing. He sighs. 'Let's start on the hotels, then. See if anyone can tell us who didn't come back to their rooms yet.'

'Good idea.' Séb picks up his phone and sits down in front of another computer, where he clicks a couple of folders then opens a file. The header is clear, in large font and caps: HOTELS-CONTACTS. He starts tapping a number into his phone.

Thierry swivels back around to the CCTV monitor and watches. They are still on separate couches. She has her arms crossed tightly, looking out towards the street. The man is staring at her. His expression is not friendly. Thierry nods his head. *Interesting*, he thinks. *Very interesting indeed.*

Thirty

They sat there for what seemed like forever. Cat, with her knees to her chest, locked in position. Tristan, one arm around her, his head leaning on her shoulder. She listened to his breathing as it slowed back to something resembling normal. She knew she was in shock. Knew that there were things that would need to be said later on, once this was over. If it was ever over. She was alone now. No parents, no sister, no husband. Just Tristan, and a brutal side that she hadn't seen before and wasn't sure she liked. She was worried about herself a little, too. She had almost enjoyed what had just happened. The sky was fully dark now, the only sounds the occasional scurry of something in the woods, the odd squawk or whoop of a bird. Eventually, she found her voice.

'So this is a fucking disaster.'

He lifted his head from her shoulder. 'I know. Here we are, stuck up a mountain in the pitch-black, and I don't even have a torch.' He turned to her, stroking her face. 'I guess we're too late for the hot tub now?'

Cat shook her head. 'It's not funny. None of this is fucking *funny*, Tristan.' She pulled away from him. 'It was all meant to be simple, you said. It'll look like a tragic accident—'

'I think you might've buggered that one up when you decided to shove your sister off the edge.'

Cat felt tears prick at her eyes again. One minute she was crying, the next she was laughing. Of all the things they'd discussed, they'd never talked about how it might feel when it was done. Not that it was an issue for Tristan, who seemed ridiculously cool about it all. Terrifyingly cool, in fact. She hadn't expected that. And she hadn't expected to feel so lost, with the two people she was closest to in the world now gone.

Even if it had been what she wanted.

How the hell were they going to get down now? She could barely see her hand in front of her face. Then she remembered . . . *Oh, thank god for corporate clients.*

'We do have a torch,' she said, pulling her rucksack on to her lap. She opened one of the long side pockets, took out waterproofs and some other small bits and pieces that she could barely see in the dark. Finally, her fingers found a small plastic box and she lifted it out of the bag and flipped open the lid. Inside was a silver mini-Maglite, branded with a company name: *Epic Solutions*. 'I know the proper torch went in Ginny's bag – which, by the way, was a very stupid decision in hindsight—'

'A lot of this was quite stupid, in hindsight,' Tristan said, 'but she wasn't meant to go over the side with her rucksack still strapped to her back.'

She ignored his jibe. 'I got this at that trade fair in Ascot, would you believe. I liked that it was in its own little case, so I just tossed it in.'

Tristan laughed. 'Oh, the irony.' He took the torch from her and clicked it on. It was small, but the beam was pretty decent.

She snatched it back from him. 'I'll have that, thank you. Seeing as I was the only one to think of emergencies.'

He took her face in his hands. Kissed her nose. 'And this, my little Kitty-Cat, is why I love you.'

She let him kiss her properly then, and as he did, she managed to push away her earlier thoughts about what she'd done. What *he'd* done, too. And about his anger and violence. Just the stress, she decided. Who wouldn't be stressed in a situation like this? She pulled back. 'I suppose we'd better get going. You know the way, right? We don't have to go all the way up these steps, do we?' She laid a hand on her stomach, without thinking. The nausea was gone for now, but it might come back.

Tristan didn't seem to notice. He hadn't mentioned the whole 'you're throwing up so you must be pregnant thing', distracted by the later happenings, but no doubt it would slot back into his mind again soon and then they'd have to have that conversation.

'I need the torch,' he said. He'd pulled the map out of the plastic pocket that was in one of his pockets. He'd taken the lanyard off when he climbed down the mountain. She sat closer to him as he shone the torch over the slightly wrinkled paper. 'OK, so we're nearly back to where we were meant to be, I think. After the diversion. We just need to get up this bit, then we're away from the edge and around the top of one of the meadows.'

Cat was confused. 'Right, so after that, we're no longer on the edge overlooking the valley? Where's the bit where we were actually supposed to . . . you know.' Despite what she'd done, she couldn't bring herself to say it. She knew it would all sink in later. But for now, it was best to stick to the practicalities.

Tristan refolded the map and slipped it back into the plastic wallet, then put it in the side pocket of his shorts. He and Paul had been wearing similar cargo shorts, with multiple pockets. She pictured Paul, slipping something into his, not long before he'd fallen. Thinking about it, did she really know what any of them were carrying? She'd brought the torch that no one else knew about.

Paul had clearly had something that he didn't want her to see. And god knows what Tristan might have stashed in his pockets and his bag. But as long as he had what they needed to get through the night, she was just going to have to trust him.

'It won't be too long until we make it to the shelter, babe. Try not to worry. Yes, things have not gone entirely to plan, but we got the job done.' He stood up and picked up his rucksack. 'You carry the torch – it'll make you feel better.'

She stood up, took hold of his elbow. 'You didn't answer my question. I said where was the part where Ginny and Paul were supposed to have the accident?'

He frowned, shrugging her off. 'It doesn't matter now, does it?'

He started walking, keeping close to the inside; away from the edge. She shone the torch so it spilled out a muted yellow path for them both ahead. She tried not to think about what they were doing. About the danger they were in. If either of them slipped . . .

And she tried to push away his pissy attitude and vague replies.

Cat didn't like the way he was being so dismissive of her. All the time when they'd been planning this trip, he'd been loving and caring. She'd seen a different Tristan to the one she usually saw with Ginny. To the one that Ginny spent her time complaining about. A sliver of icy fear slid down her back. She'd been too trusting.

That was her whole problem. It's why she'd got into this whole plan at the start. The Tristan she'd been with was the 'affair Tristan', the one who could be as sexy and romantic as he liked, because the harsh truth was – affairs were not real life. Even when they were long-term. And she could see now, that for men like Tristan, the thrill was what it was all about. He had her now. They had both lost their partners in a tragic accident. No one would find it odd if, in a few months' time, they became close. That sort of thing happened all the time.

Luckily she'd been putting some plans of her own in place, alongside the one that she and Tristan had put together, first over coffees, then drinks. Then in snatched moments after illicit sex in any place they could find. She might be too trusting, but she knew enough about human nature to know that she needed security. Just in case. Like the money, for a kick-off.

She wondered, what he would do when he realised it was gone?

Thirty-One

Saturday Night

Tristan was glad when they made it to the top of the stone steps and into the meadow. From what he could see on the map, the route was now meant to take them across the top path of a steep pasture. Yes, they could still fall, but the worst that could happen is they'd roll into a sleeping sheep. Or a sleeping shepherd.

He thought back to that guy from earlier, the one that Ginny had been convinced was at the bar in the restaurant. Tristan couldn't remember taking much notice. He'd been too busy watching Cat. He'd loved watching her trying to keep a straight face when he'd run his foot up to her crotch. Typical Ginny, getting herself worked up about nothing. So what if the guy had been at the bar? He clearly lived in the area.

After the meadow, they would have to snake a path through the woods to get to the place they planned to spend the night. No chance of falling any distance in that part, but it didn't mean there weren't any other dangers lurking in the woods at night. He would have to be vigilant. He had to look after Cat.

They were never meant to be doing this in complete darkness.

The beam from Cat's torch was helping a little. They'd been lucky, too, that the sky had remained cloudless, and the moon was casting a much-needed, yet muted, glow. But there were pockets of pitch-blackness that would make anyone's imagination run riot.

They forged on ahead. Cat shone the torch into the trees, but Tristan grabbed her hand, directing the beam down to her feet, where it shrank to a bright-white dot.

He held a finger to his lips. 'Shh.'

'What is it?' she hissed.

He said nothing. Waited. And then watched her face as she heard it for herself. A twig snapping. A faint rustling in the trees.

He held his breath, waiting for another sound. But none came.

'An animal?' She tried to sound hopeful. 'Could be a deer?'

Tristan sniffed. 'Or that shepherd weirdo is still about.'

Cat wrapped her arms around herself, and the torch beam disappeared behind her. 'Why would he be? He'll be in his hut, or his house, or wherever it is he goes at night.'

He looked into the trees, but couldn't see anything other than blackness.

An owl hooted, and he flinched. *Fuck's sake.* He was getting jumpy now.

'This is madness,' Cat whispered. 'We can't stay here overnight. How far is it to the shelter?'

He kind of agreed with her, but they didn't have much of a choice now. She shone her torch around, and the beam caught on a signpost that they'd missed earlier. She stepped away from him and walked closer to the sign, shining the beam towards the top, where arrows pointed to the left, the right and straight on.

'Cat . . .'

'Look. Which one of these takes us back down? This one says forty-five minutes. We can do that, can't we? Even in the dark?'

He walked up behind her and pulled her arm back, dropping the beam down again. 'It's too risky. It'll be pitch-black on that descent. You need to abseil down a bit using chains. No way we can do that right now.'

She shifted away from him, shone the torch back on the sign. 'Abseil? Are you sure?'

'I researched this all, Cat. Like you asked me to. It's the quickest route, but it's slippery and hazardous, even in the daytime. We're both exhausted. We need to rest a while, then tackle it at sunrise.' He wrapped his arms around her waist, nuzzled her ear. 'You need to trust me on this.'

He felt her sink into his arms.

There was another rustling in the trees, but it sounded like, whatever it was, it was moving away from them. Definitely an animal, then. Spooked by their presence as much as they were by it.

'*Was* that him in the bar, by the way? Ginny seemed pretty certain.'

'Nah,' she said, turning around to face him. 'I told her she'd got it wrong.' She looped a finger around her necklace, lifting the pendant out on top of her t-shirt. An unconscious gesture, one that he'd noticed her doing before.

He reached out to touch it, just as she slipped it back inside her t-shirt. 'What's with the necklace? I haven't seen you wear that before.'

'It's new.'

'Ginny had a new necklace on too. A flashy one with a green stone. You two go for a girly shopping day, did you?'

'I didn't even notice she had a new one.'

He frowned. 'Only you two would decide to wear fancy new necklaces on a day out hiking.' He shook his head. 'Women. Anyway,' he continued, 'we should get going. If that freak is hiding out in the woods, we need to get some distance between us.'

Tristan grabbed the torch with one hand and took Cat's hand with the other, and led them into the forest. He flicked the torch off and they stood still for a moment. The darkness had swallowed them whole; the moon was unable to penetrate the dense canopy of trees. All he could hear was the sound of them breathing, and then, after a moment, the quiet sounds of the woods around them. Things skittering in the undergrowth. The air was damp and dank, as he flicked the torch on again and led her deeper into the trees.

'It's not far. Stay close.'

He did his best to ignore the multitude of noises that seemed to be growing and pulsing around them. Like the one that sounded like a distant scream, that he told himself was just another bird.

———

Thirty-Two

He enjoyed the darkness. He enjoyed acting on instinct. Seeing where the path might take him. But he knew exactly where he was going right now. It was a well-trodden route, despite the rougher parts that might make the average day-hiker a little wary. Some people ran this route. It wasn't that hard.

But the little flock of sheep were making hard work of it. The young blonde whining her way from start to finish.

Well, not anymore.

He'd thought about hiking down to where he was sure she must've fallen, maybe to make sure that she wasn't coming back. But there was no need. That fall was enough to end anyone.

He'd been a little surprised that it had happened there. Couldn't work out if it was intentional or a nasty accident. Wrong place, wrong time.

Poor little blondie.

But he had no interest in her. It was the other one he wanted. And she was still around.

He sniffed the air, hoping she might be nearby. But he knew she wasn't. Not yet.

But soon.

He heard the sounds of a waterfall nearby and detoured off the main track. He licked his lips, tasting salt. He was thirsty.

He climbed down to the edge of the pool where fresh water tumbled down the rocks, and he cupped his hands under it and drank. It was cold. Delicious. It made his head hurt, but he liked it.

Then he found a flat stone and sat there for a while, just listening to the sounds of the water. The sounds of the trees, and the undergrowth. The scurry of small things as they darted around, searching for food. For shelter. For smaller things to eat. He cupped his hands and drank more water, letting it cascade down his chest, the coolness soothing his hot, sweaty body.

He heard voices in the distance. The snapping of branches.

They were coming.

He couldn't wait to see her again.

Thirty-Three

Saturday Night

Tristan was trying to be a hard man about it all, but in the thick, dark woods, he was just as scared as Cat. He kept a tight hold on her hand, the torchlight shining a few feet ahead of them, giving them a small arc of light – just enough to make sure they didn't trip over a protruding root, or a rock. Or something else. He wasn't convinced they were alone in this section of the woods, but he wasn't going to bring it up again. For now, the sounds seemed consistent with wildlife and he hoped that was all they had to contend with. There were no really dangerous animals in these mountains. There was unlikely to be anything that would attack them. He was just a bit worried about startling something that was out sniffing around and giving themselves heart attacks in the process.

There'd been enough excitement for one day.

He'd surprised himself with what he did to Paul, but he told himself it was a survival instinct. Paul had been on to them, he was sure, and despite his meek exterior, Tristan had no doubt that Paul would've attacked to save himself. He just hadn't been quick enough to realise the threat.

Hitting him with the belay device had been an almost-instinctive move. He'd known that the heavy steel would have an impact.

Even if he'd swung the rope with only a carabiner at the end, it would've been enough to knock Paul over. It was the element of surprise more than anything. Seeing Paul's open, pleading eyes as he'd rolled him to the edge had given him a jolt, but he'd held fast and carried on. After the blow, what else could he do? He could hardly tell Paul it was an accident. The whole thing had given him a rush.

None of it had been supposed to happen like that.

Paul and Ginny had been supposed to 'fall' during the chained descent, into an area that Tristan could control. Where he could make sure that one, they were both actually dead; and two, they were out of sight and wouldn't be found easily when the mountain rescue teams were eventually deployed. Cat pushing Ginny when she did had been a risk, but he'd dealt with it.

It was done.

They would need to find a way to scrub the events of the day from their heads, and move on.

Cat's hand felt different to Ginny's. Cat was bigger-boned than her sister – in a good way. She was far from fat; in fact, she had perfectly proportioned curves and a cracking pair of tits that he'd been more than happy to get acquainted with. Ginny was all skin and bone. Barely eating in a ridiculous attempt to look perfect for her Insta fans, while pretending to eat all the elaborate food she created on her channel. Were people really so stupid? It seemed so. He wondered if her followers would care that she was gone, or if they'd quite happily move on to the next shiny thing. She'd made murmurings about pregnancy and child-rearing influencers being the next big thing; hinted that she might want to go down that route.

He'd ignored her. He didn't want kids.

Which is why he'd had the snip, several years earlier.

It could fail though, right? There'd been that guy at work whose wife had got pregnant after a failed vasectomy. It was more common than people realised – and there'd been no chance of an accident with Ginny as she'd been on the pill too. Although he wouldn't have put it past her to stop taking it. Hence his own insurance policy.

But now . . . well, now he was kind of hoping that the procedure had failed.

He squeezed Cat's hand. 'Do you really think you might be pregnant? You know what Ginny's like . . .' He paused to correct himself '. . . *was* like, with all her bloody theories.'

He felt Cat tense. 'Paul thought it might just be the altitude and not enough food.'

'But what do you think? I mean, I'm no expert, obviously, but aren't there other signs? Don't you have to miss a period?'

'My periods have always been all over the place. When we were young, Ginny was able to track hers to practically the minute they were due, while I was always the one who ended up having an accident in white jeans.' She tried to laugh, but it sounded forced.

'That's what you get for wearing white jeans,' he said. 'Weren't they banned after the eighties?'

'I'm surprised Ginny's not still got a pair. She was much more into them than me. She was also quite happy to tell me how I was too fat to wear them. Just as well they were ruined, eh?'

Cat's tone sat somewhere between nostalgia and bitterness, and it was a timely reminder of why they were here. He felt his own tone harden. 'She was a little bitch, Cat. But you don't have to deal with her shit anymore. Neither do I. I know you don't believe me, think it's just me trying to butter you up, but I really do wish I'd dumped her the minute I realised she had a much hotter sister.'

'We might never have got together anyway, but at least Paul would've survived his fate.'

He let go of her hand. 'Don't tell me you're regretting getting rid of him? OK, so it didn't happen like it was meant to and I get that you're upset about that. But you told me he was bad news,

145

Cat. I believed you, even though you've consistently refused to tell me what he actually did. I know it had something to do with him leaving work. You might as well tell me now.' He reached for her hand again, softening his voice. 'If you tell me, then I'll be able to reassure you that we've done the right thing here.'

'Have we though? What the hell are we doing, Tristan? We're . . . we're murderers.' She stopped walking, and slid her hand out of his. 'I can't carry on with this. When we get back down there tomorrow, I'm going to the police and I'm telling them everything.'

Tristan snorted. 'You really want to spend the rest of your life in prison? Do you actually have any idea what it's like in those places?' He paused. Lowered his voice further. 'They'll take your baby away, Cat. Our baby . . . I mean. I don't even care who the father is. I can step up . . . I know you weren't sleeping with Paul, so it can't be his . . .' There was no need to tell her that there was a good chance it wasn't his own either. He didn't really want to think about what that might mean.

'I might not even be pregnant. Can we just get to the shelter? I'm so tired . . .' Her sentence trailed off as she started to cry.

Christ, not again. All she'd done for at least half an hour after Ginny fell was to sit there and cry. Then she'd laughed, and he'd been confused, but put it down to shock. Of course she'd been going through a cascade of emotions while he'd climbed down the mountain on his ridiculous, fruitless, *fake* rescue mission. And her useless husband standing there doing nothing.

He sucked in a breath, trying to calm himself down. His thoughts were all over the place. For a moment he'd thought the same thing as Cat – that they needed to hand themselves in, tell the truth. How were they going to live with it? He knew their behaviour now was irrational. They'd killed their partners, widowed themselves, and yet they were talking about having babies and . . .

He stopped his spiralling thoughts, blew out a long, slow breath, bookending the madness with air.

He'd come round to the idea of her being pregnant, though. Maybe it was the way forward for them both. If they could hold their nerve, get through the tough bits. Convince people they fell in love due to their combined grief – blah blah blah. They could fudge the dates. No one had to know. Or better still, they could just fuck off and start afresh. He could work anywhere, and so could she – not that money was an issue. He had plenty of savings – all left to Ginny if he died, but she was gone so that was no problem anymore. Plus Ginny's money, of course. Ginny's inherited trust fund that had triggered this whole little situation that they'd found themselves in.

Thirty-Four

Saturday Night

He kept telling her that they were nearly there, but she was starting to feel delirious from it all, like she was having an out-of-body
experience. There was the Cat in the woods, in the dark, blindly
stumbling along the path. Bickering then making up. Wondering
what the hell she was doing, then remembering why she was doing
it. There was that Cat, and there was the other one, floating above,
looking down. Watching this couple walk from one bad situation
to the next, trying to convince each other that it was all going to
be OK.

That Cat didn't cry. The floating Cat was hard and emotionless,
despite the shimmering, wisp-like quality. The floating Cat saw it
from the outside. Like someone trying to make sense of it all. A
police officer, a psychologist. One of their friends who just couldn't
get their head around what had happened. A journalist. A potential
client who'd read it in the news. The floating Cat was all of these,
and the mind of Cat – the one that connected the real one to the
detached soul of Cat – the mind of Cat knew that they would
have to deal with all of these people, these situations; and as in
any situation like this – no matter how fool-proof, how watertight
the story – there would be doubters. Like the ones who refused to

believe that Amanda Knox was innocent. Like the ones who were convinced that the McCanns had killed their own daughter. There would be the internet conspiracy theory groups, full of people with too much time on their hands and too much glee in uncovering the gory details at the expense of the victims. These people would hound them and hound them, until they broke. Because in this case, the hounds would be right.

Tristan and Cat were cold-blooded killers.

She had to keep reminding herself why they needed to be.

They were still in darkness, the relative silence only punctuated by their own breathing and footsteps on the mulchy forest floor – plus the rustling and crackling and occasional hoots and scurrying that she was slowly becoming used to. But something had changed. The air was lighter, in some way. Less damp and cloying. And there was another sound – something that was very much like running water.

'We're nearly at the waterfall,' Tristan said, swinging the torch around into the trees. 'Can't see it yet but you can hear it, right? It's going to open out a bit soon, and then we'll be there.'

Floating Cat dropped down and back into the real Cat's body. She felt her own form and shape, as if trying on a new suit. Her head had cleared, and she was ready to carry on. 'The money transfer should've gone through today. You didn't mention it earlier.'

His voice was wary. 'I didn't have a chance. When did I see you alone?' He took her hand and squeezed it. It felt different to before. Unfamiliar. Unwelcoming. He still wanted this, didn't he?

'I know. I just thought maybe you could've confirmed it. It's been on my mind. I appreciate all you've done sorting it out. I'm just a bit antsy.'

'Look, I deal with this stuff all the time. My clients are billionaires, and even they get funny on transfer days. Our fund . . .' He paused. '. . . *your* fund . . . it's a drop in the ocean. It's a minnow in a sea of sharks. It'll be there, and as soon as we get back to the car and get both of our phones, we'll confirm that it's gone into your account. OK?'

She nodded. 'Sure. It's fine. I trust you.' Problem was, she wasn't sure that she really did. Not completely. She'd trusted Paul completely, and that had turned out to be a big mistake. Trust was a bit of a minefield, really. She had no doubt that her parents – despite their ill-advised will change – had trusted Ginny to do the right thing. And of course, Ginny being Ginny, she had not. But Ginny never did anything by herself. She always relied on others to do the difficult thinking for her.

Cat took a deep breath, and kept walking.

Tristan let go of her hand and walked on ahead, just a little. She upped her speed, wanting to keep close behind him and the torch beam that was their only hope of making it through these trees.

'There!' He stopped walking, and she almost crashed into his back. 'See it? It's got a pale-green door. You can just make it out.' He shone the torch ahead. Started walking again.

She did see it. And as they got closer, she could see more of the whole thing. A shelter, he'd told her. Somewhere safe to spend the night. She didn't know what she'd been expecting, but this wasn't it.

He took her hand again and dragged her towards the house. Well, what was left of it. An old crumbling brick structure with broken windows. The pale-green door was battered, and half covered in moss. The stone of the building was black in places, where damp had seeped in. The rest of it was covered in ivy and other climbing things that burrowed their way in through the gaps in the brickwork. The forest was clinging on, making it part of its own. If you were to google 'horror cottage in the woods' or 'serial killer's lair', this place would be in the top five hits.

Her stomach churned and she felt ridiculously cold all of a sudden. She wrapped her arms around herself, trying to soothe her stomach and fend off the chill. The sound of the waterfall was louder now, but she still couldn't see it – although she assumed it was the reason for the dip in temperature.

'We made it.' He turned around and hugged her. 'I knew we would.' He pulled back. 'Jesus, you're freezing. Best get ourselves inside.'

She looked at him, quite amazed with how pleased he looked with himself. 'It's a bit . . . basic.'

He laughed in her face. 'Are you fucking serious right now? You sound like your stupid little sister. Basic? It's an abandoned house up a mountain. In case you'd forgotten, we're stuck up here until the morning. Do you know how much research I had to do to find this place without actually flying over and searching the place myself? So many goddamn hiking and mountaineering forums, having to chat to all those boring freaks who wanted to tell me about the route when all I wanted to know was "where can I kill someone and make it look like an accident" and "where can I spend the night to get my story straight".' He shook his head. 'You have no idea, Cat. No *idea*.'

She swallowed. Took a moment before replying to make sure she didn't say something she might regret. They were meant to be in this together, but it felt like he was turning on her. 'I don't like your tone.'

His eyes flashed with anger, and for a moment she thought he might hit her. Then his shoulders dropped, and his face softened. 'I'm sorry.' He pulled her close, nuzzled her neck. 'I'm a bit wound up. Let's just get inside, shall we?'

He stepped away from her again and directed the torch towards the building. Then he made his way through the overgrown vegetation that had sprouted all along what was once the path to the house. She followed. No matter what he did, she didn't want to be too far from him. She knew her own mood was up and down, the same as his. The aggression was just his way of dealing with it. He shone the torch on the door, rattled the handle. She'd been expecting it to be locked, but it was just a bit loose. He yanked the handle to the right, and the door opened with a creak.

'Let me check it out first. Just wait here for a minute.'

She watched as he disappeared inside the gloomy building, the light from the torch a small dot as he pressed forward. It grew dark once more, and she felt a chill run across her shoulders. The sound of Tristan's footsteps faded as he vanished further inside the house. She turned back to face the forest. The darkness was so thick that she wasn't sure if she had her eyes open or closed.

She blinked, then held her hand out in front of her, penetrating the black. There was no hint of a light from anywhere. She held her breath, listening for the noises of the forest. She tuned into the sound of the waterfall nearby. Listened to the familiar rustling in the undergrowth. Small things scurrying around. The faint call of a bird, somewhere far away.

She turned back to the house, peered inside the dark doorway. The same musty smell of the woods around her was inside the house, mixed with other things: dust, mould. Dead things.

Now that she was here, she wasn't at all sure that she wanted to venture inside. It was exactly the kind of place where something or someone might lurk in the shadows.

Thirty-Five

SUNDAY AFTERNOON

Pigalle watches the man on the monitor as he walks up to the desk and slams his hand on the intercom buzzer. The man looks furious.

The woman is still sitting on the sofa by the window, and she says something that Pigalle lip-reads as 'For god's sake, calm down!' These are the first words that she's spoken for over an hour. Pigalle is still not sure if they are a couple or not, but whatever their relationship to one another, it's not a happy one.

The man ignores her and presses his finger on the buzzer again. Pigalle sighs and gets up from his seat.

'It's OK,' Séb says, waving a hand. 'I'll go.'

Pigalle sits back down to watch the interaction. Séb has left the door open a little, and despite the TV, Pigalle can hear the conversation taking place at the counter.

'Are you OK, monsieur?'

The man's shoulders slump, as if the fight has gone out of him. 'I'm hungry. I'm tired. Is there anything you can do for us? Please?'

Séb shrugs. 'You don't have to stay here, you know. No one is making you.'

The man closes his eyes for a moment, then opens them again. His hands are on the counter and he is clenching and unclenching his fists. 'We're waiting for the embassy person. Any updates?' His voice is pinched, as if he is trying hard to stay calm.

The lieutenant shrugs once more.

The man bangs a fist on the counter, but not very hard. 'I know you're watching us. I spotted the CCTV earlier. I like the way you have it squashed up there next to the controls for the fish tank, thinking we won't notice.'

He hears Séb let out a small laugh. 'All police stations have CCTV, monsieur. We are not hiding anything from you.'

The man frowns. Pigalle really wants to know what this man is thinking. He wants him to open up. He is quite sure that it is the woman who is insisting they keep quiet, and he can't work out why. But watching them is interesting.

'Can you get us something to eat? Please?'

'Sure,' Séb says. 'You only had to ask.' He pushes the door open and steps back into the office, giving Pigalle an eye-roll. 'I don't know what is wrong with him,' Séb says to Pigalle. 'But he is not looking very well. He's getting agitated.'

'Call the café next to the bus stop. Ask them to bring in something for them. I can't ask Sandrine again.'

Séb nods and picks up his phone, and Pigalle sits back to continue watching. The man is staring into the fish tank now, as if expecting to find answers in there.

He's watching the fish, and I am watching him.

Pigalle is also drawn to the fish tank. He often spends time just watching them. Swimming back and forth, around in circles. No clue where they've been just a minute before. He envies them their short memories, because sometimes memories can break you. The seahorses, though, they're different. Intelligent. He is fascinated by them. He remembers learning that their eyes can act independently so they can see all around them. Wouldn't that be a useful skill for a policeman? And of course they mate for life, and the males carry the babies. He wonders how the human race would behave if the same was true for them?

Pigalle watches as the man walks back over to the sofa and sits down. His anger seems to have dissipated, and he flops, almost boneless, on to the seat. The woman stares at him for a bit. Opens her mouth, as if she is about to speak, then closes it again and turns back to face out of the window.

The man stares up at the CCTV, straight into Pigalle's eyes.

What are you thinking, monsieur? What have you done?

Eventually, the man turns away – following the woman's gaze to life beyond the window. Pigalle looks out. Passers-by occasionally glance in at them, mild interest on their faces. But what are they looking at? Just a man and a woman, trapped and slowly falling apart behind a large pane of glass.

Thirty-Six

SATURDAY NIGHT

The house was a lot less welcoming than Tristan had hoped for. From the forums he'd joined, he'd got the impression that the place was occasionally used by hikers who'd planned an overnight trip. He was expecting the rooms to be empty, maybe swept clean. Perhaps with some things left behind by other walkers and climbers that might be of use to the next person to come across the place. But it was not like that.

It was more like the abandoned house in a horror movie.

The first room, which the front door opened into, was *mostly* empty. The corners piled high with dead leaves and twigs, the occasional flash of white from some rubbish hidden amongst the detritus as he swung the torch into the corners. He wrinkled his nose. The air stank of dirt and dust, and something worse underneath, old and decaying.

The room leading off was the kitchen, with a wooden table and chairs that looked like they would collapse if touched. There was an old cooker, coated in a mix of old soot and grease. And a huge sink with a pool of stinking brown water and various things partially submerged. Tristan had no urge to uncover what might be in there.

He shone the torch over the filthy draining board and a family of small beetles skittered away into the cracked woodwork behind.

'Can I come in yet?' Cat's voice cut through the darkness, making him jump.

'Just one more minute. I was going to check upstairs.' He took in the narrow wooden staircase at the far end of the room. There was a faint dripping sound coming from somewhere up above. He shone the torch up to the ceiling. The beams were dark, and bowing, as if water had been dripping on them for a very long time. A leak in the roof. Probably one of many. But it made him nervous about the safety of the floors upstairs.

He walked to the bottom of the stairs, shone the torch up and into the corners. Then back down to the stairs in front. They looked mostly intact, but that didn't mean they were safe. He took a tentative step on to the first one, testing his weight. Seemed OK. He took another step, and this time the stair creaked under his weight. Maybe it would be OK, but thinking about it – did they really need to go up there?

He abandoned the stairway and went back through to the first of the rooms. There was the faintest of breezes from the open door. The torch's beam caught Cat's face. She put her hand to her brow, shielding her eyes.

'Well? Is it safe?'

'I think so. But I think it might be best if we stick to this room.' He directed the torch into the corners, then up the walls, across the ceiling. No dripping in here. It seemed more robust. It would do.

'There's a funny smell . . .' Cat said. He shone the torch back on to her and took in her unimpressed face. Christ. What was she expecting? Who knows what had crawled into this place and died, but at least if they hunkered down with the door shut, it would keep them away from anything else that might be lurking in the woods. He had no idea what time it was now, but it must be well into the night. They only had a few hours to go.

'Just come in and get the door shut. I'll light some candles.' He held the torch between his knees as he slipped off the straps of his rucksack and dropped it on the floor.

Cat came inside, pushing the door carefully shut behind her. She took her own rucksack off and laid it down beside his. 'What's through there?' She gestured towards the open doorway, the movement of her arm causing shadows to jump up the wall.

'Kitchen. It's horrible though. I wouldn't bother.' He walked over to the wall by the front door. There was a window. He hadn't noticed it before, as it was boarded up. 'Here, can you hold this?' He handed Cat the torch, then slid his fingertips under one edge of the wood. It was soft from years of damp, and it crumbled away in his hands. He slid a fist into the gap he'd made, then pulled away the rest of the boards. The window was filthy, but intact.

He turned to Cat. 'Better to have the boards off. As soon as there's a hint of light, we can make a move.' He ripped one of the dirty ragged curtains off the rail and used it to wipe a patch of grime off the glass, then he threw the filthy fabric in the corner, on top of the leaves and god knows what lurked beneath, then wiped his hands on his shorts.

Cat was shining the torch in his face, and he raised a hand, squinting at her. 'I don't think blinding me is going to be very useful, under the circumstances.'

She lowered the torch towards the bags. 'Let's get out our secret supplies, then.'

He unclipped the top flap of his bag. 'Are you OK? You sound a bit tense.'

She sat down on the floor, crossing her legs. 'I think "exhausted" is the word you're looking for.'

He laid a hand on one of her knees. Squeezed. 'It'll be over soon. Then you can sleep for a week in the most comfortable bed in the world.'

'Oh yeah? Are you taking us to the Premier Inn?'

'Funny. You know where we're going. We need to hole up for a bit. Wait things out.'

'Separately,' she said.

'Yes. Separately. But away from home. Just in case the press hounds get wind of the accident and come sniffing.'

She started fumbling with the clips on her bag. Wouldn't look at him. 'I really hope they don't.'

He pulled out a candle. One of those travel ones in a tin. She'd insisted on buying these in that outdoors shop in Reading they'd gone to, while they were planning everything. He'd wanted to go back to the hotel, but she'd insisted they get all this overpriced hiking kit that they would never actually need. He took out another candle. This one was citronella – to ward off mosquitoes and other flying pests. The smell of it even unlit was giving him a headache. He laid the candles on the floor, then took out the big box of extra-long matches and lit the wicks. The cloying smell of the citronella hit the back of his throat, and he slid the candle away.

'Can you put that one as far away from me as possible, please? It reeks.' He took out the other two candles, and lit those too. 'And we talked about the press. It's going to be a story of interest. Just don't talk to them, and we'll be fine. Even if they stand outside your house and shout through the letterbox asking if you killed your sister and her lover—'

'I'm not going to be at home though, am I?'

He opened the bottom section of his rucksack and took out the vacuum-packed blanket. As far as hiking shit went, this item was probably the most useful. He hadn't noticed until now, because he'd been too pumped on adrenaline to realise – but it was actually getting cold. 'Well done,' he said. 'You were paying attention.' He grinned. 'I, however, will no doubt have to put up with that nonsense. But I'm very good at ignoring people when it suits me. Just ask Ginny.'

He felt a small pang of something as he said her name. Like someone had pinged an elastic band against his chest. Poor old Ginny. Cat didn't think she'd deserved such a gruesome fate. But what happened had happened. The job had been done.

The way he'd spun it to Cat was that Ginny would be zonked out on Valium before she slipped and fell to her death. She might've had a brief moment of panic as she tumbled off the slippery slope, not sure what was happening. But then she'd have hit her head on a tree stump, and it would be over quickly. Simple.

As it turned out, that wasn't what happened at all. The first part, where Cat had pushed her, was similar to their initial plan. The problem was, because Cat had done it instinctively, he had no way of knowing how far Ginny would fall, and how long it would take her to die.

It was extreme bad luck that she'd landed on that ledge and winded herself so badly she couldn't call out. It had looked like her arms were broken, and at least one leg – from the strange angles of her as she lay there watching him descend in his harness. He'd had to look away from her pleading eyes as he'd smashed her head with a rock before pushing her over the side.

Poor Cat. She'd have to live with the guilt of killing her baby sister.

Except she hadn't. He had.

He watched Cat as she wrapped her own blanket around herself. Each movement making shadows dance around the room. He thought about the fact that she might be carrying a baby, and that it might not be his. Was he wrong to trust her? She was no fool. But he'd just have to give her the benefit of the doubt until they knew for sure. She was rummaging now for something else. She lifted her head, sensing him watching, and gave him a wary smile. 'Have you got any more of those energy gels? I think we finished the sweets.'

He fished one out of his bag and handed it to her. Then he took out a bottle of water from the side compartment and took a long, slow drink.

It was her turn to stare at him, now. Her gaze was intense. She was quite something, this one. Despite everything, or maybe because of it: he was aroused.

Thirty-Seven

SATURDAY NIGHT

Tristan handed Cat the bottle of water and she drained it in one go. She hadn't realised how thirsty she was – but, thinking about it, it had been a while since either of them had eaten or drunk anything. They seemed to have made it to the house on adrenaline alone. Despite the state of the place, she was glad to be under cover and out of those woods. She hadn't told Tristan just how creeped out she'd been, and she certainly wasn't going to make any further complaints about their room for the night. She'd seen his face earlier when she'd commented without thinking.

'I'm sorry about before. I was tense and angry. But I'm OK now.' He'd moved his hand from where it had started, on her knee, to halfway up her thigh. His fingers were beginning to press and probe on the soft flesh inside, edging their way up towards her shorts. She laid a hand on top of his, gently pulling it away.

Was he seriously trying to get frisky with her right now? In this place? After what they'd done? Sure, they'd kissed a little, earlier. But that had been a kiss of desperation between two people whose emotions were running high. He shuffled closer to her, tried to bat her hand away, but she held firm.

'Now? Seriously?'

He pouted and snatched his hand back. 'Jesus, Cat. No need to be so coy. It's nothing we haven't done before.' His playful pout turned into a sneer. 'I don't remember you telling me to stop before. In Ascot. In Reading. In any of those hotels in Canary Wharf that you seemed to be happy enough to turn up at during the day . . .'

She kept her voice low. 'What's gotten into you?'

Tristan sighed. Ran a hand through his hair. 'Sorry. Again. I guess I'm feeling a bit strange right now. Everything's a bit surreal.'

'You can say that again.' She took his hand in hers, stroked her thumb over the side of his. 'I think we're both still adjusting to what's happened. In fact, I'm pretty sure we're both still in shock. Even though we planned it, I still can't quite take it in.' She looked down at her feet. 'We got carried away with the plans. I don't think I ever really properly considered how it would feel.'

He lifted her chin with his other hand, looked into her eyes. She could see the light of one of the candles reflected in his dark pupils. 'Everything is going to be fine. Trust me. We're both going to be different people after this, but that's no bad thing. For me, at least. I wasn't a good person when I was with Ginny. I didn't respect her.' He looked away. 'She deserved better.'

The lump in Cat's throat was growing so big, she felt like it might choke her. She had to swallow hard to make it go away. She wasn't sure she believed what he was saying anymore. About how he'd treated Ginny. He was talking in clichés, and his tone was cold.

Cat took her hand away from Tristan's, then pulled her knees up to her chest and wrapped her arms around them, like she'd done on the side of the mountain. Maybe Ginny had deserved better. She hated her sister, that was an undisputed fact. But there was a big leap between hating and killing. And maybe Tristan wasn't who she thought he was.

She felt like Tristan didn't really care about what they'd done – while, despite everything, she *did* care. Yes, she had wanted them out of her life, but had she got it all wrong? It was never meant to be grisly. They weren't meant to suffer. She and Tristan had found themselves in a situation that had spun out of control. As for Paul . . . he deserved punishment for what *he* had done. But was death too much? The death penalty was the ultimate punishment – but was it ever truly justified? An eye for an eye, the bible said. Except Paul hadn't killed anyone.

What a mess.

Could she still trust Tristan?

She lifted her head just a bit, watching him. He was raking around in his rucksack pockets, pulling things out. He unwrapped a chocolate protein bar and handed it to her. 'I know you probably don't feel like eating but you need to keep your strength up.' He stared at her. 'For both of you.'

She uncurled herself and dropped her knees to the sides, crossing her legs. 'We don't know if there *is* a both of us yet, remember?'

He stared at her stomach. 'Let's assume, for safety's sake, that there is. OK?'

His voice was tender, and made her feel at ease. Her mind whirred through all the possibilities like some sort of super-computer. *Trust him. Don't. Fancy him. Don't.*

He was incredibly attractive, that was undeniable. *If* she was pregnant, then any resultant offspring would no doubt be beautiful.

If it was his.

But she worried about his moods. Could they really all be explained away by the stress of the day? Of what they'd done? Until today she'd thought she was sure. But the way he'd been picking on Paul, dismissive of Ginny. Then later, seemingly angry with Cat – these things had caused a small ball of doubt to begin to expand and bloom. And that worried her.

It worried her a lot.

What was to stop Tristan double-crossing her? Perhaps he had plans to get rid of her, too. She didn't know the route. He could easily lead her the wrong way. It might even look like an actual accident this time.

She watched him as he chewed his own protein bar. He seemed miles away, deep in thought. Probably thinking the exact same things that she was. He would gain the most if he got rid of her. He held the key to the money transfer, and even if he didn't move it to a different account, it would be his – with Ginny gone.

But then if something was to happen to him . . . then it would all be Cat's, wouldn't it? Not just Ginny's money that she all but stole from Cat – but Tristan's money too. And he must have plenty of it, with the job he did. The bonuses. The savings. If something was to happen to him, and Ginny was his beneficiary, then it would come to Cat, because there would be no one left in the family line.

She took a bite of the protein bar. It tasted like cardboard filled with dirt. She'd love something nice to eat right now. Cheese on toast, maybe. And a big mug of hot chocolate.

She pushed the thoughts of the money from her head. It was money that had brought them here. Money and greed. But it had to stop somewhere. It was like gambling in a casino. How much are you happy to win? How much are you willing to lose? Besides . . . it was more than money. She just wasn't sure she was ready to face the truth of her real motivation.

Tristan spoke, bringing her back into the room. 'We can get a test in the village. After we've sorted things with the police and the hotel.'

She blinked. Shook her head. She was trying to dislodge the horrible greedy thoughts. Tried to imagine a baby being the thing that might turn everything around.

And then she heard a noise outside. 'What was that?' She shrank back into herself, arms around her knees. Her heart thumped.

Tristan stood. 'I don't know. An animal?' He walked over to the window, and the shift in the air made the candles flicker.

She swallowed. 'I heard a twig snap. I think there's something right outside.' If this was a horror film, she'd wait while Tristan investigated. After a while, she'd make the mistake of going to look for him, and she'd find him hacked to death or hanging from a tree. She'd seen all of those movies. She blew out a breath. 'Maybe we should go upstairs. Get away from the door.' She paused, anticipating his next move. 'I don't think you should go out there.'

He rolled his shoulders. 'Go through to the kitchen. Stay in the corner, OK? Take the torch.' He turned the door handle. 'I'll be right back. I promise.'

Thirty-Eight

SUNDAY AFTERNOON

The man is now half sitting, half lying on one of the benches in the locker room by the toilets. There is a camera in that area too, and although the woman urged him to lie down and rest, he still looks uncomfortable. In pain. But refusing any further help. Pigalle is certain now that the woman has a hold over him, but has no idea what it might relate to. Pigalle is getting as fed up with the waiting as they are.

He insisted on turning the TV off after the second football match finished, and thus he and Séb have been sitting in the office doing very little but watching the couple as they battle with themselves over their decision to keep quiet. Séb has just got off the phone with the embassy personnel, and the news is good.

The woman walks up to the counter.

'*Excuse-moi?*' she says, not too loudly. Not bothering to press the intercom, knowing that they will be able to hear her now that the racket has been switched off.

Pigalle walks out front and greets her with a warm smile. 'Good news, madame. You must have the sixth sense . . .'

'Oh?'

'Yes. Your embassy friends are back on the road. They will be here shortly.'

She nods. 'How many of them are coming?'

'It is two. A man and a woman. I have met them before, actually. Very nice people. Despite you getting us all to work on Sunday, we do want to help you.' He keeps his voice gentle. He sees no point in showing how impatient he is for all of this to be sorted out. 'I hope that as soon as they arrive, we can all talk properly and get all of the details that we need? There is not much daylight left . . . if we need to send out the searchers.'

The woman bites on her bottom lip. 'Would it be possible for us to talk to them separately? I mean . . . I don't want to talk in the same room as *him*.' She lowers her voice and gestures with a nod towards the locker room.

'Madame, I asked you before. If you are scared of him. You said yes but then you don't tell me anything more. How can I help you if you don't tell me what is going on?'

A lonely tear rolls down her cheek. 'I will explain everything, I promise. I'm sorry.' The tears fall faster now, and she looks genuinely distressed, but he is no longer sure if she is genuine. There is too much stalling. Too much unsaid. He leans over the desk and hands her a tissue.

'We called the hotels, madame. We wanted to try to find out who is missing.'

'And?'

'No luck so far.' He gives her a terse smile. 'You could help by just telling us where you were staying.'

'I will. Soon. I just . . . I told you. I don't want anything to be misunderstood.' She pauses. Wipes her eyes angrily. 'I just want this to be over, too, you know. If you had any idea what I've been through . . .'

Pigalle nods, gritting his teeth. He tries to remain sympathetic but he has had enough now.

Even the most patient men have limits.

Thirty-Nine

SATURDAY NIGHT

She didn't want to argue, even though she was sure going outside was a mistake. She'd had a bad feeling since they arrived at the house. Something felt wrong about it. Why hadn't Tristan checked upstairs? He'd said something about the stairs being unsafe, but for all Tristan knew, someone could be up there. Listening. Waiting. She absent-mindedly fiddled with her necklace again, tapped the pendant with her fingers. It made her think about Ginny's necklace, and how she'd failed to notice it and yet Tristan had. It wasn't like Ginny to wear fancy jewellery. And what was the point of wearing it on the hike and risking it getting broken? She ran her fingers over her own pendant and slipped it back inside her t-shirt.

Then she remembered.

A green stone, Tristan had said. Their grandmother had been a fan of emeralds. Their mother had kept all of the pieces in a carved walnut box that took pride of place on her dressing table.

The period after their deaths was still a blur for Cat. She hadn't wanted their things. She hadn't wanted their money. But it was the injustice of it all, the distribution of the inheritance being entrusted to Ginny, instead of it being shared equally from the start. Ginny had been instructed to give Cat a lump sum, but she'd kept the rest of the estate, include the chattels. All the contents of the house.

Including the jewellery.

She'd worn that necklace today to taunt Cat. She realised that now. But it had backfired because Cat hadn't noticed her wearing it. Her earlier slip, and her nausea and dizzy spells, had distracted her. Ginny must've been furious. No wonder she was being so bitchy. She'd wanted Cat to notice and to pull her up on it, but Cat had been oblivious to that. Her bloody sister. She wished that Ginny were still alive so that she could kill her again.

There was a creak above her.

She looked up at the ceiling. At the gaps between the floor-boards. It could just be the wind. Or the house settling. Or an animal. This seemed to be Tristan's explanation for most things, but she hadn't actually seen any animals yet.

She stood still, waiting for the ceiling to creak again. Tristan was still outside. He'd been a while now, and a shiver ran over her as she remembered her earlier silly thoughts about horror movies.

Not so silly now.

There was not supposed to be anyone upstairs. But if there was anyone up there, they weren't moving anymore. Maybe they were waiting to hear what she would do. She picked up her mini-Maglite and walked carefully through the open doorway into the kitchen. She shone the torch up the stairs, then back down to the bottom stair, which was in a bad state of repair, as Tristan had said. She frowned. So maybe he *was* just being careful. On the plus side, if it was too dangerous to climb the stairs, then no one else would've done that either. Unless there was another way . . .

There's no one up there, she told herself. She headed back to the front room, just as the door opened wide and Tristan appeared. He looked a little dishevelled but otherwise fine. His head, at least, still seemed to be firmly attached to his body. Thank god for that.

'Nothing,' he said, closing the door behind him. He shone a torch at her, then lowered it. 'Did you go into the corner, like I told you?'

Cat felt like a multitude of angry ants were crawling up her arms. 'Where did you get that torch?'

Something flashed in his eyes, then was quickly damped down. 'Would you believe it was in the side pocket of my bag all along? I was sure I'd packed it in Ginny's bag, but I found it when we got here.' He shone the beam at the floor, to where his bag sat, most of the contents spilled out around it. 'What an idiot.'

She wanted to believe him, but she wasn't sure she could. After all, if she was capable of double-crossing him, he could certainly do it to her. She'd needed to ensure that she was getting the money, that's all. It had only taken a minute in the car, with his phone and hers – the verification codes shared to one another's phones. If it had been his money, he'd have done the same.

Except it wasn't his money. And he had no right to it.

She laid a hand on her stomach. The baby was a complication. Possibly. There was next to no chance that it was Paul's.

Tristan picked up the two blankets and took them over to the far side of the room, away from the door. 'We should snuggle up. Share the warmth. We've still got a few hours to wait it out in here.' He sat with his back against the wall and pulled one of the blankets over him.

When she didn't answer, he looked up at her. 'Cat? What's up?'

'Are you sure there was no one out there? Only, I thought I heard a noise upstairs. When you were out . . .'

Tristan sighed. 'There's no one outside and there's no one upstairs. How would they get up there, anyway? I told you, the stairs are buggered.'

'But what if they got in another way? Climbed up from outside—'

'Why would anyone do that, when there's a perfectly functioning front door and a room in here to sleep in?' He shook his head. 'You're letting your imagination run away with you. Come over here. Sit with me.'

'And there was definitely no one outside? What if that . . . shepherd—'

'There was no one out there. I promise.'

She wasn't sure if his promises were up to much in this situation, but she went and joined him anyway. For the next few hours, she would have no choice but to be with him, and the two of them might as well be warm. Once they got back down the mountain, Tristan might find there'd been a change of plan. But for now, she needed to stop overthinking it all.

Cat sat down beside Tristan and shuffled in close. He pulled her blanket up, and folded the two together in the middle, then leaned over and tucked hers underneath on her side. She was grateful for his care. The temperature had dipped considerably since they'd been in the house. The flickering candles gave the impression of warmth, but it was all fake. Just like her relationship with Ginny had been. She'd always been sad about it. The fracture had started in their early teenage years and widened over time, but although it hurt, she'd found her own ways to deal with it. Until the events of the last few months had caused her to snap.

She'd had enough of people walking all over her. Thinking they'd get away with it because she was kind. Well, maybe being kind was overrated. She'd been played for a fool by all the people she'd thought she was close to, and it had caused her to harden her shell.

Tristan had rested his head on her shoulder and was snoring gently. Typical man. Paul had been the same. No matter what had been going on, if he'd needed to sleep, he would switch off like a light, while Cat spent her time tossing and turning.

Churning everything round and round in her head. Just like she was doing now.

She decided to take a leaf out of Tristan's book. She sat back against the wooden wall, tried to brush away thoughts of insects crawling down and into her hair. Her ears. Her open mouth, even, if she did manage to fall asleep. *It's only a couple of hours.* Then they could get back down to the village, and the first awful part of this would be over.

Cat closed her eyes. Shuffled closer to Tristan. She was drifting off when she heard the noise outside. Another twig snapping. *An animal*, she told herself, half smiling in her almost-sleep. Then there was a long, slow creak, and a cold draught hit her as the front door opened slowly inwards.

Forty

SATURDAY NIGHT

He opened the door slowly, not entirely sure what he was walking in on. He knew they were in there. He'd tracked them for hours, staying hidden. Keeping his distance. There'd been a couple of occasions where he was sure that one of them had seen him, and he'd prepared himself for that. After all, he had no idea if they would even make it to safety. He'd spotted the old house before they got there, taking an alternate route through the woods with only the moonlight and the sounds of their distant footsteps to guide him. He had a torch, but it was the kind that helped you find the keyhole to get into your house when you were drunk and swaying on your own doorstep. It didn't emit any kind of beam that would help him.

He'd stayed near the waterfall when they'd gone into the house. Him first, then her. He'd sat on a rock near the pool, the sounds of the splashing water making him feel less alone.

He stepped into the house, staying as quiet as he could. He hadn't expected to find them so quickly. The flickering candles highlighted their conjoined shape, the two of them huddled together at the back of the room.

She was awake. Her eyes shining in the candlelight, widening in fear as he stepped closer.

'Hello, *Sidney*,' he said, amusing himself with his *Scream* joke. His voice was barely a croak. He'd strained it earlier, screaming and shouting for help as he'd clawed his way up over the side of the mountain.

Cat sat up straight, and her movement caused Tristan's head to slip off her shoulder. He woke with a start. Then his eyes widened, too. The pair of them were frozen to the spot. Clearly this was the last thing they'd expected.

He took a few steps closer, dragging his bad leg behind him.

'Paul?' Cat managed, eventually. She let the blanket fall off her chest, pulled her arms out from underneath. 'Oh my god.'

Despite the pain in his ankle – which was most likely just sprained rather than broken, as he was sure that no one could walk on a broken ankle – and the dull throb in his skull, from where Tristan had tried to brain him with that lump of metal from his climbing belt, he was actually not in too bad a shape. His finger-nails were mostly gone, from where he'd jammed his fingers into the smallest crevices, making his way slowly up the side of the mountain in pain and in the growing dark. Adrenaline had replaced fear. He hadn't looked down. He could've stayed on the ledge, but he might not have survived the night, so what choice did he have – and really, what did he have to lose? If he'd fallen to his death, like poor Ginny, at least he'd have died trying.

He found himself smiling at the comical expressions on his wife and his brother-in-law's faces.

Tristan bunched up the blanket and threw it off. He stood up, and attempted to shift his face into one of concern.

'Mate . . . fucking hell. Are we glad to see you!'

Cat got up, then. Walked forward to greet him. She held out a hand, ushering him in. 'I can't believe you're here. Tristan climbed down to look for you, but you were nowhere to be seen.' She burst into tears.

He had no doubt that her tears were genuine, but they were from shock, not happiness. She'd just told him a blatant lie, confirming his suspicions about the two of them being together. Sure, they could try to explain away their huddling together for warmth, but he knew for sure that Tristan hadn't climbed down to try and find him, because he'd landed on a ledge that wasn't too much of a drop beneath where he fell. He would have seen Tristan if he'd started to climb down.

Paul locked eyes with Tristan. He knew he was thinking the same. *Shut up, Cat. Don't say anything else.*

Because Paul knew what had happened to Ginny, too.

'I'm guessing you didn't know about the ledge,' Paul said, 'when Cat shoved Ginny over the side?'

Cat's eyes flicked towards Tristan, then back to Paul. 'What are you talking about? There was no ledge. Ginny fell—'

'She didn't fall, though, Cat. Did she? She was pushed. By you.'

Cat shook her head. 'No. No. It was an accident. We were fighting, yes. I admit that part. But I didn't push her. We were prodding at each other, she slipped.'

Paul's stomach flipped over. Was she trying to gaslight him now? He'd been there. He'd seen it happen with his own eyes. He shook his head, then directed his gaze towards Tristan. 'I'm guessing this was all your idea. Makes sense now with you apparently "helping" Cat plan the hike.'

Tristan snorted. 'And what possible motive would I have, eh? Ginny . . . you . . . it was all an accident. We found this place, and then in the morning we're going to get help—'

'You found this place because you knew it was here. This was all planned. I confess, I don't know why. It all seems a bit elaborate. Have the pair of you been watching too many Hitchcock films or something? In between fucking, of course.'

'Paul—'

'Save it, Cat. You're not going to convince me that this was anything other than planned.' His voice softened. 'I know things have been difficult. I know I was asking a lot of you to trust me, what with everything that happened . . .'

Tristan looked confused. He turned to Cat. 'What's he talking about?' Cat looked uncomfortable. Tristan turned back to face Paul. 'What are you talking about?'

Paul shook his head. 'You know what? It actually doesn't matter. But I'm just bewildered as to why you thought bumping off me and Ginny was a good plan? If you were having an affair, why didn't you just leave us? It's what most people do. Most *sane* people.' He muttered the last line under his breath.

Tristan took a step forward. 'Look, mate—'

'You can stop with the "mates", Tristan. I'm not your mate. I don't think I ever was.' Paul took a step back, out of arm's reach. He didn't trust Tristan not to try and finish the job. He didn't trust Tristan *at all*. He couldn't believe that Cat had been taken in by him.

He fixed his eyes on his wife. She was still crying, but he had no sympathy for her. 'So what exactly was the plan for when you made it back down to the village? And what's the plan now that I've come back to scupper your romantic night in this pretty little cottage?'

There was an unmistakable creak in the floorboards above them. They all looked up at the ceiling. It seemed like none of them were breathing. Waiting to hear another sound, but none came.

'It's an old building. It makes noises.' Tristan shrugged his shoulders. 'I checked the whole place out when we arrived.'

Paul caught a look between Cat and Tristan. Another lie? Was she also starting to doubt this man she'd put her trust in? He could exploit this to his own advantage. He was going to have to. Because he certainly didn't believe that Tristan was going to change his plans and allow him to stay alive.

Tristan extended a hand to Paul. 'Look, just come in properly. Shut the door. It won't be long until sunrise, and we can get out of here.' He gestured down at his bag. 'I've got a first-aid kit. We can sort you out. Patch you up.' He grinned, then laid a hand on Cat's shoulder. 'Cat has been so worried about you. We were so hoping you'd landed somewhere safe.'

Paul laughed. 'Bullshit.' He slid his hand into his pocket and pulled something out, keeping whatever it was clasped tightly in his palm. 'Did he tell you about Ginny, Cat? Do you actually know what this *monster* is capable of?'

'Now come on . . .' Tristan squared his shoulders. 'There's no need for name-calling.'

'Are you actually serious right now?' Paul's voice was an angry rasp. It hurt his throat to speak like this, but he couldn't believe what he was hearing. He felt sorry for Cat, despite everything. What on earth had Tristan promised her to get her to go along with all this?

'I'm deadly serious, *mate.*' Tristan's whole body tensed.

'Tristan, stop it.' Cat held out an arm like a bar across Tristan's chest. 'We're all here together now. We need to look after each other. There's been enough fighting.'

Tristan laughed. 'You killed your own sister, Kitty-Cat. At least let me keep my end of the bargain.'

He took a step towards Paul, but Paul had been expecting it and ducked to one side. 'Don't you want to see this, Cat?' He held up what he'd been concealing in his hand. A thin gold chain, with a chunky stone pendant hanging off it. 'You probably can't see the colour in this light, but I can tell you that it's emerald green. The same emerald-green pendant that Ginny was wearing earlier. When she . . . *fell.*'

Tristan stopped. 'Where the fuck did you get that?'

Cat looked terrified. She'd shrunk back into the darkest corner of the room, her arms wrapped around her chest.

'I assume your boyfriend didn't tell you about this part, Cat? The part where he found Ginny on a ledge . . . then pushed her off to make sure she was really gone?' He locked eyes with Tristan. 'Was she still alive, when you found her? Did you put her out of her misery, before you threw her over the edge?' He held the necklace out towards Cat. 'Yours now, I think.'

She shook her head. 'Stop it. Please.' Cat put her hands over her ears. 'I don't want to hear any more of this.'

'Neither do I,' said Tristan. He lunged at Paul, knocking him over on to his back. But he didn't know what else Paul had concealed in his palm. That little multi-tool that his dad had always told him would save his life one day. Useless little torch that he'd attached to the keyring, but the knives were effective. He plunged the knife into Tristan's chest, hoping that he was somewhere close to his heart – assuming that Tristan actually had one. Tristan's eyes grew wide as Paul flicked his wrist, twisting the knife in deeper.

He blocked out the sound of Cat screaming.

Then he shoved Tristan off and rolled out from under him.

'What have you done? Paul, what the hell have you done?' Cat was on him, hitting him, punching him.

Paul pushed her gently away, and she landed beside Tristan.

'He's still alive . . . Tristan, can you hear me? It's OK. We can fix this.'

Paul ignored her and stared at Tristan. A moment later, Tristan's eyes dulled. He was gone.

Forty-One

SATURDAY NIGHT

Cat crawled away from Tristan and threw up in the corner by the window. Her stomach heaved, but there was barely anything left in it to get rid of. She sat back on her heels, her hands over her face. Her eyes itched from the tears, and she rubbed them hard until she felt like she might pop out her own eyeballs. Fuck. What the fuck? She stopped rubbing her eyes and turned around. Paul was checking Tristan's pulse, but it was pointless because they had both just watched him die.

This was never supposed to happen.

Ginny was supposed to be dealt with simply and easily. There was never meant to be any prolonged pain. Tristan was meant to be alive. And Paul . . . well, Paul was meant to be dead.

She crawled over to Tristan and laid a hand on his arm, gazed at his face – which looked more peaceful than she'd expected, after the violent way that he'd died. She looked up at her husband. 'Did you close his eyes?'

Paul nodded, his shadow bouncing on the wall behind, from the flickering candles. He was staring at her, his eyes damp with tears.

What the hell was she going to do now? She'd let Tristan convince her of the plan. She'd gone along with all of it, and the deeper she'd gone in, the more it seemed to be justified. But in the face of all this hurt, the violence she'd witnessed – and been part of herself – she was starting to think she'd got it all very wrong.

Of course, she'd modified the plan a little. Tristan had known nothing about that. But she wasn't sure it was going to work now. Unless . . .

'We need to move him.' She swallowed. Stood up. Tried her best to sound strong.

Paul shook his head. 'What are you talking about? We're not moving him. We leave him here . . . in fact, we stay here with him – until sunrise. Then we get down the mountain, and we get help, and we send them up here to find him. And to find Ginny. I know where she fell. I can lead them there.' He sighed. 'It's going to be a bit of a nightmare to try and explain it all, but I think the simple story that Tristan went rogue, pushed Ginny, attacked me, and I killed him in self-defence is the best option.' He paused, tried to meet her gaze, but she wouldn't let him. 'Cat? This is our only option.'

Cat gave him a small nod. 'Maybe.'

'Did you have something else in mind?' She watched in horror as he cleaned his pocket tool on Tristan's t-shirt and slipped it in his pocket. It all seemed so matter-of-fact. She had expected Paul to crumble. She'd underestimated him, it seemed. She'd managed to get a lot of things wrong. She thought back to the bar in the village, when she still had a chance to stop all of this. The whispered conversation with Tristan in the dingy basement toilet.

He'd pushed her up against the wall of the cubicle. His hands caressing her breasts, fingers sliding inside her bra. 'We can forget about the plan,' he'd said, his breath hot in her ear. 'Just carry on having fun together.'

She'd let herself get carried away. The lust overtaking all rational thought. This is how it had been from the start, and she'd been drunk on it. But he'd been the one saying they should sort out a permanent solution. He'd been the one who suggested murder. Hadn't he? She'd been the one starved of affection, pushing her husband away in disgust after the things he'd done to another woman. Things he denied, but that she knew were true. Tristan had taken her away from all that. He'd helped her to deal with the messed-up situation with her sister. Ginny's thirtieth birthday and the release of the inheritance funds. Tristan. It had all been Tristan.

Now, in the dark, stinking house with the smells of death and vomit in her nostrils, Cat closed her eyes tight, trying to push the memory back into her head. She fidgeted with the hem of her t-shirt, squeezing her hands into fists. Digging her nails into her palms, protecting herself from breaking the skin by pressing them through the fabric. Tristan might have planted the seed, but she was the one who had let it grow.

Paul was watching her. Reading her mind. His voice was like stone. 'So what was the plan, by the way? Before it all caved in. Are you going to tell me?'

She swallowed. Should she tell him the truth? Possibly, but not right now. The longer they left Tristan, the harder it was going to be for them to get rid of him. And they had to get rid of him. This was the only part of the new plan that she was formulating fast in her head that would make any sense.

'I'll tell you everything. I promise. But you need to help me out here. We need to get rid of Tristan. There's a waterfall nearby. If we can just—'

Paul started laughing. A cold, harsh laugh that lacked any humour. 'Can you hear yourself, Cat? What the hell are you talking about? I've just said – the only way out of this is to tell the truth—'

'You suggested I blame Ginny's death on Tristan. That's not the truth.'

'That *is* the truth though. Isn't it? This was all Tristan's idea.' He waved his arms around the room, the breeze causing the candles to flicker. 'You didn't even know where this place was. I *heard* you, remember?' He stopped talking. Dropped his arms back to his sides. 'Unless . . . No. You weren't bluffing, were you? Did you plan to dupe him?' He looked up at the ceiling, then back to her. 'Is there someone upstairs? That man from earlier . . . ?'

It was Cat's turn to laugh. 'Now who's being ridiculous? There's no one upstairs. Tristan checked.' She looked towards the kitchen. 'It's not safe.'

'Maybe I should just check again . . .'

She grabbed his arm, pulling him towards her. 'I need you to trust me on this, Paul. If the last few months have been anything to go by, I think you should start listening to some advice that might get you out of a tricky situation.'

He stared at her, but said nothing. She knew she had him. She always managed to maintain the upper hand with him, in the end. He was weak. That was why he'd got himself into a mess, and that was why he needed her to help him. And that was why he was going to do exactly what she said.

'Thank you.' She knelt down and started to empty Tristan's pockets. The map was still inside the plastic wallet. She took the lanyard and hung it around her neck. She grabbed whatever else was in there and threw it into the top of his rucksack, kicking it out of the way. Blood was starting to pool underneath Tristan's body. There would probably be blood spatter all over the room, but it was too dark to see, and she couldn't think about that right now.

She turned to Paul, who was standing in front of the window, watching her. His body was silhouetted by the candles, but around the side of him, she could make out a change in the light through the dirty window.

'We don't have much time. Hikers will start to climb up here at sunrise. We need to sort this out before then.' She took her torch out of her pocket. 'This is all we've got. But I don't think it's far.' She slid the torch into the plastic wallet beside the map and turned it upside down, twisting the neck-cord to force the wallet to lie flatter; the torch pointing slightly ahead, instead of straight to her feet.

Paul sighed. 'Let's get it over with, then.' He opened the door wide before walking over to her. 'I'll take the top end. It'll be heavier. You face front with the torch beam. Hold his legs either side of you like you're carrying a stretcher.'

She crouched down at Tristan's feet, looping her arms under his calves, trying to support them in the crooks of her elbows. Paul grunted as he lifted Tristan up behind her, and she was glad she couldn't see Tristan's dead face anymore. Her biceps burned as she took the weight. So much more than she'd expected. She looked out into the woods. The pitch-dark from before had started to lighten to a thick reddish-brown. Where there had been nothing before, shadows of the trees now appeared in front of her. The torch swung out as she stepped down out of the cottage and on to the path.

Somewhere to the right, the waterfall battered down; a comforting cacophony. They walked slowly, staying on the path, following the sound. The noise of the water mostly drowned out Paul's heavy breathing behind her. They didn't speak. She tried not to think, either, about what they were doing. About what they had done. Husband and wife. Murderers.

After a few minutes, as the tumbling water grew louder, they walked through a swarm of tiny flying insects. She wrinkled her face, trying to flick them off. Felt them landing on her skin. Biting at her. They were close to the water.

As the trees thinned, the light from the waking sky hung over them. Indigo, with purple shades pushing through. They had to hurry. The water gushed louder.

And then they were there.

'Lay him down,' Paul said, softly.

She felt the weight shift behind her, then crouched down as she lowered Tristan's legs to the ground. She let go, then walked to the edge of the path. There was a steep drop beneath. A muddy bank, with the dark shadows of gnarly tree roots. Straight ahead, the waterfall dropped in front of them, foaming into the depths of the dark-blue pool beneath.

She took a deep breath, inhaling the scent. Damp, wet trees. Fresh water. Something dark and mulchy beneath.

'Ready?' Paul said from behind her.

Cat turned. Paul had lifted Tristan's shoulders again. His head was flopped to one side. She looked down at him. At the man she'd shared plans with. Plans for a new life. Then she looked up, at the man she'd married four years ago. The man she'd somehow, in her mad moment of revenge and lust, wanted to kill. She felt sick. And then she remembered the baby. If there was even a baby. And she thought of her sister. Of that moment, etched into her brain forever, where she pushed her off the side of a mountain.

She stayed where she was, facing Paul. Facing Tristan. 'I'm sorry,' she said, quietly. She wasn't sure what she was even sorry for. For wanting him dead? For a moment of regret?

Her words were impossible to hear over the sound of the cascading water. She lowered herself down, keeping her weight back on her heels, and lifted Tristan's legs.

Cat locked eyes with Paul. His mouth was set into a hard, straight line. He gave her the smallest of nods, then she matched his steps as he shuffled slowly sideways towards the edge. Her arms, her shoulders, her stomach – every part of her burned, as she followed

Paul's lead. They swung Tristan back to the left, just enough, then to the right. Over the edge. Then they let go.

They stood together in silence as Tristan plunged into the pool beneath with a distant splash. Then Paul reached for her hand, and she let him take it. And together, they headed back to the cottage, as the light in the sky took on a deep, rosy glow. Morning was upon them, and there were plans to be made.

Forty-Two

SUNDAY, DAWN

Paul shivered as they reached the doorstep. They'd walked back from the waterfall slowly, gripping on to each other with a new urgency. If they made it out of this . . . if they got away with this . . . Paul knew that everything he'd once thought, believed, done, would be different.

They would be different.

The house was different too, changed by the dawn's light. The sky above them had turned from black to blue, with tinges of pink from the haze. The house was still bathed in darkness, hidden amongst the thick canopy of trees, but the light from the sunrise cast new, altered shadows.

It was the start of a brand-new day. Somehow they would put the events of the last twenty-four hours behind them, and they would be reborn. They might fall back in love. Start over. Together.

Wishful thinking.

Paul could tell from Cat's demeanour that nothing was going to be that simple. There had been a *plan*. A plan in which he was dead, and Ginny was dead, and Tristan was still alive. He was curious about Cat's *new* plan. Very curious indeed. But she had always been someone who could adapt quickly. She'd told him countless stories from her job, about venues going bust and whole weddings being moved at the last minute. She had never let anyone down when it came to changes of plans.

She let go of his hand and entered the house in front of him, heading straight to the rucksacks.

'We need to get everything together. We'll be able to leave soon.'

He looked at her sadly. If she'd softened for a moment, after what they just did together, then the moment was short-lived.

They'd left the candles burning when they'd taken Tristan away, and three of the four still burned. One of them gave off a strong, cloying scent, like toilet cleaner and cheap perfume. To keep away bugs, he assumed. Cat would've brought it. Cat would've thought of everything. He wondered again what she was thinking right now.

'Can we sit for a bit?' he said. 'Please? I'm kind of done in.' He took a breath and his lungs burned. It felt like something was stabbing him in the chest. A broken rib, probably. So far, he'd managed to deal with everything via the wonders of adrenaline, but now it was fast wearing off.

He sat down and propped himself up against the wall under the window, wincing as his ribs protested. 'I really think I need a rest before we try and make the descent.'

Cat ignored him. She'd repacked everything into the bags, except for the candles, and she was sitting on her heels, the map spread out on the floor in front of her. Tristan's map. She directed her small torch over the crumpled paper with one hand, and with the other she was tracing a finger across the dotted lines of the trails.

'I know where we need to go,' she said. 'We passed a sign for the fastest route down last night, but we couldn't go in the dark, so—'

'By "we", you mean you and Tristan,' he cut in.

188

She ignored him again. 'He said it's a bit tricky. You need to use chains to lower yourself down parts of it. Plus it'll be damp and slippery, as it's right in the trees where no natural light can penetrate.'

'Sounds like the kind of place where someone might have an accident.' He coughed, and it hurt. Tristan had clearly done his homework planning this route for them, he thought. The pair of them would have made quite a formidable couple. Shame Tristan wasn't quick enough to escape his deadly knife attack.

Cat was still doing her best to ignore him, but he noticed that she flinched a little when he mentioned the possibility of an accident, and he suspected that this was the real location where he and Ginny were supposed to have met their sticky ends.

'I suppose all the plans got scuppered when Tristan took us on that wrong path early on, eh? Where you nearly slipped over the edge and Ginny saved you.' He tried to laugh, but it was too painful. 'Oh, the irony. He didn't plan *that* bit very well, did he?'

Cat let go of the map and swivelled around to face him, dropping down on to her knees. She shone the torch in his face and he flinched, squinting his eyes. *Well*, he thought, *that got her attention.*

'What you have to understand, Paul, is that Ginny completely fucked me over.'

He raised an eyebrow. 'OK. And this is the first I'm hearing about it, why?'

She sighed. 'You were kind of *distracted*.'

He knew what she was referring to. Of course he did. But that shit was going to have to wait. He needed to know what had brought them both here, first. To this house. To this mountain.

'The sun's not quite up yet, Cat. Why don't you start from the beginning?'

Cat stared at him, biting her lip. Contemplating. He didn't know the story yet, but he suspected she had little left to lose, now that Ginny and Tristan were out of the picture. He thought back to the start of the hike. Cat snapping pics on that little instant camera. Was that all just part of her game? Deflecting them from the fact that she'd made them leave their phones in the car? What an idiot he'd been to go along with that.

She opened up the side pocket of one of the rucksacks and pulled out two bottles full of blue liquid. It looked like that stuff runners drank to replace fluids. Full of sugar. She'd had this all along, and never offered it before? Wasn't meant for him though, was it? This was Tristan's drink.

Bastard.

She handed him a bottle and he popped the cap and drank greedily. He hadn't realised how thirsty he was. His stomach groaned and cramped, as the sweet, sugary liquid hit its empty depths. He realised he was starving, too.

'OK.' She took a sip of her own drink, then recapped it and laid it down. 'You know Ginny turned thirty back in April?'

He nodded. There had been a party. Bloody awful place in Mayfair where you had to buy a bottle of vodka for £200, then it came in a suitcase filled with ice and four different mixers. The music was R'n'B at ear-splitting decibels, and the blingy bouncers had wanted to punch him in the face just for the crime of him being a rich, white male customer. The women were treated differently. Especially the ones in the spray-on dresses with the hair extensions down to their plumped-up arses. Why the fuck Ginny had wanted to go to a place like that was utterly beyond him.

They'd gone, and they'd stayed over in that overpriced hotel on Park Lane too, but then next morning at breakfast there had been an atmosphere between Ginny and Cat that was not fully attributable to a hangover, or even the ill-advised coke they'd all snorted in the ridiculous mirrored toilets at 4 a.m.

They'd checked out shortly after breakfast, and Cat had refused to say what had gone on between the sisters. And because they were sisters, Paul had seen it all before and wasn't interested enough to ask. More fool him.

Besides, as Cat had just pointed out – he'd been *distracted*, back then. Well, he couldn't deny that. Having a 'sexual harassment in the workplace' accusation hanging over you would be distracting for anyone. But that was over now and, as far as he was aware, Cat had believed his version of events. She had no reason not to. There was no evidence.

But she had been cold with him recently, and he was going to have to get to the bottom of that. Go over it all again, continue to protest his innocence. If he ever got off this mountain.

'Is this something about what you two were arguing about at breakfast, the morning after her party?'

Cat blew out a long breath. 'If I'm dispensing the truths here, I expect you to do me the same honour.'

Shit. He felt trapped now, but, given the circumstances, didn't think he had much choice. Plus, he was actually desperate to know what this was all about. An illicit affair seemed too cheap for the effort that had gone into bumping off the surplus partners. 'Seems fair.'

'Ginny somehow convinced my parents to change their will. They left everything to her. She was supposed to allocate something to me. She showed me a letter, where there was this sum of money. It was meant to represent half of the house . . . But she got everything else.'

Interesting. 'Your parents had the house valued, then? They definitely wanted this new will put in place?'

Cat nodded. 'Ginny spun them some line. Well, lots of lines. It had been going on for years. Behind my back. Slowly eroding their trust in me, through mistruth and misdirection. Discouraging them from questioning me on things.' She shrugged. 'I guess if you feed someone enough bullshit, with nothing to contradict it, eventually they'll swallow it.'

This felt like a direct dig at him, but he let it go.

'I just can't imagine your parents going for all this. They weren't stupid people, Cat . . .'

She whirled around to face him. 'Are you calling me a liar, Paul?'

'No. Of course not. It's just . . .' He let his sentence trail off. Was he calling her a liar? He'd known her parents, or at least he'd thought he had . . . Of course things had taken a turn for the worse for them, when the economy collapsed and they'd had to re-evaluate their import-export business. But to be coerced into changing their will was a bizarre concept that he was struggling to process. Had stupid little Ginny really had the power to make that happen? Maybe she'd been brighter than anyone had given her credit for.

Cat was staring at him. 'Well?' she said, her eyes like steel. 'I think it's your turn now.'

Paul swallowed. 'OK,' he said. 'Give me a minute.' The shadows in the room had shifted. He glanced around, taking in the scene outside the dirty window and the half-opened door. The sun had risen, casting a muted mustardy glow. The cluster of ferns lining the ramshackle path had changed from black to dark green.

They could leave now. They could make their way back down the mountain. To their lives that had been irreparably changed by this trip. Their new lives, then. Whatever those might be. He stood up, lifting one of the rucksacks and throwing it on to his back, wincing inwardly at the pain. 'Let's get going. I'll tell you everything. I promise.' He forced a smile so hard that it hurt his cheeks. 'Then you can tell me about your plan to get us out of this mess.'

Forty-Three

SUNDAY, EARLY MORNING

They took the path towards the signpost, walking in silence. Cat knew the way instinctively, after following the path to the house the night before in the dark. In the morning sun, she realised that the path was quite well trodden, not as deeply hidden in the woods as she'd imagined. Something fluttered in her chest. People might be here soon. They might go to the house. Despite the state of it, maybe people did use it for shelter regularly. The place would be covered in Tristan's blood. His DNA. Traces of all of them. They had to hurry. At the signpost, they turned right, heading towards the descent.

'Are you sure this is the right way?' Paul said. His voice was thin. Pained. The adrenaline that had got him through their earlier exertions gone now. Cat felt weak, too. She would love nothing more than to curl into a ball and sleep. But she was determined. With all she'd been through to get to this point, she wasn't giving up now.

'I'm sure.' She pushed a couple of branches out of the way and walked through the gap in the trees that led to the way down. Despite the morning sun, it was dark and cool on this part of the mountain, and she was glad they hadn't tried to attempt it last night. Although, if they had, might Tristan still be alive? That would bring its own problems. Having Paul back on the scene was causing her to have to think through things in ways she'd never envisaged.

She made her way down the first part of the slope, and then saw the next part, and stopped dead.

Paul came up beside her. 'What's the matter?'

Cat pointed.

Paul sighed. 'Right. OK. Well, to be honest, I'm not sure this is anything worse than we've already endured. I'll go down first, and you can follow. That means I'll be beneath you if you slip.'

Cat noted the heavy chain that was bolted to a rock, and to other rocks further down. The path underneath was thick, churned mud. The gradient was Black Run level. If only they had skis. It was clearly enough of a hazard that someone had seen fit to attach the chain, to help guide people down.

That flip in her stomach again. She'd forgotten about before. The dizziness. That strange feeling low in her abdomen. Ginny's taunts. If there was a baby in there, then it was making itself known once again. She sucked in a breath, let it out slowly. She could do this. It was so close to the finish line now. Just one final push . . .

Paul walked carefully down the slope backwards, gripping the chain. Practically abseiling. She thought of Tristan then. His equipment in his bag. Him scaling down to find Ginny . . . and then what had Paul said? He'd found her and pushed her further? He couldn't know that for sure. He was only guessing that Ginny had fallen on a ledge because *he'd* fallen on a ledge, and Ginny's necklace – well, that could've fallen off regardless, couldn't it? She closed her eyes for a moment, squeezing them tight. She didn't want to think that Tristan could be so cruel. So . . . evil.

But she was hardly one to talk. It wasn't like she hadn't planned all this. *Shut up, Cat. Stay focused.*

194

'Clear!' Paul's voice seemed to come from very far away, and she realised that he'd made it down the steep, chained descent and was standing on a flatter area, a hundred metres or so down. He waved up at her. 'Come on. It's fine. If I can do it . . .'

She turned to face into the mountainside, stepped across and took hold of the chain. Then she made the mistake of looking down at Paul. From that angle, it looked very, very steep. A wave of dizziness passed over her, and she blinked it away. Took another breath in fast, then out long and slow.

She took small steps, keeping her toes pressed hard into the mud. She ignored Paul's encouraging calls. Tried to zone him out. She was sick of hearing his voice. She wasn't sure she wanted him to reveal the truth now – about what had happened with the woman at work. As far as everyone was concerned, there was no case, and therefore no evidence. *He said, she said.* And he said he didn't touch her. That *she* was the one making it all up, because her job was on the line and she needed to distract the company into keeping her on. They'd hardly sack a woman who'd accused a male employee of groping her in a lift after the work Christmas party. Not in these times. As everyone was always pointing out – a court case for something like this would drag the woman's reputation through the mud. Why on earth would anyone lie and put themselves through that?

The verdict from the employer's investigation had implied that she did lie – or, at least, she had misremembered. Paul was a model employee. They were both drunk. It was all just a bit of fun. So he said. Just *bantz*. A bit of flirting, from both sides. It was nothing.

He absolutely did not touch her. *He* said.

Cat remembered exactly what she'd been doing when the photograph had popped up on the screen of her MacBook. She'd been looking into luxury breaks in the Maldives. She'd thought the two of them needed a bit of time away, after the pandemic had scuppered their travel plans for so long. Her finger had been on the 'Buy Now' button on the ridiculously overpriced flights. Then the image had appeared, stopping her in her tracks.

'That's it, you're nearly there.'

Paul's voice broke through her thoughts, and she blinked the image away. But it was timely that she'd been thinking about it now. Because it was going to help explain things when they made it to the police station.

She slowed down, keeping her toes pushed into the mud. She slipped a couple of times. It was so damp and wet under the trees. No sun made its way in there. But she kept her hands tight on the chain.

The photograph had been perfectly clear. A selfie. Two people in a lift. The man in a white shirt, partially unbuttoned. His hair mussed, his eyes a little unfocused. He was holding the phone up high in his left hand. In his right, he was holding the woman. Her face was pressed up against the mirrored wall of the lift, slightly to the side. Her hands were pressed on the mirror. Her blouse was loose, her skirt pushed up at the back. She was wearing a thong. But only the top string was visible, as the one that went underneath her was obscured by the man's right hand.

It was the faces that Cat remembered most clearly. His, grinning: the cat that got the cream. The woman, wide-eyed. Shocked. Pained.

Scared.

Another photograph appeared straight after. The woman sitting in the corner of the lift, hands over her face. Knees pulled up to her chest. The man in close-up, his tongue poking out of his mouth in a suggestive manner.

Cat been stunned. But she'd acted quickly, screenshotting both of the images – before a few seconds later, they had both disappeared from their shared Cloud.

Rookie mistake, Paul, she thought, as she recalled it. *Make sure you know where your phone is sending things.*

'Well done. That's the hard bit over.'

She'd made it to the bottom.

She flinched as his hands touched her shoulders, steering her on to the flatter part of the path. The fresh memories had brought her revulsion back to the surface.

'Look, Cat . . .' He turned her to face him. 'I know you want me to talk about all that stuff that happened at work, and I promise you, I will. But can we just get down, first? I think we've survived the tricky part, but it looks like there's still a bit to go to make it to the bottom.'

She peered down at the winding, rocky path. She didn't want to listen to his version of the truth, anyway. He'd had plenty of opportunity for that, and he'd lied. So then she had lied back, saying that the truth would set them free. Well, it wasn't going to. She was stuck with him now, and they were going to have to stick to the same story to avoid both of them being arrested for murder – but that was where their relationship now lay. The thought of staying married to him made her feel sick.

The new plan that she had been formulating as she made the descent was starting to take shape in her head.

'Sure,' she said. 'We can talk about it all later.' She set off ahead of him, taking careful steps. There were lots of loose rocks on the path, which itself was slippery and uneven. The gradient was still fairly steep, too. She wished she could walk faster, but it was going to be an arduous journey back to base.

'I mean, like I said before . . . it's all in the past now, right? I left the job to make things easier. I didn't want *her* feeling . . . I don't know . . . embarrassed about it all. About her mistake.'

Cat kept walking. Heat was starting to build in her veins. He couldn't even say the woman's name. He wanted to keep her at a distance. *The woman*. That mysterious woman who had a few too many, and took the elevator with a colleague she thought she trusted. The nameless woman who would never stop blaming herself for the actions of one creep. One creep amongst many creeps. It was just the fucking way of the world. Not all men, no. *But we don't know what the bad ones look like.*

'Her name is *Samantha*!' Cat wanted to scream it, but her voice remained low and steady as she fought to keep her anger in check. 'That woman whose life you ruined, and who no one fucking believed, is called *Samantha*.'

Paul said nothing.

Cat's head pounded with fury. Her vision blurred.

She stumbled.

Felt her ankle go. She reached out blindly, but there was nothing to grab on to. Dank air whooshed past as her centre of gravity shifted, and she fell.

And this time she had no little sister to reach out and pull her back to safety.

Forty-Four

SUNDAY MORNING

Cat had a vague sensation of falling and hitting her head, but when she opened her eyes, she was no longer on the mountain. No longer with Paul. She blinked a few times, trying to force herself awake. She knew she was dreaming, but she couldn't lift herself out of it. She was vaguely aware of the sounds of the forest, and then she let herself succumb. Her eyes closed.

In her dream, Cat opened her eyes and found she was in a very different place. Morning sunshine hit her face and she lifted a hand to shield herself from it, rolled herself over. Her head was banging. Her mouth dry. She was desperate for a sip of water. A glass appeared in front of her as she tried to shuffle herself into a sitting position.

'Morning, sleepyhead.'

Her dreamy vision swam, and it took her a moment to work out where she was. The voice that spoke to her was slightly unfamiliar. Unexpected. And somewhere far away, she thought she could hear another voice, too; a familiar one, calling her name. But then it was gone, and she was firmly back inside her head.

Dream Cat sat up and took the water, gulping it down, spilling a cold trickle down her naked chest.

'Possibly the third bottle of fizz was overkill.'

She watched as Tristan climbed out of the bed, heading towards the bathroom. His arse was smooth and toned. His whole body was like that, in fact. So different to Paul's. She finished the water and put the glass on the side table. The third bottle had *definitely* been too much.

The night before came back to her in segments. Pieces of a jig-saw slowly slotting together. The conference ending, Tristan send-ing her a message with his room number on it. Her sitting in the bar alone, downing a vodka and trying to decide if what she was about to do was brilliant, fun and wholly justified . . . or if she was nothing but a clichéd bored wife, ready to blow up her marriage for a bit of fun. Her choice of 'partner' was a consideration, too. Her brother-in-law. Her little sister's husband. Surely this was peak nastiness on the scale of affairs, from blurry one-nighter to years-long second-family adultery?

Tristan came back from the bathroom carrying another glass of water. His face broke into a grin. 'Heyyy,' he said, slow. Sexy.

She felt a stirring down low. Familiar. Urgent. She remembered the rest of the night, too. Champagne, lots of it. Her sucking on an ice cube then taking him in her mouth. Fucking. Lots of fucking. Laughing. Music. More champagne.

The sight of him made her forget her headache. He climbed on to the bed, his eyes locked on hers. His hands all over her.

'Hey, yourself,' she managed. Then they stopped talking, their mouths busy elsewhere.

Afterwards, he got out of the bed and walked over to the coffee machine, a swagger in his step. She watched his arse again. The room smelled of his sandalwood aftershave, and their hot sweaty sex. She sunk back into the pillows, watching him. After a few minutes, the aroma of coffee hit her.

'Never say I'm not a fucking genius,' he said. Cups and saucers rattled.

She closed her eyes, opened them again. She was still there. In that room. King-size bed, antique furniture. Gilt-framed oil paintings on the walls.

'How did we get here?' She sat up quickly, holding the sheet up to her neck. At some point she had removed her wedding ring, and she momentarily felt sick at her own betrayal. She shook the sensation away, remembering why she was doing this.

'Well, I took the M3, mostly, then I cut down by the—'

He stopped talking when the pillow hit him on the back of the head.

'Oi, careful. Got your coffee here, lady.'

He kicked the pillow up into the air like a football, then lifted the cups and carried them over to the bed. He didn't bother with the saucers.

She took the offered cup from him and inhaled the steam. 'You know what I mean.'

'Bit late to get contemplative now, isn't it? I've already shagged your brains out.'

She slapped his arm. 'I'm serious, Tristan.'

He put his coffee down and sat on the bed, facing her. He crossed one leg in front of him and pulled the sheet over his lap, covering himself up. Funny how serious conversations and nakedness could leave you vulnerable.

'I was bored, you were bored . . . now we're not bored?'

She bit her lip. Frowned.

He carried on. 'I sent you that message after Ginny's thirtieth. Well, after the argument the two of you had at breakfast. Awkward.' He shrugged. 'I didn't like the way she treated you. I thought it was shitty.' He laid a hand on her leg.

'What, you? Ruthless Banker of the Year 20-whatever? You thought someone enacting some financial shenanigans was – and I quote – "a bit shitty"?'

He squeezed her leg. 'There's business, and there's family. She conned you, Cat. She seemed quite proud of it too. When I asked her about it, it seemed like she'd convinced herself that she deserved that inheritance in lieu of having your brains.'

Cat forced out a laugh. 'She had our parents wrapped around her little finger. They would have done anything for her. She probably just snapped her fingers and they happily changed the will to make her executor and cut me out without a second thought . . .' Her sentence trailed off when she saw the expression on his face. 'What is it? Did I get a bit of that wrong?'

He took his hand off her leg and looked away. 'We should probably leave it. If you wanted revenge, you've already had it. Just make some smug comment someday to make her wonder if something's happened between us, and you'll fire up her paranoia. That's enough, right?'

Cat pulled her knees up to her chest, wrapped her arms around them. 'What aren't you telling me?'

Tristan pulled on his boxers, then ambled across to the chair where his shirt had been hung over the back. Flung, in fact. Cat remembered unbuttoning it and throwing it there.

'Tristan?'

He buttoned his shirt, still not looking at her. 'They were on to her, Cat. They wrote another will.'

A cold shiver crept across her shoulders, icy fingers pressing into the flesh. 'What?'

Tristan was buckling his belt. 'I swore I would never—'

'Never what?' She threw the sheet off and jumped out of bed, grabbing at her own underwear and hastily stepping her feet through the holes. She threw her dress over her head, not bothering with her bra.

'They were on their way to the solicitors to finalise the *new* will. They were changing it back, Cat. Ginny overheard them talking. Seemingly they'd seen through her plan, realised that she was trying to push you out. They were planning to fix the will, then call round to see you, take you to dinner. They felt bad for listening to Ginny's lies. Believing her when she said you weren't interested in them, or her. That you thought you were better than them all . . . that you didn't need them.' He hung his head. 'She only told me this the day before the party. That's why I kept trying to get your attention when I saw you. I wanted to talk to you . . .'

'I thought you were being sleazy. I thought it was a wind-up.'

'I know you did.' He ran a hand through his hair. Sighed. 'She had to stop them, Cat. She couldn't let them change the will. Couldn't risk them bringing you back into their lives. What if they cut off her allowance, too? She wasn't working then, remember?'

'What did she do, Tristan?'

He sat down on the chair, hard. 'She cut the brake cable on that old car of theirs. Said she had to look up a video on basic car maintenance just to find out where the cable was.'

Cat thought she might be sick. She'd been on her way to see them. Her mother had left a message that morning that Cat had thought strange, so she'd jumped in her own car and was on her way. She replayed the message in her head, realising now that she'd got it so, so wrong.

We're so sorry, darling, please forgive us.

Cat had been the one who'd found them. Their car was concertinaed into a bridge at the sharp bend at the bottom of the private road that led to their house. Ginny would have known there was no way they could have made that bend without braking. She would

203

have known that their dad always drove too fast down that private road.

If I can't speed on my own land, then where can I!?

By the time Cat had found them, it was already too late. The car engine belching smoke, the shapes of her parents hunched over the crushed dashboard. There were no airbags in those old cars. She'd called an ambulance straight away, but she knew it was pointless. And all the time, Ginny had been behind it. Sweet Virginia – the naive, innocent one.

The deceitful little bitch.

'I think you should leave now.' Cat didn't want him to see how much she was shaking.

Tristan nodded. 'I'll message you, OK?' He kissed her on the cheek, whispering, 'You don't have to deal with this alone. I can help you, Cat. With Paul too. Whatever it is that he's done.'

Another piece of the jigsaw slotted into place. Another conversation from the night before. Tristan asking, 'So why did Paul really leave? I never bought that burnout story . . . calmest trader I knew, that one . . .' And she had told Tristan that Paul had had a one-night stand – still protecting Paul from Tristan learning the whole truth about the sexual harassment claim – and now Tristan must think her pathetic, to have her sister and her husband both betray her, and she just accept it. *Well*, she thought. *Maybe I don't have to accept it at all.*

He turned to her once more, his hand on the door. 'I like you, Cat. Let me help you. We can work on a plan . . .'

And then he was gone. But the seed had been planted. She laid her head back on the soft pillows, pulled the duvet up over herself again. Within moments, she was fast asleep.

And then the dream faded away, and she was cold, and in pain.

'Open your eyes, Cat. Please. Wake up!'

A familiar voice. Urgent, in her ear.

She opened her eyes, and she was back on the mountain. The sky was cloudless and blue, the sun high and bright. She laid her hands flat, grasping for something. Hoping for soft sheets but finding dirt and parched grass. Her head was pounding.

'What the . . . ? Where am I? Tristan?'

A face loomed over her. Battered, bruised. One side of his head was matted with blood and hair. Bloodshot eyes. A strong smell, like a frightened animal's. 'Cat, it's me – can you see me? How many fingers am I holding up?'

She blinked, trying to make him go away. She tried to float herself back into that huge, soft bed with the crisp white sheets. That room in the hotel where she and Tristan had started all this. But she couldn't get there. Her mind wouldn't take her there. She knew where she was. This was the end. A literal rock bottom.

'Paul . . .' She felt a tear trickle out of one eye and slowly slide down her cheek and into her ear. 'How did we get down? I think I tripped—'

'I carried you. Shush now. Take a minute, then we'll see if you can get up and walk. We're at the foot of the mountain, Cat. We made it!'

She closed her eyes again. Opened them. It was no use. She was stuck in reality, and she was going to have to deal with it. She pressed down hard into the muck, pushing herself up so she was sitting, then let Paul take her hands and pull her to her feet. She felt a little wobbly, but when she took a couple of steps, she seemed to be fully intact.

'You hit your head, Cat. Knocked yourself out cold. You'll need to take it easy.'

She lifted a hand and ran it across the back of her head. A large egg had already formed. But this was good – an external lump hopefully meant that nothing bad was happening inside. You heard of those people who hit their head then got up like nothing had

205

happened, and twenty-four hours later they were dead from a brain haemorrhage.

Could happen. But it could happen to Paul, too – after that crack that Tristan gave him, and god knows what else had happened when he fell on to the ledge. Both of them might be on borrowed time. So all they could do was make their way back to base and take it from there.

But the dream had galvanised her. She felt bad about Tristan. He was merely collateral damage in a situation that he'd triggered into action. But there was nothing she could do about that now. She had to think this problem through, just like she had done so many times at work. *Change of plan, Cat, that's all. You've dealt with this before. You can deal with it now.*

She let Paul take her elbow, and allowed herself to lean on him, just a little. Just enough. They hobbled out from the clearing towards the road, and not too far in the distance, thankfully downhill, was the village.

Paul held out an arm, thumb pointed upwards.

It would soon be over.

Forty-Five

SUNDAY MORNING

Paul knew that it was quite normal for people to hitch in the Alps, because of the quiet roads and irregularity of buses, and not something to be wary of like back home, where you might be wary of travelling serial killers. He laughed a bit at his own thought, but it sounded like a cough, so Cat didn't notice. Besides, it was instinct that made him flag down help. He wasn't sure that either of them could walk much further at that point.

The truck driver who picked them up had looked concerned, but Cat, somehow, using French skills that he hadn't been aware that she possessed, had reassured him and he'd dropped them off just outside the village, instead of taking them to the hospital.

They'd discussed this, in the brief moments of them trying to walk down the road to the village. Cat had been insistent that it was police first. That they weren't in urgent need of medical help. He'd thought her wrong about that but he was far too tired to argue. And he'd meant to ask her, as they climbed out of the truck, about how it was that she spoke such good French when the night before, and all day, she had acted like all she knew were some schoolgirl phrases, rusty from years of underuse.

Ginny had been wittering on about Cat's time in France as a student while they'd been having lunch, but Paul had barely paid any attention. Perhaps Cat's recent bang on the head had reset her vocabulary. You heard about those people who woke from comas speaking fluent Mandarin, right?

God, he was tired. He would kill for a comfortable bed and a twenty-four-hour sleep. But they had to stick to Cat's plan – report the others missing, absolve themselves of any blame. Go home. Would they be able to do all this before their 8 p.m. flight? Twelve hours to go. No chance.

He shook his head, letting out another cough of a laugh. *You're not going to be allowed on that plane, Paul. Let's face it. Not when they find out what you've done.*

In the stark normality of the village, everything that had happened on the mountain felt unreal – like it had played out in a movie they'd all watched.

Tristan was dead. He knew that for sure, because he'd killed him. Ginny was also dead.

OK, he didn't know that last part for sure, but he was under no illusions. Tristan had found her and finished her off. The man was a stone-cold psychopath. That was the difference between them. Paul's *own* actions against Tristan had been self-defence. And Cat's action against Ginny had been a stupid, angry accident. She couldn't have meant to kill her sister. None of this could really have been her plan, could it? That plan, of course, where he was supposed to be dead, and Tristan was supposed to be alive.

Part of him wanted to tell the police all of this. But part of him still trusted his wife . . . despite everything. After all, she had stuck by him through his own unfortunate actions. The Christmas Party Incident. That stupid bitch Samantha had never been able to handle her drink. What the fuck did she think was going to happen when she got in that lift with him? If it hadn't been then, it would've been back in his room. Or hers. He wasn't fussy.

It's not as if it was the first time he'd done it.

He used to laugh when Cat told him about Ginny and Tristan, her sister crying over Tristan's latest infidelity. Tristan had wanted to be caught, that was clear. Another item for the psychopathy collection. Paul had always been far more discreet. If only bloody Samantha had been the same, instead of freaking out and running to HR as soon as she got into work on the Monday.

God, he was so damn tired.

'We're here,' Cat said, knocking him right out of his day-dreams. She seemed to have found some energy since the trucker picked them up, although her face was looking a bit puffy from a recent bout of crying.

She was peering at the sign on the wall.

He grabbed on to the railing next to the steps. He really needed to sit down. A wave of tiredness had hit him hard. A heavy weight was pressing him down towards the ground. He needed to try and stay alert. Needed to make sure he knew exactly what was going on. Cat sat down on the step, and he lowered himself down too. 'What now?' His voice was ragged, hoarse. His breathing laboured. He needed medical attention.

Cat stood up and wiped a hand across her face, smearing mud and tears. She walked carefully around him, peered closely at the sign next to the door. 'There's a phone number here. For emergencies.'

Paul laughed, but it was that cough again. It hurt his chest.

'We don't have phones, remember?'

Cat sighed. Walked away from him, glancing up and down the street. 'Something must be open.' She paused. 'I could go to the hotel.'

Paul shook his head. 'Not sure that's a good idea, is it? You said we need to stick to the plan.'

Cat was hesitant. Unsure. 'Yes, but . . .' Her eyes travelled over him. His injuries. His pain. Did she care? He wasn't sure anymore. 'I could go somewhere else. Get help. We need assistance now, not in three hours . . .' She walked further away from him, taking in the street filled with closed shops, hotels still sleeping, no public phones in sight. She started to walk slowly along the street.

Paul's chest tightened, fear gripping him. He pulled himself to his feet. Called out, his voice barely a rasp. 'Don't leave me here, Cat. Please.'

We need to stick together, he thought. But he knew he'd already lost her.

Forty-Six

He climbed down the stairs carefully, avoiding the couple at the bottom that he'd smashed up earlier to stop them from going upstairs. He went through to the front room, where the morning sun was streaking through the filthy window.

The place was a mess.

He'd heard the struggle from upstairs, but he hadn't been able to see what was going on. Then he'd heard the voices, heard their plan.

The floor was covered in blood.

Even if there was anything to clean it up with, was there any point? If they sent up any rescuers they'd be sure to find the mess. Then they'd send Forensics, and it would be game over.

He walked back into the kitchen. There was an old broom in the corner. He opened the cupboard under the sink and it fell off its hinges. He shoved it away. A family of beetles scurried out and disappeared into the gaps in the floorboards.

He took the broom and went into the front room again. He brushed a pile of leaves over the blood. Then he took the broom and tossed it back into the corner in the kitchen. There was no point in what he'd just done, but somehow it made him feel better.

He disliked mess.

He wasn't happy that the blonde and the man had left the place like this. But they'd panicked. Made stupid choices.

He could relate to that.

But it would all be OK soon enough.

He thought about the blonde again. Wondered if she had made it down the mountain, and what she had planned for her companion now.

Forty-Seven

Sunday Evening

Paul shifted in his seat. He glanced up at the clock. 5 p.m. Jesus. He couldn't believe they'd been there all day, pacing about, saying next to nothing to the police. Watching those stupid fish swimming round and round. Waiting for these people from the embassy to come and help them out of this mess.

His various aches and pains had dulled, somewhat. Probably due to the strong painkillers that the police had given him from their first-aid kit, and that he'd swallowed without question. After all, Cat had been quite insistent that they had to stay here and not go to the hospital to be checked out. He'd been surprised to find that there were two interview rooms at the back of the station, but he hadn't been surprised when they'd eventually asked to interview him and Cat separately. They might not have been under arrest, but he could tell that the police had been suspicious the whole time – especially with them refusing to speak until the embassy reps arrived. He knew Pigalle had been watching them. He had a strong feeling that the man didn't like him, and he didn't know why.

The door swung open and a flustered-looking man in a crumpled suit appeared. He had floppy blond hair that he shoved behind his ears impatiently before slapping his briefcase on the table in front of him and sitting down hard on the plastic chair opposite Paul.

'Not a good journey, then?' Paul said, trying to lighten the mood.

The man stared at him. Frowned. His eyes scanned Paul's bashed face, travelled down to his filthy t-shirt, his scraped and bruised arms. They'd given him a blanket earlier, but he'd taken it off when he'd come into this stuffy, windowless room. He had it draped on the back of the chair now, acting as a cushion against the hard plastic.

'Probably not as bad as yours, by the look of you.' The man reached across the table, offering a hand. 'Matthew Dobbs. I'm a Diplomatic Services Officer with the British Embassy in Bern.' He pulled his hand away, and flipped open his briefcase. He was still staring at Paul as he sat back down. 'So . . . Captain Pigalle says your friends are missing. Want to tell me what's happened?'

'Do you know if they've sent out a search party yet?'

Dobbs shook his head. He looked annoyed. 'No. From what I've been told, the pair of you have been refusing to cooperate. I'm really not sure I understand what's going on here.' He took a notepad out of his briefcase, followed by a silver pen. He clicked the end a couple of times, turned it upside down and peered at the nib. Then he scribbled on his notepad until the ink started to flow. 'So . . . the woman you're with. She's your wife?'

Paul nodded.

'Let's start with your names, shall we?'

'I'm wondering why they've insisted on separating us. We're not under arrest . . .'

Dobbs looked up from his notepad. 'Pigalle's a suspicious sort. He acts like the type who can't be bothered coming in to work, but underneath it, he's taking everything in. He told me he had a funny feeling about the situation right from the start. Couldn't understand why you were refusing medical help and being cagey about what happened.'

Paul put his elbows on the table. 'Look . . . Cat speaks a bit of French, but—'

Dobbs started writing. 'Cat? With a C or a K? Short for Catherine, I guess?'

'Yes. Yes. It's Catherine Baxendale. I'm Paul. Same surname.' He sighed. 'We wanted to make sure nothing got lost in translation.'

The embassy man looked up, his face pinched. 'Pigalle speaks fluent English, Mr Baxendale.'

Paul felt a cold sweat start to form on his back. He'd thought he was calm, and the man opposite the flustered one. But they seem to have changed positions. He'd expected the embassy representative to be supportive, but now he was looking as suspicious as Pigalle.

'I'd like to see my wife.'

'Of course. She's talking with my colleague at the moment, but once we're done we'll all head back through to the bigger room and hopefully get something to eat. I'm bloody starving.' He glanced at his watch. 'I like to eat every three and half hours. Keeps my blood sugar in check.'

Paul hadn't eaten since the second chewy sandwich they'd been given earlier, and he had no appetite at all now. He just wanted this over with. He wondered how Cat was getting on. She'd seemed resolute when he'd last seen her about half an hour before. Ready to tell the people who could help them their version of the truth. They'd rehearsed it as much as they could, sitting on those steps outside, waiting for the police station to open. They'd gone over and over it again and again, Cat doing a role-play where Paul had to state several times what had happened on the hike. She'd coached him on his emotions, making sure that he was going to be believed. He'd offered to do the same for her, but she'd assured him that she was fine. It was all in her head. She'd had far longer to prepare for this than he had, she insisted, even if the plan had changed somewhat.

Dobbs was clicking his pen on and off again, his eyes still fixed on Paul. Paul swallowed. A small voice whizzed into his head and he had to blink several times to make it go away. *You could just tell the truth*, the voice taunted. *Maybe that's what Cat is doing right now . . .*

No, he thought, shaking his head. *No. Cat will stick to the plan.*

'Is everything OK, Mr Baxendale? It looks like you're having a conversation with yourself there.' Dobbs had stopped clicking the pen and was still staring at him intently.

Paul felt beads of sweat break out across his brow. He was far too hot, all of a sudden. A fever, maybe. An infection setting in. *Just tell the truth*, the voice in his head chirped, more insistent now.

Paul put a hand to his brow. It felt clammy. He closed his eyes slowly. Opened them again. 'There was an accident. They fell—'

Dobbs sat up straighter. 'Who fell?'

'Ginny. Cat's sister. She was feeling faint, and she slipped, and . . .' He paused. Rubbed his eyes with his fists. 'Tristan tried to help her, but it was no use. We couldn't even see how far she'd fallen.' He took his hands away from his face and fixed his gaze on Dobbs. 'We had no way of getting help.'

Dobbs frowned. 'You couldn't call for help? You were on the Argentine, is that right? That's what Pigalle told me. The signal is usually fine there. I've done that hike myself.'

Paul sucked in a breath, felt it catch in his throat. 'We all left our phones in the car. We were using a map. Cat thought it would be more fun.'

Dobbs bit his bottom lip. Sighed. 'Bit irresponsible, don't you think?'

'In fairness, it didn't seem too arduous. We were expecting to be up and down within five hours . . .'

'I sense a "but" . . .'

'We met a couple of hikers early on, right at the start. They said there'd been some rock falls. That some of the paths were loose. They tried to tell us to take another route, but—'

'But you didn't listen.'

Paul shrugged. 'It really didn't seem so bad. Tristan—'

Dobbs clicked his pen. 'Tristan? Who is he, then? Where is he now?'

'He's Ginny's husband. My brother-in-law. He's . . . he's gone too.' Paul felt the sweat start to pool at the top of his shorts. It was cold. Despite the heat in his body, he was freezing all of a sudden. He shuffled in his seat, grabbing the sides of the blanket behind him and pulling it up over his shoulders, wrapping it around and gripping it tightly across his chest. 'He . . . he went crazy.'

Dobbs's mouth dropped open. He let go of his pen and it rolled across his notebook and on to the table. He took a moment to compose himself before picking it up again, his finger poised on the top, ready to click. 'Go on . . .'

'You've got to understand . . . we were all exhausted. We were in shock about Ginny. None of us knew what to do.' All of this was the truth, at least. There was no need to act out the emotions for this part. He had definitely been in shock when Ginny fell, even if the others had been somewhat expecting it to happen. Given that they'd planned it. 'Tristan was mad with grief. Cat went almost catatonic for a while.' The lump in his throat was growing like a tumour. He remembered Ginny bickering with Cat. Calling her by *that* nickname. He swallowed the lump down. 'But Tristan . . . he just flipped. After he tried to climb down and find Ginny, he just started rambling nonsense. Then he ran off.' Paul lowered his eyes, trying to avoid Dobbs's gaze during the lie.

When he looked up again, Dobbs was looking sceptical. 'Ran off where? Did you see him again?'

Paul took a moment. He had a choice. He could still tell the truth. Ultimately, he'd done nothing wrong. He was a victim. He'd acted in self-defence. Cat was the one behind it all. Cat was the one who would go to prison if the truth revealed itself.

But they had an agreement. They would both lie to save Cat from prison, and she would stay quiet about the other business. She knew the *real* truth, she'd said. And it would ruin him if it got out. If the police re-opened the case and he was found guilty, he would never work again. No one wanted a sex offender in their workplace. Even if it was all her own fault.

Bloody Samantha.

The whole situation sucked, but if they could both get out of it and remain free, then he'd find a way to live with himself. He wondered how Cat was getting on in the room next door. These same questions. These same answers. He hoped she wasn't cracking under the pressure.

'Mr Baxendale? Paul?' Dobbs's voice was softer now. Some sympathy edging in. 'Did you see Tristan again?'

Paul shook his head. *Decision made.*

'No. We never saw him again.'

Forty-Eight

SUNDAY EVENING

Cat wiped her eyes with a tissue from the cellophane pack provided. Her hands were shaking as she balled the tissue up, clutching it tightly in her fist. 'I'm sorry.' She sniffed, then wiped at her eyes again with the back of her hand. 'It's just been so difficult, having to share space with him while we waited.'

The woman on the other side of the desk took a pen and a notepad out of her leather satchel. She'd already introduced herself as Lydia Pearson, from the British Embassy in Bern. She'd travelled with her colleague Matthew Dobbs. She apologised again about the delay. Her face was smooth in the way that only someone who's never abused their skin with alcohol, smoking or sun can boast. Her blue eyes were sharp but kind. She was looking at Cat with sympathy and, so far, she hadn't pressed for Cat to say anything about what had happened.

If she thought it strange that Cat and Paul had refused to go into detail about their situation prior to now, she didn't show it. Cat smiled, and the woman smiled back.

'Take your time, Catherine. I'm sure this is very difficult, but please be assured that I am here to help you. OK?'

Cat nodded. 'Call me Cat. Please. Only my parents called me Catherine.' She glanced away. 'I don't want to think about them right now.' Another sob escaped. 'They'd be devastated about Ginny.'

'Your sister, is that right?'

Cat nodded again. She'd blurted out most of the story earlier, but it had been garbled and mostly incoherent, and now it was time for her to take things calmly. She needed to get this right. Her future would depend on what she said next.

'We often went on weekends away with Ginny and Tristan. They were good company. Obviously things were difficult for a while, you know, when we were all locked down and couldn't really travel and what have you. This was actually our first trip abroad for about two years.' She stifled another sob.

Lydia pulled another tissue out of the packet and handed it to her. 'And things were going OK? No issues to be concerned about before you started the hike yesterday morning?'

Cat shook her head, the lies flowing effortlessly. 'Nothing. Ginny and Tristan were happy. It was nice to see, as I know they'd had a bit of a rocky patch with Tristan being stuck working from home and Ginny feeling a bit like she was messing up his usual daily routine.' She looked down at the table. Sighed. Then lifted her head again. 'As for me and Paul . . . well.'

'Problems?'

Cat forced out a small laugh. 'You could say that . . .'

'Is it something you want to bring up here?' Lydia's voice was sympathetic. 'I mean . . . is it relevant to what happened?'

Cat sniffed, rubbing her nose with the tissue. Nodded. Then she pulled herself up straight and laid her hands on the table in front of her, the balled tissue squashed underneath. 'I thought I knew Paul. I thought I knew every nuance of his being. But recent events made me realise that I didn't know him at all.' She paused. Sucked in a breath. 'Such a cliché.'

Lydia was leaning back in her seat now, one leg crossed over the other. Her expression quizzical. 'I think it's fair to say that no one really knows anyone else, do they? No one can read anyone else's thoughts. No one knows how people will react when they're faced with something difficult or frightening. Stress and pressure can do a lot to people, you know. You shouldn't think you've failed because you didn't spot the signs.' She uncrossed her legs and leaned forward. 'Sometimes there just aren't any signs to spot.' She shrugged. 'I've met a lot of people in my line of work and, I'll tell you, no matter what I think I know about human psychology, people will always do things that surprise me.'

Cat shifted in her seat. This was going exactly how she wanted. She glanced up at the camera in the corner of the room. 'I know you said the cameras are off, but . . . well, maybe we should have one of the police in here with us now anyway. I'll only have to say it all again otherwise.'

Lydia picked up her pen and flipped her notebook open. 'So you want to make a statement? I thought you wanted to talk to me first, to explain everything? About the accident?'

'I did.' Cat sighed. 'I do. But . . . well. Maybe we should get it all over with. Formally, I mean. We've already delayed things a lot. But as I said to the captain before, I was scared of doing this alone. I don't want anything to get . . . misunderstood.'

Lydia reached across to the wall and pressed a green button on the phone that hung there. It made a buzzing sound that could be heard both in the room they were in and the room that it was connected to. The walls were paper-thin. The captain and his lieutenant had probably been listening to every word anyway. She had a sudden flash of Captain Pigalle leaping back from the connecting wall, holding a glass and wearing a guilty expression.

'*Oui?*' His tinny voice came through the intercom speaker.

'Can you come through, please, captain? Catherine would like to make a formal statement.'

'I am coming in now.'

Cat locked eyes with Lydia. 'And by the way . . . just to be clear? What happened was not an accident.'

'OK . . .'

Captain Pigalle entered the room just as Cat started to cry. The stress of keeping her story straight was starting to get to her. But more than that, she was tired. She wanted to sleep. She wanted to drink too much wine, and pass out, and wake up and act like none of this had ever happened. She was trying her best to keep Tristan from her thoughts, but somehow he kept creeping in. And Ginny . . . oh god. Ginny. She had to keep remembering what Ginny had done, and why this whole thing was justified.

She wiped her eyes with another tissue. 'It was Paul,' she said, trying to keep her voice strong. Trying to deliver the lie as steady as she could make it. 'It was all Paul.'

'Please, madame . . .' Pigalle raised a hand, gesturing for her to stop. 'Before you carry on, I would like to record this conversation. That is OK?'

Cat nodded, then Pigalle said some spiel about recording the interview, and who was present and what time it was. Then he sat down next to Lydia, and the two of them looked at Cat expectantly.

'I'm not under arrest, right? This is just me telling you what happened?'

'Of course,' the policeman said. 'But it will help us all if we record this. You understand?'

Lydia placed a hand on top of Cat's. She smiled gently. 'We can stop anytime that you like, Cat. We just want to understand exactly what happened.'

'And Paul?'

Lydia and Pigalle glanced at each other. Pigalle frowned. 'Paul is doing the same in the other room. With my colleague, and Monsieur Dobbs. But maybe we should all talk together?'

Cat shook her head. 'No, it's fine. As I said before – I'd prefer to talk to you on my own.'

Pigalle pressed his hands together. 'I think it will save us some time to do this all together. Don't you agree?'

Panic started to build in Cat's chest. 'But we already agreed. I asked this before. I told you I was . . . I was scared of him.'

'Nothing is going to happen to you, madame. We are here for you. But I want to understand all of this so that we can proceed. We still need to find your sister and your brother-in-law, am I right?'

So he *had* been listening in. Because she hadn't revealed any of this to him yet, only to Lydia. Unless . . . Paul. Maybe Paul was getting ready to stitch her up.

Cat looked down at her hands. The palms were dirty and scratched. She curled her fingers and inspected her broken, filthy nails. Then she took a deep breath and looked up at the man and woman before her.

'Please. Let me start this on my own, at least. He'll have his own side of the story and I won't get a chance if he's in the room with me.'

'Let's do it your way,' Lydia said. 'OK, Captain Pigalle?'

'Fine. Let us see where things go.'

Cat smiled at them gratefully, her heart rate beginning to slow back to something approximating normal. 'It all started in January.' She paused. 'After Paul sexually assaulted one of his colleagues at the Christmas party, a week before.'

Pigalle raised an eyebrow. 'This does not sound good. Was there an investigation? Was he charged?'

'And what does this have to do with what happened on the mountain?' Lydia looked confused. Cat couldn't blame her.

It was a risk going down this route, but it was all she had. 'It was concluded a couple of months ago. It really dragged on. He wasn't charged with anything. He was suspended on full pay, but he decided not to go back. Everyone was happy enough with the outcome.' She paused. 'Everyone except Samantha. But I'm not sure there was anything else she could do. Both the investigation by his work and by the police came back saying the same thing – that there was no evidence.' She looked down at her hands again. Saw the marks on her wrists from when Paul had grabbed her earlier. He'd gripped them hard when he'd pulled her to her feet at the bottom of the mountain, and she'd always marked and bruised easily.

She held up her wrists for them to see, hoping they would see it as evidence of his ability to be rough.

They were both looking at her sympathetically, so she ploughed on. There was no going back now.

'I believed him. The whole way through. I stood up for him. I looked after him when he broke down, terrified it would go to court, that he'd end up in prison.' She put her hands back down, palms flat. Her wedding ring was scratched and dull. 'Then, a few weeks ago, I found the photos.'

Forty-Nine

SUNDAY EVENING

Dobbs frowned at him. 'OK, just so we're clear . . .' He looked down at his pad and read from his notes. 'Ginny fell. Tristan tried to help her. You didn't see him again.' He looked back up, straight into Paul's eyes. 'How did he manage to climb down the mountain? Was he an experienced climber?'

'I didn't know this until yesterday, but yes, it seems so.' Paul felt momentarily buoyed to be able to tell the truth about something, and the words flowed easily. 'He said he'd been doing some courses. He had all the kit. He climbed down, and he climbed back up – but he couldn't find her.' He folded his arms. 'It was after that he went mad . . . he shouted at me, blaming me – when he was the one who'd planned the route—'

'Tristan planned the route? I thought this trip was your wife's idea.'

'It was . . . but he helped. Maybe he told her he'd been doing some climbing. I don't know.' Paul shrugged his shoulders. 'Anyway. He was yelling at me, then he swung his rope at me. It still had that big metal clip thing on the end of it, from where it attached to his harness.'

'The belay device?'

'If you say so.' Paul uncrossed his arms and lifted a hand to the side of his head. He gingerly peeled back a piece of his matted hair and turned his head to the side, giving Dobbs a clear view. 'He cracked me across the head.'

'Nasty. Then what?'

Paul turned his head, looked away. 'He ran off.'

When he turned back, Dobbs's expression was sceptical.

'I assumed he'd gone for help. Or he was heading back down. He knew the way, after all. I thought he'd be here, in fact. When we arrived.'

Dobbs's expression had become unreadable.

Paul was about to start adding in something more, ready to start babbling, when the intercom buzzed. He'd babbled just the same when the police had questioned him about what happened at the work party, and he'd tried to rein it in since then, but it was hard to curb his natural tendencies to talk himself out of a hole using far too many words. Saying that, he'd managed to lie his way out of that mess fairly convincingly. Mostly due to a fuck-up with things being deleted from phones that worked in his favour.

Thinking about it, why was he defending Cat? Going along with her stupid plan? She could say what she liked about what had really happened that night in January. But without evidence, and with him denying the whole thing, what could anyone do? The intercom buzzed again, and this time Dobbs picked up the phone. He kept his eyes locked on Paul as he listened to the caller, then he sighed and put the receiver back in its cradle.

'Captain Pigalle would like to speak with you,' Dobbs said.

'Now?' Paul felt a flutter of unease in his belly. The plan was that he and Cat would tell their stories separately, then the police would go and find the others. Why was Pigalle interrupting now? This did not sound good.

The door opened and Pigalle appeared. His face was flushed, his jaw set. 'Thank you, Monsieur Baxendale. I just have a couple of questions then you can carry on.' He sat down next to Dobbs and slid a couple of papers across to the embassy man.

Paul watched Dobbs's face as he started to read. He lifted up the top sheet and, underneath, Paul could see what looked like a printout of a photograph. Dobbs's expression rippled and morphed from impatience to something else quite different. He glanced up at Paul, and anger flashed in his eyes.

'Have you had any issues with . . . aggressive behaviour before, Mr Baxendale?'

No calling him "Paul" now. Something had shifted. He'd heard rumours of the French police tactics before. Was Pigalle going to pin all this on him?

'What's this about?' Paul's stomach was doing small somersaults, but he was trying his hardest to keep a neutral expression.

'How was your relationship with your sister-in-law, Mr Baxendale?' Pigalle asked.

The somersaults were getting bigger. 'What's this about? What has my wife said?'

Pigalle smiled, but it didn't quite reach his eyes. 'We would like to hear this from you, monsieur.'

Paul looked from the police officer to the embassy representative – the embassy representative who was meant to be helping him out. Not making things worse. 'Am I under arrest?'

Dobbs's expression was pained. He looked away briefly, then glanced back at Paul before looking down at his notes, as if there might be something in there that had given him a clue to this disaster. Because that was what this was, Paul realised now. Something had happened. Something had changed.

Someone was not sticking to the plan.

'Do you think you should be under arrest, monsieur? From what you've led us to believe, you were in an accident along with your friends – who are now missing. *Non?*'

'Yes!' Paul slammed a hand on the table. 'That's what happened. So why does it matter if I got on with my fucking sister-in-law or not? Has Cat said I didn't? Because if you must know, no, I didn't like her very much. But I also didn't really give much of a shit about her. I zoned her out, mostly. Cat dealt with her.' He paused, blew out a breath. 'You should ask Cat how she got on with her sister. You'll find that much more enlightening, I'm sure.'

Dobbs laid a hand over Paul's. 'I know this is distressing, Paul. You've had a terrible time—'

Paul pulled his hand away, ignoring him. He faced Pigalle. 'What's my darling wife been saying then? Go on.' He crossed his arms, closing himself up.

Pigalle leaned into Dobbs, whispered something in his ear. Paul heard Dobbs say, 'I suppose so . . .' but he sounded uncertain.

'Maybe I should have a lawyer. Are you able to act in that capacity, Mr Dobbs?'

Dobbs shifted uncomfortably. 'I'm afraid not. I can make some calls . . .'

Paul waved a hand at him, dismissively. He knew when he was being stitched up. But whatever Cat had said, she didn't have any actual evidence. Two could play that game.

'Right, well—'

Pigalle raised a hand. 'One moment, please.' He slid a piece of paper across the table. 'Can you tell us what's going on here, please, monsieur? That is you in these photographs, am I correct?'

Paul flipped over the paper. It took him a moment to focus. To register what it was that he was looking at. He pushed the paper away in disgust. 'How the . . . ?' Burning bile made its way into the base of his throat and he thought he might vomit. Of all the things he'd been expecting, this one was way down on the list.

'I don't understand.'

'Your wife passed this on to us, monsieur. She had it saved in her Cloud drive. We let her access it here.'

He had a sudden flash to the day that he'd tried to delete the photos from his phone. He had no idea why he even took them. He'd thought it was funny at the time. He'd thought he might even show Tristan. But in the cold light of day, they hadn't looked funny at all. And then Samantha had made the complaint, and he'd immediately gone to delete them. But in his panic, he'd tapped the wrong thing and they'd saved themselves to his and Cat's joint Cloud account. The one where they saved wedding photos and holiday photos and stupid things that were meant for each other to see. He'd deleted it straight away. It was just his stupid luck that Cat had been online at the time. She must've seen them pop up and taken screenshots immediately. And she'd kept quiet. This whole fucking time. That . . . bitch.

'I don't see what my photos of me and a friend messing about in a lift have got to do with my sister-in-law.' His arms were still crossed. He was not going to yield.

'I think you are an intelligent man, Monsieur Baxendale. You can connect these dots, *oui*?'

Dobbs cleared his throat, but said nothing more.

'Your wife has told us about the allegations back at home, Paul.' Pigalle raised a hand to silence Paul, who had his mouth open, ready to object. 'We know that the case was dropped due to lack of evidence.' He pulled the printed photographs back towards himself. 'But they did not have *this* evidence.'

Paul glared at him. 'I still don't see what that has to do with—'

'It paints a picture. Not a pretty one.' Pigalle stood up. 'Please come with us now, Monsieur Baxendale.'

Dobbs stood too, gesturing to Paul. 'Come on,' he said. 'Better that we get to the truth sooner rather than later.'

Paul stood up and followed them out of the room. He kept his mouth shut, because he had a very bad feeling about all this. And he was pretty sure that anything he said now would only make it worse.

Fifty

SUNDAY EVENING

Cat's hand shook as she picked up her coffee. She took a sip. It was thick and strong, like the cup that Pigalle had made for her earlier. It was helping her stay focused. She placed the cup back on the table in front of her. 'He'll deny it, of course.'

'I suppose we'll find out soon enough.' Lydia was scribbling notes. The two of them were alone in the room since Pigalle had left them to confront Paul with the photographs.

Cat took another sip of her coffee. 'What will happen to him?'

'I—' Whatever Lydia was about to say was cut off when the door swung open and Pigalle walked in. He was followed by a furious-looking Paul, and a man that she didn't recognise.

'Matthew Dobbs,' the man said, sitting down next to Lydia. 'I'm also here from the embassy.'

'Hello.' Cat tried not to look at Paul, but she felt his gaze burning into her.

The lieutenant appeared a moment later, carrying extra chairs. Pigalle and the lieutenant spent a bit of time rearranging things so that they could all sit around the table – pulling it out from the wall and placing a chair at the end, where they gestured for Paul to sit.

She was separated from him by Lydia and Matthew, who had now squeezed in beside her – and opposite them, the two policemen sat down. They were stony-faced now.

Like everyone, Cat assumed they just wanted this dealt with without any further delay.

She felt her stomach churn. Those butterflies in her chest again. This was it. She had to get this right, or she wasn't going to be walking out of this station today.

Pigalle switched on the recorder and said a few words about who was present. Then he fixed his gaze on Cat. 'Madame Baxendale,' he said. 'Perhaps you would like to explain these to us.' He slid the photographs across the table towards her, but she didn't look at them.

'These are photographs that I found on our shared Cloud. They show Paul with a woman . . . a work colleague. Her name is Samantha Jones—'

'We were messing about. She's a *friend*.'

'Please be quiet, Monsieur Baxendale.' Pigalle was still watching Cat as he spoke. 'Please. Carry on.'

'Well . . .' Cat's voice started shaking. 'You can see what's going on here. She doesn't look happy about it. She doesn't look like she's messing about with a *friend*.' Cat cleared her throat. 'In her statement to the HR department, and to the police, she said Paul grabbed her, forced her—'

'This is fucking bullshit!' Paul stood up quickly, knocking the table forward. They all jumped back. The lieutenant stood, facing Paul.

'Monsieur, you need to calm down. You are not under arrest. We are trying to establish the situation. Now please. Sit down.'

Cat hadn't realised before how physically intimidating the lieutenant could be. Earlier, he'd been all smiles and shrugs – and she realised she'd underestimated him. Pigalle too. These were no fools. She took a deep breath, trying to keep herself calm.

'The point is,' Cat said, her voice steady now. 'This just proves what kind of man he is.' She glanced at Paul. His mouth was set in a hard line. His fingers gripping the table. It was clearly taking great restraint for him to keep quiet. 'The truth is . . . he came on to Ginny. While we were on the hike.' She stared down at the table, managing to squeeze a tear out before she raised her eyes again. 'She rebuffed him.' She paused. Bit her lip. 'And then he pushed her.'

'You fucking lying bitch!' Paul was up out of his seat, flipping the table over. He grabbed her by the throat and they both fell back on to the floor with a thud. She felt the breath go out of her. She raised her hands, grabbed hold of his, trying to pry them off her neck. His face was bearing down on her, and he was swearing, blasting a diatribe of pure hatred. Globules of spit landed on her face.

Cat felt like she was about to pass out, then just as quickly as it had started, the pressure was off, as Paul was yanked away from her. She put her hands to her throat, started coughing. And real tears, now. Shock, mostly. But for a moment, she had really thought she might die. She couldn't quite believe he had it in him.

Lydia and Matthew helped her to her feet, as she tried to block out the sounds of Paul being dragged out of the room by the policemen. A door slammed. But she could still hear muffled sounds of shouting, in English and French. It occurred to her that that Paul might suffer at the hands of the police for what he had done, but she realised quickly that she really didn't care.

This had gone much better than she could ever have envisaged. She hadn't known that Paul had it in him to be so violent. Maybe he wasn't the wet blanket that she'd come to believe he was after all. She had to admit she felt a grudging respect for what he had just done, in the face of her betrayal.

But it was his own stupid fault for trusting her, given that the original plan was to get rid of him on the mountain.

Lydia and Matthew were looking at her carefully. She'd said nothing since the attack, lost in her own spinning thoughts.

'Are you OK, Cat?' Lydia said, eventually. 'Can we get you anything?'

'Maybe just some water.'

Matthew left the room and Lydia continued to stare at her, as if unsure of how to deal with this.

'You're safe now, Cat.' She turned away and started to pick up the papers that were strewn across the floor.

After a few minutes, the door opened and Matthew returned, a paper cup of water in his hand. Pigalle followed close behind.

'I am very sorry, madame,' Pigalle said. He bent down and flipped the table up the right way again, pushing it back against the wall. 'It was my idea to talk to you both together. Now I understand why you wanted to stay away from him.'

Cat pushed her chair in closer to the table then lifted the cup of water, taking a sip.

'Your husband will not be upsetting you again,' Pigalle continued. 'My lieutenant will make sure of that.'

Cat coughed and took another small sip of water. Her throat hurt, but it would ease.

'Perhaps we can continue now?' Pigalle's voice was gentle. 'There are still a few things we need to understand.'

'You've seen what he's like now. But I suppose he'll continue to deny what he did to Ginny.'

Pigalle shrugged. 'He said earlier that it was you who pushed your sister.'

Her voice was sharper than intended. 'And why would I do that?'

Lydia tilted her head to the side slightly, reached for Cat's hand across the table. 'Try not to get upset, Cat. It's what we'd expect him to say, under the circumstances . . .'

'We don't know the full story yet, though,' Pigalle said, pressing himself back into his seat and crossing his arms. 'I feel like something is missing. Like what happened to your other friend, Tristan.'

Cat looked away. 'Tristan fell.' She started picking at her cuticles.

'Go on . . .' Pigalle urged.

'When I say "fell" . . . this was also down to Paul. After Ginny. They fought. I thought . . . I thought they were both going over the edge at one point.' She choked back tears. She hadn't expected to cry so much, but she couldn't help herself. But she had to try and pull herself together. There had been a moment up on the mountain, when Tristan had tripped on a tree root walking towards the shelter, where she'd thought she might end up there alone in the dark – and the thought of that still terrified her, even though she was back down here, in the daylight. Safe.

With Paul – back from the dead.

Whatever had happened up there . . . ending up on her own – having to make that descent alone . . . that had never been part of the plan. That fall she'd taken on the descent . . . if she'd been on her own . . . well, then the whole thing would've looked like a tragedy, with all four of them missing.

Maybe that would've been better. Easier, at least. She wasn't sure how much longer she could carry on with her lies.

'I'm very tired.' She sat back in her chair, and for a moment she thought she might fall asleep. She'd had so many adrenaline peaks and troughs in the last thirty-six hours, it was a wonder she hadn't had a heart attack.

'You can sleep soon, madame,' Pigalle said. 'We just need to get all the information first, OK? Remember . . . you wanted us to look for your friends? We need to know where to start.'

Cat took in a fast breath, let it out slowly. She needed to stay calm. But she really didn't want a search party going up there. Not yet. Not while she was still here. She had no idea how quickly they might find the bodies, but she wanted to be long gone before they did.

Surely they would let her leave soon? She wasn't under arrest. They didn't see her as a danger to anyone. Unlike Paul. She had to drive the final nail into his coffin. She was taking a risk with her next revelation, but she'd had hours to go through it all, making it work in her head. It would work. It had to.

'I have something else that might help.' She sat forward again, pinching the skin beneath her thumb with the thumb and forefinger from her other hand, trying to dig the ragged nails into the soft skin. Trying to stay alert.

Pigalle, Matthew and Lydia were watching her intently.

'It's a recording . . . I got it by accident, really. I got this little recording gadget at work. I get lots of stuff like that. I work in events management?'

They nodded at her, urging her to continue.

'I was playing around with it one day. I left it out, switched on. When I plugged it into my computer later, there was an audio file on there. I listened, expecting background noise of the house. The sound of the TV, maybe. But there was more than that. There was a recording of Paul.'

'And? What was he saying?' Lydia's eyebrows shot into her hairline.

'He was talking to someone on the phone. I don't know who. But he was talking about Ginny. I'd told him that I was angry with her for the way she'd handled our parents' estate . . . they died three years ago. A car accident. Ginny was executor—'

Lydia cut in. 'And she didn't give you your share?'

Cat nodded, finding her flow. 'Right. It was all a bit messy, but I was sorting it out. Jeez . . .' She sighed. 'What with that, and Paul's work thing . . . plus still trying to get back on track after I lost so many event bookings during the pandemic . . . anyway, yeah. Paul was angry. I heard him asking someone what would happen . . .'

'To what?' Pigalle rested his chin on his fist.

'What would happen to the money if both Ginny and Tristan were to die.' She looked away, blinking back tears. They weren't even fake. She was better at this than she'd thought she would be.

'Do you have this recording?' Pigalle demanded, sitting up straight again. 'Did you keep it? Is it on the Cloud, like the photographs?'

Cat shook her head. 'I have it, yes, but it's not in the Cloud. It was a new device, you see. It saved a local file automatically. It's on my laptop.'

Pigalle sighed. 'And where is your laptop, madame? Is it in the UK? Back at home?'

She shook her head again. 'No. It's in the hotel. I can go and get it right now . . .'

Fifty-One

Sunday Evening

Paul was in a cell, alone. Another room he hadn't expected to find at the back of the police station. Quite a labyrinth it was, this building. Or a TARDIS. He wasn't really sure. He *was* sure that another of his ribs had broken, when that lump of a lieutenant had thrown him into the small room like he was throwing a steak to a dog.

Paul tried to keep his breathing in check, but his heart was still thumping hard in his chest. They'd formally arrested him after his outburst in the interview room, and he supposed he couldn't really blame them.

Fucking Cat. She had stitched him up good and proper.

Dobbs, the useless fucker, had come in briefly to explain that they would be referring all this to the main police station. He would be taken there soon for more questioning and, in the meantime, they would start to assemble a search party. No one had actually accused him of murder. Yet. But it was only a matter of time. Nobody believed that Ginny and Tristan might still be alive, and they were right, because that pair were both most definitely dead. He knew that Tristan had finished her off. He could tell from the look on his face when he'd confronted him in the old house.

What the hell had Cat been thinking, trusting that psychotic bastard? And why the hell was she pinning all of this on him now? What did she have to gain? She'd made her fucking point, that was for sure. A woman scorned, and all that.

OK, so maybe he should've told the truth about what had happened with Samantha – but the best-case scenario was that he'd be exposed as a cheat. Did he really want that?

It hardly mattered now.

He wondered where Cat was. Were they still talking to her? Was she in there now, trying to suppress a smirk while she played the distraught wife and sister?

He'd *tried* to tell them the truth: Cat and Tristan planned this. Cat pushed Ginny in a fit of rage – not part of the plan . . . Tristan had pretended to look for her but actually finished her off, then he'd tried to kill Paul by whacking him over the head and rolling him off the same section of the mountain. Then the two of them had thought they'd got away with it . . . until Paul had reappeared, having fallen on to a ledge and found Ginny's necklace. That fucking necklace didn't help. He'd tried to give it to Cat, but she'd refused to take it, and so it had gone back into his pocket, along with his Huntsman, and now the police had taken both and they'd just made him look guiltier. He'd told them, too, about the second fight with Tristan, and how he'd accidentally stabbed him – and that it was Cat, again, who had decided what to do next. They'd thrown him in the waterfall, and then they'd come up with a plan where it was all a big accident . . . and they were going to stick together.

They hadn't believed him.

He tried to explain about the deal that he'd made with Cat. That she had agreed to continue keeping quiet about the real version of what had happened with Samantha, and that he would lie and say that Ginny and Tristan had fell.

But they didn't believe that either.

His actions in the room had sealed his fate. Cat had told them he was a predator. That he was violent. And all he'd done was back her up.

Well done, Paul.

He still didn't understand why all of this had happened.

Why would Cat sleep with Tristan? Was this all just about revenge on Ginny for the mess-up with the inheritance? Or was there more to it? And what about the baby. *Was* there even a baby?

He would love to know.

He slumped back in his chair. His heart was still thumping. His head fizzing and buzzing with thoughts.

'I'm fucked, aren't I?' he shouted towards the camera above the door. 'Thank you, Cat. You've done a sterling fucking job here.'

He stood up quickly, pulling the thin mattress off the cot bed. He swung it hard, and it flew across the room, crashing into the door. He grabbed hold of his hair, twisting it in his fists. And then he screamed, loud, long.

No one came.

He walked over to the far corner of the room and sat down, pulling his legs up to his chest. The position was uncomfortable, making the pain in his chest sharper. He pulled his legs up tighter, absorbed in his agony. Then he dropped his head and screamed silently into his knees.

Fifty-Two

Cat couldn't quite believe that they'd agreed to let her leave the station. She stood outside, gazing at the village where she had spent so little time. Ginny had wanted to browse the shops this morning, before they packed and drove back down to Geneva to catch their flight home. Cat shook her head, trying to dislodge thoughts of her sister. That was something she was going to have to face, of course, but not right now. She had to remain focused for just a bit longer.

She'd missed that flight, of course. The day was still warm, but the sky was already darkening. The bright blue veering to indigo, the air thickening. A storm was coming. The shops already starting to pull in their outside displays.

'Ready?' Lydia stepped out of the building and on to the street. She glanced up at the sky, frowning. 'Looks like rain.'

Cat nodded. She started walking across the wide road towards the hotel that sat on the bend, the front not much to look at, but the other side was where it drew in its guests, with the magnificent views of the snow-capped mountains. The hot tub was on that side. Something else she hadn't managed to make use of this weekend. Ginny, again, in her head. She balled her hands into fists, letting her ragged nails cut into the flesh of her palms.

'I'm so sorry that all of this has happened to you,' Lydia said, walking by her side. 'I think the police failed you . . . with Paul's case.'

'I feel partly to blame,' Cat said. 'If I'd taken the photographs to the police instead of keeping them for myself.' She shook her head. 'I'm not even sure what I was going to do with them. I mean, I would have left him, of course. After this weekend . . . I guess I just thought maybe I needed to give him a final chance to tell me the truth.' The lies came thick and fast now. Cat was fully immersed in this latest depiction of events.

'And he didn't . . . but you can't blame yourself for what he did to Ginny. Or to Tristan.'

Cat swallowed. The air mixed with saliva had formed a hard lump in her throat, trying to choke her. She coughed. Lydia placed a gentle hand on her back, and Cat wanted to cry, then, but she held back. She'd done enough of that today. She needed to keep it together now.

'It's really quite incredible that he planned all this, Cat. You can't blame yourself. People get hoodwinked by charming psychopaths all the time. They walk among us, you know. Until they snap and do something like this, it's usually impossible to tell.'

Cat said nothing.

They stopped outside the doors of the hotel. 'Do you think you can give me twenty minutes? I just want to freshen up a bit. Chuck some stuff into my case and put it at reception. I hate to think of them having to pack up our room.'

Lydia frowned. She glanced back at the police station, then to the hotel, as if she was calculating the distance. Working out the risk. 'Sure, OK. Remember to bring your laptop with you though! Don't chuck that in your case.'

'Of course.' Cat cast her eyes down, then back up to Lydia's face. 'I need you to hear the recording. I wish I'd put it on the

Cloud, like those bloody photographs. But, to be honest, I thought it was a joke . . .'

Lydia tried to smile. 'I don't think I'd believe it either, if my husband said he was going to try and murder my sister and her husband. It's just lucky you were recording at the time.'

'As I said, I was just mucking about with that little gadget I'd picked up at a trade fair. I wasn't even convinced it would work. I left it on the hall table to see what it would pick up. I never imagined it would record something like that, or that it would end up being real . . .' She let her sentence trail off. *Don't overdo it, Cat. Stay strong*, she told herself.

Lydia opened the door of the hotel. 'Go on then. Get sorted and I'll see you back here. I'll try and grab a coffee from the restaurant.'

'Thank you,' Cat said. 'The restaurant is down there.' She pointed Lydia towards the place where they'd all sat for breakfast yesterday, planning their day, and the lump in her throat grew bigger. She swallowed hard.

The woman at reception appeared unmoved by Cat's dishevelled appearance, and the fact that she was supposed to have checked out several hours ago. The woman handed Cat a replacement key card and told her that an extra night had already been charged to her card. For both rooms. She'd made the booking, after all. The woman turned away and continued to talk to someone sitting out of sight in a back office.

Cat glanced down towards the restaurant and saw that Lydia had seated herself at one of the tables and was gazing out at the view.

Perfect.

She hurried to her room and opened the door. Thankfully, she was a well-practised hotel traveller, and the room was neat and tidy, with only the minimal amount of items removed from her case.

Paul's stuff was hanging in the wardrobe and she contemplated pulling it all off the hangers and tossing it into his wheely-bag, but, on balance, she couldn't be arsed. She collected her toiletries from the bathroom and looked at herself in the mirror.

Fuck. She looked rough. But did she really have time for a shower? She stuck her head back around the door to check the bedside clock. She'd already been five minutes. She didn't want Lydia coming down to check on her.

She quickly washed her face, then pulled her hair back into a ponytail. She yanked off her shorts and put on a pair of black leggings, then replaced her t-shirt with a soft, pale-blue hooded top. Her boots were filthy, but they would be fine. She threw the ruined shorts and t-shirt into the bin, then stuck on her plain grey baseball cap and pulled her ponytail through the hole at the back.

Better.

She grabbed her travel bag, then did a final sweep of the room. Nothing lying around – nothing of hers, anyway. No phones, iPads or laptops. She hadn't even brought her laptop with her this weekend, but the story of the recording had rolled off her tongue and made perfect sense. The only questionable part was why the 'recording' wasn't in the Cloud, but that was easily explained by the fact that she'd told them she plugged in a new device, which had stored the files on a local drive. If only she *did* have a recording. It would have made everything a lot easier.

She was glad she'd managed to transfer the money in the morning, using her and Tristan's phones. Otherwise she'd have to go back to the car now, and she wasn't sure she could risk any more delays. She was already much later than she'd planned to be.

She lifted her bag, hooking the straps over her shoulders. The multi-functional travel bag had turned out to be a godsend – multiple compartments, expandable, wheels *and* straps. It could literally carry anything and go anywhere. And it had a rain cover, too, which changed its colour from red to blue. There was nothing she was wearing or carrying now that anyone from this hotel, or the police station, had seen.

Not that they'd notice. The distracted reception staff wouldn't bat an eyelid if she walked out past them now. But she wasn't taking any chances.

She closed the door of her room quietly and headed in the opposite direction to the one she'd come from; away from reception, away from the restaurant. She'd chosen this hotel carefully, requesting a room on this floor specifically. She pushed open the door at the end of the corridor, and of course no alarm went off. They always said that fire doors were alarmed, but she'd stayed in many hotels in many places, and she'd never been caught out yet. Of course, there was always the chance that one door, somewhere, might actually be alarmed – but even if it was, she wouldn't be hanging around for a reaction from the staff.

She hurried down the metal stairs of the fire escape, out to the side of the hotel. Away from the main street, and the police station. She walked quickly, wincing slightly, as a stabbing pain in her ankle started up. Bump on her head aside, she thought she'd got away with that tumble down the mountain, but perhaps she had broken a little bone. Or maybe it was just a sprain. She'd experienced pain like this before. She could walk through it.

She had to.

She walked quickly, knowing that her twenty minutes must be nearly up. Hoping she still had enough time. She glanced back at the police station, thinking about Paul. She shuddered. The thought of his hands on her, after what he'd done to Samantha. Just the thought of him sleeping in the same bed was enough to cause a wave of nausea. She'd had to draw on all the strength she'd ever had to deal with him, and Ginny's betrayal. The last few weeks had been hell.

She stood at the bus stop, keeping herself back from the road. She glanced down to the hotel a couple of times, expecting to see Lydia bursting out. Hopefully she was taking her time with her coffee, letting poor Cat shower and pack and come to terms with her horrible, evil husband.

Lydia really needed to work on her people-reading skills.

After a moment, a truck pulled up. She knew it wouldn't take long. Of course there wasn't going to be a bus at this time of day on a Sunday, but thankfully in these Alpine villages there was always someone happy to help a stranded traveller.

She jumped into the cab of the truck, shoved her suitcase under her feet. The driver talked to her in rapid French and she replied, asking him to slow it down a bit so that she could understand, then she told him to drop her as close to the train station as possible. He nodded, then turned the radio up. The latest Euro-pop hit was blasting through the speakers as he pulled away from the kerb. She kept her eyes straight ahead as they passed the hotel, and then the police station, and fought the urge to look back.

Fifty-Three

He stood under the departures board, checking the train times again. He'd arrived hours ago, showered and changed using the station facilities. He'd eaten a sandwich, drunk two coffees.

Waited.

He was bored now.

The game had been fun for a while, but now he just wanted it to be over. He looked at his watch. Stared up at the train times again. Frowned.

Had he got it wrong?

The Tannoy announced the next departures. Then told everyone to mind their luggage. He only had a small bag. He would buy everything he needed when he got there.

After it was all over.

He walked across the station concourse towards the entrance, watching the smattering of people coming in and out. The station was quiet this evening. It was Sunday. People here were lazy on a Sunday.

He looked at a small monitor showing the times. Glanced back at his watch.

Then back to the door.

And then he smiled so wide that he thought he might split the corners of his lips.

She was here.

Fifty-Four

SUNDAY NIGHT

Cat slid across the double-seat, positioning herself next to the window. She was looking forward to the train journey. Geneva to Zurich was around two and half hours, and then not long to wait for the connecting Nightjet train that would take her deeper into Europe. That was going to be the most fun part – she'd always loved a sleeper train. Not that she had any intention of sleeping tonight. She'd gone past tiredness into a wired state that would keep her buzzing along for as long as was needed, and then, no doubt, she would crash.

The man opposite bundled his jacket into a ball, laying it on the seat beside him. The reflective strip on the sleeve caught a flash of light from the overhead strip-lights, sending a sparkling silvery streak across the table for a moment, then he folded it again and the light was gone.

Cat shook her head. 'A bright-red jacket? With a reflective strip? Did you want to be seen in those trees? What were you thinking?'

He shrugged. 'It was the only jacket I could get hold of. I grabbed it from that shop next to the police station in Villars – it's for *layering*, apparently. I hadn't really planned to wear it, but it was much cooler in those woods than out on the path—'

'Ginny was all over it. You took a risk. What were you doing, anyway?' She pulled out her pendant and turned it over in her fingers. 'Wasn't my GPS tracker enough?' He smiled at her, and she lost herself for a moment in his huge green eyes, like sparkling magical pools – she remembered the first time they'd met. His eyes were the first thing she'd noticed about him, when he'd turned to her in that dingy dive bar and grinned. Before it turned out that he was her new tutor. Her new *married* tutor. 'And maybe you should drop the accent now. We don't want anything to connect you to that mountain. You were getting far too friendly with the locals in there.'

'But you love French Frank, *non?*' He grinned. 'It's such a shame we have to change our names. Besides, I'm not sure anyone born after 1985 could even name the French currency before the Euro. Coming up with that moniker was quite clever of your sister, considering you always told me what an idiot she was.'

Cat ignored the slight. It didn't feel right to take the piss out of Ginny. Not now that she was dead.

Frank slid the new passports across the table towards her. 'I was starting to think you weren't coming . . .'

Cat picked up the passports and flicked to the ID pages, taking in their photos and their new identities. She held them up to the light, watching the colours of the holograms shift and swirl. 'Pretty good. Let's just hope they stand up to scrutiny.'

'I told you – working in Asia gets you many good contacts. My friend who did these for me is basically a pro. Oh,' he said, pointing to her pendant, 'and the GPS on that thing is shit, by the way. Why do you think I had to hide in the house?'

The train pulled away from the station with a lurch, and Cat sank back in her seat. 'Another crazy risk. What if one of them had gone upstairs?'

He grinned. 'I knew they wouldn't. Not after I kicked the stairs in to make them look unusable. Besides – you were lucky I was there to clean the place up. You and hubby made a proper mess with Tristan.' He paused, waiting for her to react. When she didn't he shrugged and carried on. 'My only real fuck-up was getting spotted in the woods . . . I thought I was far enough back from the track. But your bloody sister must have the ears of a bat.'

She took him in, his easy smile. Her mind went back again to that first night they'd met in France, over ten years ago. Then the night in London, later on, when she'd told Ginny about him, and Ginny had just assumed he was French. For some reason, she hadn't bothered to correct her. Cat had quite liked the idea of having an exotic, sexy French boyfriend – and, to be fair, he spoke French impeccably, and his accent was spot on. She'd be surprised if anyone would have suspected that it wasn't his native tongue.

'You know,' he continued, 'she didn't look quite as I expected. None of them did.'

'You were checking out their social media though, weren't you? Saying that, Paul doesn't post much. Ginny's is so heavily filtered that it's basically fiction. And of course Tristan doesn't use it at all. Well, except Messenger, sometimes.' She took a breath, realising what she'd just said. 'I'm still talking about them in the present tense . . .'

He reached across the table and put his hands on top of hers. 'Until they find the bodies, they're still technically *alive*.'

The train picked up speed and she glanced up at her suitcase, squeezed into the rack above her head. Frank was looking at her expectantly, but something had changed now. Now that she was there. Apart from a few hiccups, things had mostly gone to plan. Paul was meant to be dead, of course, but he'd come in handy at the end. She was still a little sad about Tristan, but that part couldn't be helped. That was all Paul's fault. The original plan was that they would go back to the car and drive to the train station, and then she would give Tristan the slip, there. It's not like he would go home and tell anyone what they'd done. He wasn't an idiot. He'd report them all missing and leave it at that. He'd already shown that he didn't care about Ginny and Paul. So it wasn't too much of a stretch to imagine that he would soon get over Cat's disappearance. Even if she did have the money.

Anyway, that was all irrelevant now. And Paul was going to get what he deserved in prison.

'Do you want a drink?' Frank said, leaning across the table. 'I can go to the restaurant car . . . you look like you need one. I mean . . . you've had a mad time. You're clearly in shock.'

'I'm OK,' she said. 'I think I'll wait until we get on the sleeper. I could do with a little rest though, you're right.'

'Of course. You shut your eyes. We've got a couple of hours to go.'

When she woke up, the light was different. They were in the station. She'd slept for the whole journey but it felt like five minutes. Her eyes were gritty and dry. Frank was pulling the bags down from the rack.

'Hello, sleepyhead,' he said, leaning down to kiss her. She turned her head at the last minute. Her mouth felt disgusting. And those words had given her a little flash to that room in Ascot, Tristan's face above hers.

She blinked, rubbing at her eyes, trying to dislodge the image.

She let him carry the bags off the train.

'Do you know which platform it is?' he said, glancing around. The station was huge and quiet. Bright lights and Tannoy

251

announcements in German now that they'd moved into another of the Swiss cantons.

'She's just said it's 5e.' Cat started walking, following the sign.

'You speak German now, do you? I didn't even catch that.'

'Oh . . . I did one of those little apps during lockdown. Paul spent his time shooting people on his PS4, so I thought I'd do something a bit more useful with my time. I was never a baker or a crafter, and, besides, you can never know too many languages, can you?'

He said something to her that sounded like it might be in Mandarin, then laughed. 'I said: you're right. Well done. You can sort everything out for us in Berlin then.'

The train was already waiting at the platform. She couldn't see how long it was, but it was double-level and it was bright and shiny – and a flutter of excitement fizzed around her stomach. This was really happening. She wondered for a moment about Paul. They would be taking him to another police station, where no doubt they would be far less polite now that he was accused of murder. At least, she hoped that was what was happening. He would crack, she knew. He might've been strong enough to lie his way through what happened with Samantha, but there was no way he was getting out of this one. Not without a very expensive lawyer. Tough to pay for that on his delivery-man salary.

They'd want to talk to her, of course. But they'd have to find her first.

She let Frank carry the bags on to the train. 'Let's get these in the cabin and then we can relax,' he said, reaching for her hand. She let him squeeze it.

'Why don't we head straight to the restaurant car?' she said. 'I could really do with that drink now. Plus, they need to do all the check-in stuff for the cabins. The host will come and find us.'

He frowned, but then she squeezed his hand back and he relented. 'Alright . . .'

They walked along the train until they found the restaurant car. There were a few others in there, with the same plan. The bar staff were already serving them drinks. Frank pushed the bags up on to the overhead shelf and she glanced up at hers, making sure it was in there securely and wouldn't fall down. And making sure she could lift it down herself, if she needed to. She was letting Frank help her because she was tired, but she wasn't about to become complacent. He slid into his seat and started rummaging around in his bag.

'I'll get us some drinks,' she said.

He looked up. 'They'll come to us . . . it'll be table service.'

She ignored him, but a flash of irritation hit her. This was how it had started before. A bit of advice here, a bit of help there. Then he was calling twice an hour to check where she was, who she was with. Turning up at her room in the halls of residence late at night, on nights where she said she couldn't see him because she was studying. Checking if she was there.

It had been supposed to be a bit of fun, but he'd become obsessive. Which is why she'd known he was the right person to help with her big plan. He'd always said he would do anything for her, and when she'd emailed him out of the blue a few months ago, he'd been so excited to hear from her. And so ready to start a new life with her. 'The one who got away', he called her. Yes, she had. As soon as she had realised what a control freak he was. But he was exactly what she needed now. They'd finalised the plans in London, him coming to meet her. And that was the night they'd slept together, after all those years.

She laid a hand on her stomach, still wondering about the implications of that.

The woman behind the bar was more than happy to serve her there. She asked Cat what she would like, and Cat replied in perfect

German. The woman smiled. She'd made out to Frank that she'd just played around on an app, but actually, she was almost fluent. Another string to her bow. One that was coming in very handy right now when she had to explain to the woman that she wanted a large gin and tonic, and just a tonic – but please make them look exactly the same. Ice, lemon. A packet of salted pretzels.

'*Danke*,' Cat said, smiling.

The woman smiled back.

Three drinks later, and Frank was slurring his words. 'Did you sort out the money?'

She nodded. 'It was easy. The phone thing was a piece of piss. For someone who works in banking he's surprisingly lacking in security. I saw the fingerprint smudges on his keypad. Ginny's birthday.'

'So you've got the money?'

'Yes,' she repeated, patiently. 'Codes entered via both of our phones. All set up like he said it would be.' She smiled. 'If only Ginny had come to me when the inheritance came through, instead of her stupid, cheating husband. Then none of this would have had to happen . . .'

'But then you wouldn't be here with me,' he said. His eyelids were starting to droop. 'I might need a little nap. Shall we go to the cabin now?'

She glanced up at the digital display, telling them which station they were due to stop at next.

'Maybe one more drink?'

'OK . . .'

He fell asleep before he finished it. The crushed-up Valium had started to work after the second drink, but she thought it would make it look more obvious to the woman behind the bar if he'd sunk four large gins before passing out.

His head fell to the window, his shoulders dropped. He snorted a couple of times, then seemed to settle.

The Tannoy announcements were off, because people were sleeping. Part of her wanted to go along to the cabin and climb into bed. She could probably sleep for a week, if she gave into it. But she was so close now. She couldn't lose sight of the plan. She'd lost count of which plan this was now. B? C? D?

Or maybe it had always been A – just with a few variations along the way.

She watched Frank as the train slowed and the station sign appeared on the platform.

Karlsruhe. She'd no idea what was there, but she knew there was a connection to Munich. Frank might be going to Berlin to start his new life with his new name, but she wasn't going with him.

She reached up and pulled down her bag. Nodding at the woman behind the bar, saying a silent *thank you* as she left. A quiet understanding passing between the two women. The woman had not commented on Cat's injuries, but she couldn't have failed to notice them, despite the baseball cap and the long sleeves.

The train stopped and Cat climbed down on to the platform. She waited for a few minutes, until it pulled away. No one was getting on at this stop. No one else was getting off. As the restaurant carriage passed, she saw Frank's head against the window. He was sound asleep. Completely out of it. He probably wouldn't wake until he reached Berlin – and by then she would be long gone.

She pulled out the handle of her bag and flipped out the wheels. Then she reached into her pocket and took out the mini-Maglite torch.

Epic Solutions.

The woman at the trade fair in Ascot had been so impressed with Cat's skills, organising such a complex event – she'd offered her a job on the spot. She had many companies, she'd said. Her headquarters were in Munich. Cat turned the torch over in her fingers, smiling at the email address on the back. She had contacted the woman a couple of months ago, asked if it was a genuine job offer. Explained that she needed to get away . . . and that she might have to change her name. The woman had understood. She'd said she had big plans. Couldn't wait to work with her.

She remembered Tristan, in her bed, at the end of that long working day. His offer to help her with her problems. Help her sort things out. *A plan*, he'd said. But she already had a plan.

She had always been very good at making plans.

Cat walked across the quiet concourse, looking for her platform. Another connecting train, and a little while to wait first. Luckily there was a café open, and she went in and ordered herself a peppermint tea.

She really wanted a proper drink. She would've loved a gin on the train. But she couldn't risk it. Not until she did a test. She laid a hand on her stomach, wondering if there was a little life inside there, a tiny bean, already starting to grow shoots and form itself into a little human. She would do a test in Munich. And she would tell her new boss straight away. This didn't have to be a blocker to her new life. In fact, it might even enhance it.

Another slight change of plan, perhaps. But certainly nothing she couldn't deal with. She sipped her tea, inhaling the minty steam. Glanced up at the departures board.

Not long now, until her brand-new life was ready to begin.

ACKNOWLEDGEMENTS

The idea for this book was sparked during a real-life hike on the trail described in this novel. It was while I was standing on the scary steep ridge, too tired to carry on, trying not to look down into the valley for fear that I would tumble to my death, when one of my companions said, 'Look, isn't that a red kite?' and I looked on in awe as the incredible bird hovered there, while wondering to myself – what if one of us fell right now? And the inevitable afterthought . . . what if one of us was pushed?

Haha! Luckily none of us fell or were pushed, and we miraculously did make it back before the hot tub closed for the night. Moral of the story: never go to dangerous places with a crime writer.

Thank you as always, to my brilliant agent Phil Patterson. I pray every day that he doesn't become a victim of friendly fire while out walking his dog near the rifle range because I really do need him.

Huge thanks to Victoria Haslam, my Thomas & Mercer editor and champion. It's so much fun working with you and I love everything you've done for me and this book.

Possibly the biggest thanks ever go to my developmental editor Russel McLean – who pulled the charred bones of this book from the wreckage and helped me to see what it was meant to be. Me and Jessica are forever in your debt.

I probably wouldn't have finished this book without the support of my crime writing crew, who shall remain anonymous in case I forget someone.

Thank you to my readers – the bloggers, the reviewers, the reading champions. Everything I do, I do it for you . . .

Massive thanks to Catherine Baxendale, for generously bidding for her name in the book via last year's CLIC Sargent auction, and for her lovely seahorse gift that I know was very traumatic to purchase. Two things I love about Cat – she has a phobia of seahorses (try wedging *that* into an Alpine-set thriller), and her maiden name is Holliday!

As always, thank you to my friends and family for their constant love and support.

And finally, to JLOH . . . from the bottom of my pencil case.

FREE *DARK HEARTS* BOX SET

Join my readers' club and you'll get a free box set of stories: 'As Black as Snow', 'The Outhouse' and 'Pretty Woman'. You'll also receive occasional news updates and be entered into exclusive give-aways. It's all completely free, and you can opt out at any time.

Join here: sjihollidayblog.wordpress.com/sign-up-here

ABOUT THE AUTHOR

Susi Holliday grew up near Edinburgh and worked in the pharmaceutical industry for many years before she started writing. A lifelong fan of crime and horror, her short stories have been published in various places, and she was shortlisted for the inaugural CWA Margery Allingham Prize. She is the acclaimed author of nine novels and a novella. The film adaptation of her Trans-Siberian-set psychological thriller *Violet* is currently in development.

As well as working, reading, writing, walking and drinking tea, Susi provides mentoring for new crime writers via www.crimefictioncoach.com.

You can find out more at her website, www.susiholliday.com, on Facebook at www.facebook.com/SJIHolliday, on Twitter @SJIHolliday, and on Instagram @susijholliday.

Made in the USA
Las Vegas, NV
21 September 2022